Althenopis

FABRIZIA RAMONDINO

ALTHENOPIS

translated from the Italian
by Michael Sullivan

CARCANET

First published in 1988 by
Carcanet Press Limited
208–212 Corn Exchange Buildings
Manchester M4 3BQ

British Library Cataloguing in Publication Data
Ramondino, Fabrizia
Althenopis.
I. Title
853'.914[F]

ISBN 0-85635-743-X

The publisher acknowledges financial assistance from the
Arts Council of Great Britain

Typeset in 11/13 Bembo by Paragon Photoset, Aylesbury
Printed in England by SRP Ltd, Exeter

For Laura Gonzalez

who, in urging me to this adventure
and accompanying me, was Don Quixote
to me and also Sancho Panza.

Contents

I

Santa Maria del Mare

Sancho amigo, has de saber que yo
naci' por querer del cielo, en esta
nuestra edad de hierro, para
resucitar en ella la de oro.*

* 'Friend Sancho, you should know that I was born by the wish of heaven, in this iron age of ours, to resuscitate in it the age of gold.'
— Cervantes, *Don Quixote*, I.20

1
Grandmother

She was always dressed in black, but when she passed through the piazza of Santa Maria del Mare, colours would flare around her like the flames of hell – yellows, violet, sometimes even reds and greens; she wore no bracelets and yet gleams of gold seemed to shimmer around her wrists.* She had a rapid upright walk, her great mass of piled-up hair wagging to the rhythm. She had dash and height; under her black skirt as far as the thigh, the elegant line of her leg; her dress was cut deep on her thin, reddened chest; a wide ribbon of black velvet clasped the nervous arteries of her neck.

And the glisten of other sumptuous colours surrounding her in the dark room – the candles were lit as late as possible – gleaming scraps of damask, found who knows where in war-time; yellow, pink, cardinal red, violet, even orange damasks, richly trimmed, out of which she sewed comb-cases, mirror-cases, pen-cases, wallets, note-cases, book-jackets, diaries, ledgers, pincases; and there was a heart-shaped one in red damask – to encase what? She sewed them for a beloved grandson of hers, a prisoner in the Indies; she put them back jealously in a drawer after showing them to me.

Flares of hell, of luxury and luxuria around the poor woman.

I once opened that drawer of hers, inside there were oint-ments of mercury and arsenic. I don't know why, out of what adult prompting, since I didn't know anything about anything

* Visions, which are revealed truth, like obsessions, which are truths not yet revealed, cannot be forgotten; nor yet explained.

then,* but something sinful was given off by those ointments. Perhaps my mother had once vaguely explained their purpose: irritations, eruptions of the skin, sores perhaps, on certain parts of the body; still, some knowledge told me that ailments of the skin were a sin of luxury and luxuria . . . There was also that little book of Granny's, the story of Job with all his boils, for which he blamed God and to which he later resigned himself, but all those festering boils against God . . . Even her black missal, with the red border and the gold letters on the cover, had a strange thick odour of things stored away, which weighed on me with its mystery. I connected it with my times of pallidness, with my little sicknesses and night-time anguishes, perhaps even with my warm and voluptuous bed-wetting; against which – untrammelled and luminous – stood the daytime joy of racing about the piazza with my playmates. Colours familiar to me were pink, green, brown, yellow, sky-blue also; black or white never. Sometimes red, but never that red with black. And gold never! Gold then seemed to me the height of the arcane, and of evil, not least because I didn't know how to read and struggled to make out the gold lettering on the missal . . . Our parents were atheists, atheists of a fatuous kind, so that religion itself was a sin in my eyes. Whereas Grandmother belonged to a period when it had been possible to make the eternity of history coincide with that of life, so that life went by as progress – but that was men's business – and earthly life passed into eternal life – and that was the business of women, praying at the bedside of the dying.

At seven they entrusted me to Granny, and took me with a suitcase to Santa Maria del Mare where she lived in a house that faced on to the piazza. The house was unassuming enough, but must certainly have once belonged to a local lawyer, or the pharmacist at least, with its sculptured stone lions at the ends of the banisters.

* Not to know 'anything about any anything' obviously means to be ignorant of sex and money, i.e. life, in the language of grown-ups.

As I passed inside that first time I was welcomed by the fragrant vision of a shrine to St Anthony and of a cake baked from chestnut flour set in front of it; Granny had created a little shrine just for me. There was the Saint, a beautiful young man framed in gold, with white lilies in opal-blue vases either side; the scent was that of visits to the cemetery on All Souls where we children went in a happy band: the smell of hyacinths and lilies, gross flowers, and of cakes grown stale in tins, like that old, earthy odour of chestnut cake mingling with the scent from the flowers which pressed on my temples. And there were four lighted candles in front for the saint – and the dead – which in the evening were carried into the other room where one ate. And there was an embroidered doily, solemnly stained with wax, and strings of white beads hanging from the corner of the picture. For a child who willingly wore white* – my summer dresses came from torn sheets – skinny, with large brown eyes, who everybody said looked like a madonna and would get to see the Pope when she was a big girl, that little altar gave coquettish allure to her future as a nun, a refuge not for the spirit but for touch and smell. A future more alluring than that of librarian, for which my father had destined me from the time I was six, when he began to show me his incunabula and other rare editions in the vain hope of stirring me.

The voluptuousness of that altar became one with that of the chestnut cake and the custards that Granny made in little saucepans, just for me, from a drop of tinned milk and thirty grams of sugar spared from her coffee in those days of wartime scarcity.

There was also on my arrival the fascination of drawers full of bobbins, loose threads, trimming, coloured wool, gold thread, scraps of lace, like remnants from the family history and the legends which my grandmother narrated. The evocation of those past glories and the pomp of Catholicism at times quieted my night fears, whereas the hygienic, mist-dispelling

* The will of my mother and other women in the family.

upbringing that our mother imparted swelled their diapason into the strident range. Granny's hand, which smelled of incense, oil, dust, wax and flowers, was calming, while my mother's disquieted instead. Cool and smelling of soap, it seemed always to wipe out 'nonsense', to wash something away.

Granny also had long skirts and vast and various odours around her, while even my mother's sunburnt legs smelled of soap – soda soap in those days. Certainly at times and regularly there were large board-covered basins in the toilet full of cloths and red water. I knew that they came from my mother, but I couldn't find the connection between those barbarities and her ascetic fragile body. Blood, in my memory usually on knees and elbows, came from playing, was mixed with earth, and was washed and staunched with alcohol, while you gazed at the door, frantic to get back to the game. That blood in the basin, though, had nothing whatsoever to do with playing, nor with alcohol, nor with soap. And then my mother, despite that blood, didn't have a body, she had gestures and above all she had 'things on her mind', she had headaches. That blood couldn't come from the 'things on her mind' or from what loomed over her. Perhaps from her headaches, or the headaches from the blood, but the headaches were also linked to the 'things on her mind'. Yet I caught the smell of that blood, like a bleached-out memory, even on Grandmother's skirts.

The evenings while we were eating bread soup, which apart from the rare and festive chestnut cakes was our staple diet, or while she led me by the hand across the piazza to visit her sister – more fortunate than she in those wartime days* – in the big house at the far end of the village, she would tell me the

---

* Because she had her son with her and not in Albania. And hadn't invested her money in shares and state bonds which would then be devalued. Good fortune, like misfortune, always had something to do with money. Contrary to the popular saying: 'Only for death there is no remedy', death, sickness, war or earthquake were not true and proper misfortunes unless accompanied by grave financial loss.

marvellous stories of the holy martyrs and of the girl martyrs in particular. Less frequent were those about the holy founders of Orders. Or she would tell me about the poor. When she spoke of the poor her tone was brutal – the old pauper asleep on the pisspot – taken, it might have been, from Zola or Matilda Serao; but since she was only semi-literate, she drew instead upon her familiarity with all the miseries of the alley-ways which I first encountered in her tales. For the poor she would beg a job, implore assistance, demand a pension, beseech the landlords to wait a while, bustle about to get someone into the TB hospital, solicit fuel and olive-oil, make lace doilies to sell to her acquaintances, queue in front of offices, write letters to the newspapers – on those occasions making use of her more educated sister – and in wartime collected woollies and blankets which she personally handed out at the station to the soldiers leaving for the Front, since she did not trust in the Red Cross. For the poor she would do the rounds from office to office, pass hours of indignity in anterooms, soft-soap and abuse armies of hall porters, burst into the office of the mayor, the councillors, engineers, doc-tors, lawyers. Never of notaries. She exploited the friends and acquaintances of relations, sons, sons-in-law and all the men of the family who would exclaim: 'What a spectacle you make of us!' but then would meekly yield. During air-raids she would pray publicly, *coram populo*, in the shelters or the Caporetto Tunnel.

Though she spoke of the poor realistically, she evoked around them a shining and celestial aura. If it weren't for the poor, so she let me understand, the world would be much poorer off, for it would mean that the high-handed had won, the great ones of the earth, that the world was ruled by chance only. Who then would be a brother to her, a sister?

And then she was predestined to take it on. Was she not indeed a descendant of St Clare? Hadn't her father's poor sister been torn away from her mother and sisters, from the ancest-ral castle of Sterpeto, to be enclosed with the Poor Clares? And had not the hazards of life and those of the family com-

15

bined so that from mystical Umbria she had come to serve as far away as *Althenopis*,* the city blessed in the great number of its poor?

The poor, however, lost their virtue if they became better off; they left the kingdom of heaven for that of earth, to become part of the low, of people in a small way, those ill-disposed, mean-minded, dirty, common, disrespectful, envious, vicious folk who, given the chance, would have turned as overbearing as the rich. And so they became a bestial subspecies, ferocious as upstarts, ape-like as the small impudent maids who came from the country to serve in the house.

Country people though, could never be the poor; only when they left the land did they become really poor; the fertility of the land extended to mankind, whereby country girls had milk in such abundance they could act as wet-nurses.

Of these low and ill-disposed people she nevertheless spoke little by then, herself impoverished and deprived of any previous power by her daughters, no longer having servants and factors to lord it over; few occasions remained to her of encountering insubordination or slovenliness. Instead with the passing of years she spoke more and more of the truly poor, making claims for the ancient family tradition which went back not just to her ancestors, or rather, her ancestress Clare, and all the young women of a papist family forced into

* The name of my native city. The origin of the name means 'eye of the virgin'. But it appears that the Germans during the Occupation, finding it did not come up to the descriptions of Mozart (to be found also in a novella of Mörike's) and Goethe, changed its name to Althenopis which simply means 'eye of the crone'. Certain literary apologists for the city hazard the meaning 'eye of the sage'; against this interpretation however stands the observation on the one hand that flashes of wisdom are still too tenuous in our city, as elsewhere, to be considered lasting and, on the other, the German dictionary itself, where *saggio* is given as *weise* and not *alt*. The Tourist Board, finally, prompted by a city councillor, suggests the following etymology: *alt* would be a Greek root, from *althea*, the plant with a red blossom. Althenopis would therefore be the city of the 'eye of the aurora'. All this, though it may gull the tourists, lacks philological foundation of any kind.

16

the convent each generation (she would show the photograph of the most recent Poor Clare taking leave of her family and the world: between father and mother the young girl stands, and on either side of her, in rows of diminishing height, her twenty-four brothers and sisters), but even to her mother, to her father and her only brother. During the cholera outbreak in '84 the two men had gone into the Decumani district to succour the dying, along with other followers of Garibaldi come from elsewhere, while her mother, herself and her sisters had let down baskets of medicine and victuals from balconies. Her mother helped the poor out of her Christian faith, while her father did it out of secular civic duty. As his tombstone stated, in fact, her father had 'abandoned the comforts of a noble family to share the destiny of the Unification of Italy'. After Unification, deprived of title and possessions by his papist family, turning to the magnificent destiny of industrialization and public works for Althenopis and its poor, he set up a flourishing business in public pay-toilets, as well as showers and baths, thus uniting the requirements of profit to a civilizing mission. But it was only much later that I was able to learn about this business, since his five daughters, including my grandmother, preferred the ancient splendours of the family to what followed on the Unification. The more so as they knew – and these things always have a way of coming out – that the young men in the clubs of Althenopis were in the habit of saying that those splendid blossoms, Grandmother and her five sisters, owed their beauty to the excellent manure in which they had grown.

When, because of the air raids, our mother joined us at Santa Maria del Mare, the mythic image of Grandmother began to crumble before my eyes. From goddess and holy martyr, she became outlandish, muddled, culpable. More than anything else culpable, in some obscure way. In many families in the village the old people were culpable because they could no longer work on the land. The ones in the Santa Maria old people's home were culpable because they were dirty; when they ate their soup they dribbled; once a year, at

17

Easter, when they had macaroni with meat sauce, they got it all over their chins; and they wet their beds. But Grandmother had particular faults. At that time I could only guess at them.

Her chief fault was to have frittered away the family possessions, inherited in part from her parents and in part from her husband who had died leaving her a young widow of twenty-five. Punctually, always a few weeks before a currency devaluation, she sold houses and lands; she gave lavish wedding presents to farm tenants and maids; when her tenants presented their apples, she didn't look to see how thickly lined the bottom of the pannier was with straw, or leaves when it was figs; and when she polished the furniture she didn't rub it over with wax but washed it with soap and water so that after a year or two, away went the veneer, away went the shine which was what gave dignity to those rustic pieces and made them worthy of a place in town apartments. And I watched this Grandmother of the great cleansing as she flurried about, hair piled up, cheeks flaming, the artery palpitating in her slender neck, her black dress covered in grease-stains, as she aired and mopped the rooms like one possessed, setting china and silver out in the spring morning sun on window-sills within reach of the thieving hands of maids and farm-hands. A festival of sun and water, and a ritual of expropriation. She became very beautiful on these occasions, with a surge of the spirit, and no longer of the flesh; as a young woman she had been gorgeous, not one of her daughters could match her – nor stand against that impetuous sluicing. And this wasn't something that took place merely at Easter, but whenever the spirit took her. At other times the urge would be to play the piano, or to take over the kitchen.

She lived surrounded by indignation: that of her daughters, that of the other women of the family, and of their husbands, who nevertheless rejoiced in their hearts whenever any crack appeared in the matriarchy of the five sisters. The indignation of entire generations of grown-ups, professional men or rentiers, in the face of that frittering away in the sun of income, shares, treasury bonds, furniture, silverware, at that revel of water and light in the house, of draughts that were forever assailing the delicate chests of children, at her scorn for share portfolios, for the financial consequences of wars and for the use of wax on furniture! Wax which protected, which preserved, and even gave a shine; in which men loved to mirror their undying spirit! But she wanted water, wanted the festival of water, and just like water money ran through her fingers.

Along with this palpable fault went another, more obscure. And of all things this had to be kept from me, though I sensed it in the penetrating odour of her clothes, in the luxury of her religion, in the dash of her step, in her restless siestas in the cool dark of the house in summer, in the ill-disguised sniggers that surrounded her. Once I managed to overhear one of my aunts telling my mother that the priest had broken the seal of confession to pass on the fact that Grandmother was afraid of being seduced by my father. The poor priest had done it against his will, fearing for Grandmother's reason. And I remember this tale of my aunt's making my mother laugh.

Grandmother had not got on with her husband. The word was that she had not been a good wife from any point of view, except that of fidelity, which went by the name of seriousness. For example, she was continually losing track of, or could never lay hands on, their papers, their scissors, their keys.* In the last months of Grandfather's life – and in the years following – Grandmother administered the family possessions, frittering them away, and, paralysed, he would whine impotently from his bed. She didn't fritter them away on luxuries, this wife of his, but she took in good faith the complaints of the farm people about the bad harvest or their family troubles, and so contented herself with what they brought, and even at times went so far as to hand back part of their dues. The new-laid eggs, for instance, handed back to a farmer's son invalided out of the war with tuberculosis, so disgusted with life and the world as to have lost his appetite; so to get the

* Their, i.e. his. Grandmother never had anything of her own. And Mother would complain that Grandmother, never having anything of her own, didn't sufficiently consider that other people's things were not hers.

young man to sup the eggs, Grandmother would give his grumbling father a kilo of sugar and a little cocoa, and even Marsala, if there was any in the cupboard.

She frittered things away on charity to her poor, heaping their daughters, grandchildren, cousins, with gifts. Or on gifts for the maids, or on paying her son's gambling debts, and those of the priest for sacred vestments.

Grandmother had not been happy, so they said, with her husband. It wasn't clear whether the blame lay in not having been happy with a husband or only in the fact of not having been happy. In those days not to be happy was more culpable than not being healthy. The gentry ought to be above such things, which were for the common people and the debauched. And at no time did women have the right to be unhappy; that was for men, and very few at that.

In wartime the complaints of the farm-hands always turned into insolent demands. Not only did they rummage round the house but, so it was said, up her skirt as well. The result was that she sold almost all her lands, the last piece in 1943 for three hundred thousand lire, and for years those three hundred thousand lire would come up, on a rising note, in every row between my mother and grandmother.

And the love she had for the grandson imprisoned in the Indies, wasn't that morbid, sinful even? A great love, a flaunted love, in the name of which didn't she every now and then, for all seven years of his imprisonment, steal a little of Mother's money, or her own sisters', or the prisoner's mother's, her other daughter, to put in his post-office book? And wasn't it sinful that, in the drawer along with the comb-cases, wallets, bookmarks, pincushions embroidered for her grandson, she would have locked away an old edition of De Musset's love-poems, and in the margin of the *Chanson de Fortunio* should be written in French – slightly ungrammatical, but her Italian was no better – 'Voila comme on aime en poesie, mais, dites-moi, y-at-il quelque homme qui aime comme ça?'. The edition was bound in red leather, with the title in black and gold; it gave off the scent of irises: romantic thoughts in a young girl, but was it right to preserve them as a woman, not to say old woman?

And what to say about a certain ambiguous generosity of hers? Wasn't it perhaps an ambiguous, almost equivocal, generosity she had shown as a girl when waiting up for her brother to slip back into the house through a window, and one time came on him asleep on the bowl, and led him lovingly to bed, after reminding him to wipe his arse? Wasn't that comprehension for the young man's vices bordering on connivance? And hadn't she herself despaired of the plaits her severe mother wove too tightly, undoing them, once out of the house, with the complicity of all her sisters except the eldest? And her intimacy with priests! And then with the poor! The poor whom her relations declared were not poor at all but idle spongers, if you give them a finger they take an arm – and who knew what else besides!

Along with these great guilts, one evident and explicit – the squandering of the family possessions – the other hidden, guessed-at, overheard, magnified, poor Granny had a great many small faults – oddities at least.

Like cooking. Grandmother loved to cook but it was years since she had been mistress in her own house, and thus her urge led her to violate meal-times and the shopping budget. She mostly cooked for the only members of the family who could appreciate her, the children, among whom we stood, the youngest of the grandchildren. In years past she had cooked for the one far-off, the favourite gone to the war, then for the other, gone to the TB hospital; now she cooked for us. It was her cooking we loved best, for it had nothing to do with pennypinching or modern rules of health or diet, but only with the imagination. The family derided her cooking methods, the women indignant at the riot of custards, oil, pans that had to be tidied up, while the men felt distaste, or suspicion at least – those men of southern families who suspect a fly in every tiny sprig of parsley, who fear the moving sands of sex in the quiver of a custard and spend their whole lives babbling about their Mummy's cooking, for from her hands

21

alone can custard and sprigs of parsley be trusted.

In those post-war years when Grandmother was no longer mistress in her own house, she would suddenly wake with a precise urge to cook some particular thing: croquettes, for instance, or puff pastry, or snaps *alla siciliana*, or perhaps only bread soup. When this fervour took hold of her no one could hold her, and she made great quantities of everything, as if still in the big house surrounded by children, grandchildren, sisters, relations, people calling in. Her bread soup seemed miraculous to me and I ate it with her, hidden away in a dark corner when the house was deserted, as if it were a stolen delicacy. She also had a real flair – it was a time of dearth and ingredients were scarce – for making certain fabulous custards at which others turned up their noses. My father in particular would put on a *mareado*★ air and try in vain to persuade my brother, the male of the family, to imitate him. Our mother's distaste was different and entirely cerebral; she disapproved of the irrationality of the cooking procedure, the contempt for a balanced diet of proteins, carbohydrates, vitamins, the money wasted and the mismatch between what the cookery book led one to expect and the actual results.

When this urge came over Grandmother and she came out of the kitchen in her great white apron, my mother would make a dash to stop her, and not succeeding, would then try to contain the impetus in the kitchen. Grandmother went straight ahead with whatever the urge prompted, all sweaty and stained from the rising smoke and oil, red in the face, her sleeves rolled up, having a go at washing the pans in soda to avoid clashing headlong with Mother and the grumbling maid, who, rather than poking up the fire, would take Mother's hint to leave the kitchen and go and linger at the

---

★ Castilian – queasy. The word occurs because the language of my early childhood still comes forcefully to the surface for things connected with food or with the body. This word surfaces even the more strongly because all I remember of it is the sensation of sailing in a slightly rough sea in a small boat steered by others, not knowing where or why, and feeling my stomach turn, *mareado*, precisely.

22

pump or plump up the pillows.

Grandmother's presence transformed the kitchen into a fairy-tale cave, and out from the cupboards came all the cooking pots and the ladles, which she would never put to their proper use – often enough these utensils were of English or German make, old presents to the women of the family from the males who trusted in progress. Meantime Mother would march around the house proclaiming: 'It's arteriosclerosis', hoping to exorcise the enormity with a scientific term. Father, having little respect for women in general, and especially for women of that family – a community, he used to say, from which he had saved our mother by marriage – would give an amused smile at the weaknesses and destructiveness of the female and head off over the fields to the village café! On our return from school with our pinafores stained with the grass we'd been chewing and our clogs full of mud, we would find Mother lying down in the dark with headache and a vinegar-soaked rag on her forehead, and Granny in sparkling form over the fritters and creamy pastries. And we dived into those gorgeous offerings, which dripped and smelled so good, which had neither beginning nor end, and which mocked at questions of expense and vitamin count.

And what didn't she manage to do in those wartime years with chestnuts and bread and garlic, and even with salads, sending us into the fields to gather rocket! Bread fried up with garlic, bread roasted with garlic, when there was no oil, salads of potato, onion and rocket; and the white bread got from the Americans she fried and dusted with sugar and cinnamon, a gift from the priest who had them from the Allied Command along with spelling-books straight off the press.

For herself she rarely cooked. Nevertheless every morning, even when things were prosperous, she stubbornly made bread soup, and on the occasions she ate in the evening she would make it again. And in spring, without fail, she always made a bean soup as a purge.

There was yet another wicked art she practised: medicine. The grown-ups had things to say about that too; it wasn't arteriosclerosis they invoked here but superstition. She would bind wounds with slices of potato or strips of medick which she grew in a pot on the balcony; for swellings, lettuce leaves; for warts, the milk of figs. She was outraged by women using infusions of parsley, and cured colds with decoctions of dried figs, althea root, the flower of the prickly pear and eucalyptus leaves. In the evenings she would bring us camomile in bed; on feverish foreheads lay rags soaked in vinegar; for worms make us inhale the smoke from burning pine, or give a drop or two of the pressings of rue. When aspirins lost their effect even our mother sought relief in the vinegar-soaked rags, but was still not prepared to accept the use of tomatoes and potatoes on wounds.

There was a further extravagance still: Granny composed love-songs at the piano and wrote poems in the local dialect – though her mother had been Genoese and her father from Umbria. The dialect she had chosen as a minor art, she who hadn't even finished the fifth grade in elementary school and hadn't got as far as Italian, for dialect was the medium of the first love-songs she had ever heard, the language of the poor, and especially of the servant-girls of her childhood, the only people who ever told her things about real life. Now dialect might be tolerated for the purposes of art, but it was not to be borne that she should use it with us children, and every time a slurred or brazen word escaped us, Grandmother was blamed.

On top of this, Grandmother was responsible for a thousand daily annoyances: if the scissors couldn't be found, if the sewing scissors had been used to clean the fish, if the sorb-apples had been hung up to ripen in the drawing-room, if the hens had been let out on to the road and were laying in the ditch, if a piece of silk belonging to Mother had been taken from the wardrobe to make scarves for the Christmas party, if the hammer had been left on the window-sill to get rusty . . . everything was laid to her account.

In the little house at Santa Maria del Mare where we had taken refuge from the air raids, there was no piano. Nor were there any poor people in the village. Depressed by the war, she couldn't bring herself to write poetry and instead wrote interminable letters to her prisoner grandson in the Indies. She wrote him everything, as if confiding to a diary or addressing a faraway lover. This she did by candlelight, to save electricity, hoping to economise, thinking to prevent her consumption of electricity from going on to the horrendous bill which plunged the house into penury, dire straits and bad humour for several days on end until our mother, after days of what seemed like penance in bed, with the vinegar-soaked rags on her forehead to drive away the 'things on her mind', would start moving again.

Some years later Grandmother's arteriosclerosis began to manifest itself in an acute form. The elections of 1948 came up. No one managed to convince her that to vote Garibaldi meant to vote for the Communists.* People were trying to cheat her – she told us – with their political squabbles, and despite them she was going to vote for the Liberator of Italy and the People of the South, for the man – and on 'the man' her voice went up, and she lifted her face, hand, index finger, hair – whom her father had followed from Umbria. And then also Garibaldi looked like St Joseph, the male saint she most venerated and whose name was borne by her son. And off she went on her own to vote, shaking her stick and calling down wrath on the enemies of Italy, the Fascists and the Communists, and on us children who came behind her, mocking.

I felt some remorse at mocking her, and remember her now at the end of the path as she turned the corner, her piled-up hair in disorder, the trembling artery held in by the velvet band, stiff and straight in a dress slightly low at the neck, shaking her stick and alternating 'ill-bred children' with 'enemies of the people', the handbag – with her voting form and a picture of Garibaldi torn from a newspaper – tight under her arm.

It was then that the family decided she had entirely lost her

* During World War Two, the Communist partisans had been loosely grouped as the 'Garibaldi Brigades'. – *Trans.*

reason and in the two last years of her life the indignation, the irony, and the mockery gave way to pity. Though not with us children, in whom a stubborn veneration took turns with derision. The attitude of the village children to old people was generally mocking. Every now and then our gang would swarm out of the piazza to visit the old folks' home in the village nearby. There the old men let themselves be made fun of, laughing toothlessly at the young visitors from the world outside, and one of them might undo a screw of paper and offer us a chestnut, or take out a photo of a bride or a soldier to show us. Then in Holy Week the priest would come and wash their feet and we lined up silently in a row with our chests out and the objects of our mockery became unexpectedly vulnerable. They sent us to pick flowers and when the macaroni with meat sauce was set upon the table, the nuns would shoo us away. It was Easter.

With the old people from the home and with Grandmother we had, in spite of our mockery, an intimacy not to be found with any other grown-ups; to them, as to us, shit and spit were familiar, they were treated badly by the nuns as were we, they jealously kept small fetishes and objects of worship as we did, for them as for us a lira, a sugared almond, a chestnut were precious. Our derision was also a way of playing together. Like the time we offered the half-blind old man at the home a bunch of broccoli instead of flowers. 'Put them in front of your dead daughter's picture,' we said. And when he caught on he threatened us with his stick and then took hold of our elusive hands and laughed toothlessly. Or when we went to Granny with me cuddling a bundle wrapped up like a baby and pretending it was going to slip out of my grasp, and Granny became alarmed while the other girls laughed. When Granny understood, she flushed angrily, but quickly calmed down, smiled at us, and began to show us her embroidery. Or when she made us sit down round the table in the dusk to do magic with the cards; she made them dance in the air in twos, in fours, in sevens, in a line, in a ring. We soon found out that she tied them together with white strands of her long hair; still we pretended to believe in the magic. But in the very middle of the game one of us would get up ever so quiet and suddenly switch the light on and betray the trick, and Granny would let all the cards drop with a start and her eyes would glisten with tears, and her hair would look like something sad and finished with, still knotted to the cards and lifeless on the table. And yet every time that trick would astonish us, so that with kisses and hugs we implored her to begin again. And she would recommence, humming and singing to the rhythm, until the dark swallowed up the dancing cards and Granny's song and, scared, we would run for the light-switch.

Two months before she died Grandmother moved to a tenement in Althenopis. Our aunt, wanting to do what was decent, offered to take her in, but Grandmother's confessor backed her decision: it was a question of a penance for the salvation of her soul, a penance, as later emerged, to mortify the flesh. She was looked after by people who had frequented her house and who lived near the alley where 'she had done good works'. At the first hint of paralysis my aunt took her in, and she died in one of the rooms of the large apartment, then up for sale.

2
The piazza

A most civilized piazza, sunlit, Mediterranean, poor but never mean, smiling with flowers on window-sills, the area outside each house swept every morning; conceived and built, it seemed, in a single moment, from a single plan, such was its harmony, usefulness and grace. A notary, a pharmacist and a landowner had built, it seems, the three large houses that bounded it, and which stretched or spread loosely beyond the piazza into other buildings rich in stairways, arches, gardens of orange trees and courtyards. Pink, yellowish, washed-out blue were the colours of the houses. The other side of the piazza was bounded by the church and the priest's house. From the villages higher up, Monticchio, Schiazzano, Termini, L'Annunziata, Aiello, Anteselva, Nocelle, and from the villages lower down, Metamunno, La Marina, Sistri, Alisistri, Marciano, you could see the round and familiar asphalt-covered dome of the church brooding lovingly over the village. And thick around the village the straw mats that roofed the lemon and orange groves.

We lived in what had been the notary's house. Stone lions ornamented the balustrade of the stairway. Facing ours was the house that must have belonged to the pharmacist, with a pink façade, where some old women lived upstairs, while below there was the bakery. The house continued on from the bakery in more genteel form, and this wing was occupied by spinsters who lived by sewing. Their balconies, with sharp-pointed railings, always had geraniums in flower. Next to the bakery was the tobacconist's where our mother used to send us to buy Nazionali cigarettes, and once in a while for a few pence we would buy large white knobbly comfits or pink ones like shells or mint caramels thin and round as lentils. The tobacconist's was a place of perdition, for it also sold wine and the whole day long three or four men would sit drinking inside, in woollen vests, their lean white arms covered in flies. It also sold postcards with pictures of loving couples: they sat beside a trellis of roses or an ivy garland; the girls wore flowered dresses and their lovers had jackets and ties with a gold stripe; their cheeks were painted pink. The tobacconist also sold black exercise books with red borders, pens and pencils, little bottles of ink, and those 'Giotto' coloured pencils whose points were forever breaking, or would slip out whole from the wood, and served better for cleaning our teeth than for drawing.

In the house that had belonged to the landowner – the largest in the piazza, almost a palace, divided into two wings by a central arch leading to the rest of the village which terminated, as rosaries do with the crucifix, in the ruins of the castle – there lived dozens of families, most of them heirs of the one-time owners. One of these families was very influential and the father, among his many other dealings, looked after the interests of the Gargiulos who lived in the capital. The wife, who was ever so fat, was a seamstress and they had an only daughter, rotund and blonde. Mariarosa was treated better than we other children, always had impeccable flowered dresses, gleaming hair, carefully combed, washed with shampoo and not soap like ours. They gave her dolls taller than herself which she kept on top of the wardrobe, laid out in cellophane boxes like fairytale tombs, or propped up on her mother's bed like oddly dressed visitors. One wasn't supposed to touch them. She seemed like a doll herself and was careful when she played, so hardly ever scraped her elbows or knees. She was an only child, in line with her mother's decision when a second child was born dead and deformed. Now and again Mariarosa would tell us that her mother had taken an infusion of parsley and was in bed with a colic and shitting a lot, all soft; at times she would shit blood or angels, little angels, she

29

would tell us, like the cherubs in the big painting at the foot of her bed who played the harp and, glorious and triumphant, blew on trumpets and flutes.

When birthdays came round in Mariarosa's house, lavish parties were held and guests streamed in from the nearby villages. The feasting took place in the lemon grove where the clustered trees thinned out towards the vineyard; the father sat on a plank with his legs crossed and his white shirt open down to his hairy belly; the women went in and out with *guantiere** heaped with pastries ordered from the pastry-cook in Corento, and handed round glasses of vermouth or lemonade. Mariarosa's father would laugh indulgently and lend an ear to the confidences of his guests. He made his money managing property, in setting up deals and acting as middleman. Occasionally he would go off to Althenopis in a trap, his pockets bulging with bundles of thousand-lire notes tied with string. On his return he brought presents for his wife and daughter, filling the house with bric-à-brac: a music-box ballerina, a huge painted shell, fans, glass balls in which snow fell when you shook them. After the war he brought a photograph in a silver frame of an actress called Shirley Temple. Once he turned up with some canaries; another time he promised a monkey but his wife was afraid and didn't want it.

Next door to Mariarosa was the cobbler. The cobbler was skinny and sad – all the family was skinny and sad – and wore glasses; in the village only he and my mother wore glasses. He had six children; the older ones were tainted with consumption and were being looked after in a hospital in Althenopis, though even when they got better they never worked in our village but only in the neighbouring ones. Every now and again the house was whitewashed; through the open door one could see the interior: large green plants near the sewing-machine in the living-room lapped the sisters in shadow as

---

* Althenopis dialect: salver for gloves. Because it was on this that gloves were handed to the master. The Spanish grandeur in the offering of food and drink wouldn't be conveyed by the Italian term.

they worked. The village girls did not go there for their Easter dresses, but every fortnight a woman would appear, puffing and perspiring, with a lad who took away trousers in a bundle humped on his head. Once out of the piazza, just before turning the corner, he would look back and stick his tongue out. We weren't allowed in that house because they all spat blood. The mother wore a hair shirt under her dress to punish herself and expiate the malady; but we played in the piazza with the two youngest girls, Anna and Immacolatella, and sometimes, to spite my mother, I would go into their house to drink a glass of water and then spit to check the colour of the saliva.

Next to the cobbler's, in a house that looked out on a shady lemon grove, lived a young woman who had been evacuated from Althenopis because of the air-raids. She was about thirty years old, very beautiful, with a large bosom and wavy hair, who was said to have worked in the land registry and to have lost her job when the offices were moved underground because of the bombing. Signorina Angelina lived with her invalid mother and was very fond of geraniums. Hers was a true passion. She didn't like simple geraniums – or at least she despised them as commonplace – and looked instead for complicated hybrids, violets and reds, white and purples, pinks and lilacs, with black stripes, with colours that blended into one another, with pointed or jagged petals. When we returned with a rare species from our sorties in the countryside or the villages or deserted villas roundabout she was delighted, and rewarded us with sweets or thirty lire; and if the species flowered we were called to inspect it, while she looked on, her eyes shining with a moisture that seemed anointed and perfumed. She would bend over the plant with her large bosom, not like that of the other women, compressed by a bodice, but wearing an indecent brassière, my Mother said, which supported each of her breasts singly instead of squeezing them together. Coral pendants tapped lightly against her cheeks, and the strange shape of the geranium seemed to expand into the shape of her ears. She took care of the geraniums at dawn after cleaning out the hen-coop, and she used a special fertilizer which required that Signorina Angelina crap not in the toilet but in a little pisspot which she covered with a chipped flowered plate to keep off the flies.

In the house adjacent to Angelina's lived three young men, probably with their families, but we knew nothing about them. They rushed through the piazza smoking cigarettes, and occasionally gave an idle kick to our ball. We began a relationship with the young males only when one of them died. There was one whose house lay in the stretch between Santa Maria del Mare and Metamunno. We all went into the bedroom: he was lying on an iron bedstead against the wall, a white damask cloth strewn with comfits covered him chest-high, all around there were lilies, sprigs of jasmine, freesias, and a profusion of roses with worm-eaten petals. He was as beautiful as could be, dark-skinned, his hair cropped because he was a soldier, the face plump and tranquil. He seemed to be lying there waiting to become part of one of those loving couples in the postcards; all he needed was his cheeks to be painted red; or, with that elegant suit and tie, he might have been ready to set off on a rapid trip to the Americas.

In front of the landowner's house were the three church buildings: the façade of the church itself, the bell-tower, the house of the parish priest. A single gateway led to the priest's house and to that of Antima and her children. Don Candido, always up and about, went through the village umbrella in hand even on fine days, as if to give himself standing; in fact almost nobody had an umbrella and when it rained they shielded their heads with bits of waxed cloth. Donna Antima was in service with the priest; and the word was that her daughter, Antonia, was having it off with him. Antonia was blonde with curly permed hair and washed-out blue eyes in a pale and bony face. Donna Antima and her daughter would address us in honeyed tones and almost always in Italian. And when they drove us away, they never used bad language like the other women, but said 'Shoo, shoo' as if we were chicks. Criato, Antima's other child, was the village idiot; he would leave the piazza in the early morning with five sheep and come back in the evening. Sometimes as we played we came across him in the countryside and made fun of him; his blurred and guttural voice would follow after us.

When Criato was very unhappy he would take his clothes off in the fields and shake them threateningly in the direction of the village. We liked to watch him piss. 'Go on, have a piss!' we would say. He would pull out his part★ – which was what we children called it – and point it upwards to make as high a jet as possible, then he would hold it in his hand smiling proudly, catching the last drop on his fingertip and putting it in his mouth.

The interior of the church was in that rustic baroque one finds in the fondant-covered biscuits the nuns make in those regions, or in certain Easter cakes covered in meringue and tiny coloured comfits. On the right of the high altar, balancing the pulpit, towered a large white marble statue of the Madonna, donated in 1915 by the mother of a minor aristocrat from the village, sister to our grandmother, as an offering for the safe return of her son from the war. Above the high altar there was a fresco showing an extraordinary young man with an azure tunic and blond hair, hugging a lamb in his

★ It has cost me much fatigue to go through all the facts recounted in this tale. Then to revise the text, so that it satisfies memory and the reader, has required a certain labour. Here, for example, in the first draft I had written 'prick'. That was a lazy accommodation to fashion, a sign also of a certain senility of thought, but above all a serious mis-use of language because in those days this part of the body, like many another thing, had for us no name. It was in fact called 'the fact', 'the whatsit', or 'the this', or 'the that'. Correct, in fact, was 'the part' or 'the piece', at least for us girls, while the remainder was the body. Part, therefore, not of a boy's body, but of a cosmic and mysterious body. With this 'part' was associated a numinous quality which therefore cannot be rendered by terms like 'penis' or 'prick'. The first because of the obvious limit of the exact sciences, the second because, as with all obscene language, it reduces the numinous to a merely base and infernal force, whereas an essential feature of the numinous is its ambiguity.

arms, who seemed intent on informing me that I wasn't fit to live.

All the flowers in the village and the surrounding area, apart from the geraniums, seemed to be grown for the cemetery or the church which were always decked out with them: white, blue, purple irises, stupid and puffed-up calla lilies towering over the other flowers, hawthorn, jonquils and carnations, dog-roses and garden roses, yellow, white, sometimes of an emphatic red, swollen, soon blown and drooping, wasp-eaten and infested by ants, no sooner open than the petals would fall. In the half-shadow there would be a busy coming and going of old women changing the water, trimming stems, stripping off rotten leaves and replacing the flowers in the vases of blue opal or frosted glass; a heavy odour always hung about inside, putrid and sweet.

At Easter, corn-stalk wound round with strands of red wool germinated in dozens of vases; on the side-altars bizarre compositions appeared: pine-cones in which, weeks earlier, lentil seeds had been set and which germinated with a Germanic gentleness; or twisted and dwarfish succulents in small vases, the childish sports of the old women. The church would be hung with black and silver and banners of varied and conflicting colours. When newly-weds left the church the fathers threw sugared almonds to the watching children – coins even, if they were rich – and we would dive into the scrimmage to grab them. The smaller children cried since they never got anything.

On Sundays everybody went to church in their best. In spring after the war the young women and the girls were a gala of clothes. A young man came from Metamunno to play the organ.

For its flowers, for its scents, for its splendours, for its moulderings, for its stucco, for its frescos, for its hangings and its embroidered cloths, for its gilded missals, for the solemn fervour of its sermons and its music, for its festive flowered dresses, the church was a magical sphere enclosing all the luxuries and secret unbridledness of the world. And in

34

this fulgid great sin which was the church, each Sunday I had
to confess my sins. On the first occasion I said to Don Candido: 'I haven't committed any sins.' I was kneeling in the
confessional, my eyes in the half-dark screwed up in an effort
to make out his face behind the grille, where it sometimes
seemed like a beast's in the shadow of the stables or of certain
dreams. 'It's a sin of pride not to have any sins,' said Don
Candido, and from then on, scared by the long silences between us, and by that horrible verdict, I went round my friends
asking for sins. And then I would say: 'I stole some beans, I
stole some money or some sweets.' Or: 'I've been envious,
I've been gluttonous.' But all these things didn't seem like sins
to me. The only great sin that I knew I daily committed was
that of being different from the marvellous youth in majestic
movement over the high altar. My swarthiness, my dark
eyes, my skinniness, my nocturnal frights – those, for example, were sins.

And sins, too, were my pelting races in the rain to meet my
father from the motor-coach on the New Road, running till I
dropped breathless and lay abandoned with my cheek on the
road surface; or when I ran in one breath from the rock of the
Annunciata to the piazza, with my arms over my head, never
stopping; or when at nine in the evenings I wouldn't come in
from play in the piazza and heard my mother's futile calling,
mingling or alternating with the other women's. Each window had its voice, whether tired and tame, or imploring and
nagging, or furious, or sharp and peremptory, or uncaring
and distracted, or loving and fetching. These were sins. They
were not sins of disobedience as I confessed to Don Candido,
but of incontinence, even if I didn't know how to say so
because it was not among the words I knew then.

Also a sin was my terror of lightning, when I hid trembling
under the table in the kitchen, which looked out on the open
country where the storms crossed the valley.

Certainly Don Candido had no understanding of sins: in the
great sin of his church he moved about like a book-keeper,
ministering the sacraments and quick slaps to the children.

35

With the profound contempt that I felt for him, contenting himself with silly little sins and fooling himself every Sunday when he thought he was absolving my torments and my unconfessable rapture, there was mixed a kind of social contempt inculcated by our mother, who was sceptical about church matters; and, with opposite motives, by our grandmother, who compared Don Candido to altogether different priests and especially to the saints. So going to church on Sundays became part of one's social duties, from which, by a privilege reserved for grown-ups, our mother was exempt.

Flanked by the bakery and the wall of the church was the opening of the little street that led to the New Road. On the right was the carter who sold vegetables and slept in front of his store in the early afternoons. He was fat with a large belly half uncovered – he could never find vests his size – and had a son as fat as himself called Totore, who was one of our playmates. The carter was a jovial man and a great gossip. It was he who brought the news from Althenopis where he went one night a week to sell his vegetables in the market. Beside him on the cart he would set a basket with his bite for two days, a flask of wine, and two copper pans that he used in the city as helmets against the bombing. We gave bits of carrot and mouldy fennel to the donkey and he patted it and promised it a fabulous harness if it would take him quickly into town. The least ornamental was to be red with brass buckles, but he also promised twenty-four-carat gold with silver bells and velvet cloth. 'When the war is over I'll buy them for you,' he would say in a singsong.

One time he brought back a large blonde doll with its belly torn open and a missing leg, almost as big as my sister; he had come across it in a bombed-out house. Once a week he took a soup made from seven particular vegetables to a woman in Althenopis. Should he add *borrana*★ and a bit of pig's skin she

★ Althenopis dialect: borage, medicinal herbaceous plant, with oval leaves covered in rough hairs. It has a blue flower and the tips and leaves can be cooked. The Decumani midwife used to prepare her 'married' soup even in wartime, to comfort the offence to her bowels of so many deaths – she, who would give him a tip with tears in her eyes. 'It's as if the war were over,' she would say; and she tipped him almost every time with a *bonbonnière* for she was the midwife of the Decumani district and everyone took her sugared almonds. After the Liberation the tips were more substantial because an American soldier, the son of her brother who had emigrated, kept heaping her with tins of stuff, cigarettes and candies.

The carter also took baskets of lemons to a place in Via del Serraglio where the lemons were just a front for anti-Fascist propaganda. He would laugh till his belly shook as he told us this but we couldn't understand the reason for his chuckles. Often in the city women ordered large bundles of parsley and on those occasions also he would laugh and chant: 'It's not bad, it's not bad, parsley and *purchiachella*★ salad!' When he loaded the lettuces on the cart, in neat rows with the hearts all opening one way, he would sing a song about a lettuce on the bottom of the sea, pat the donkey on the back, do the same for his son, and then make a waltzing twirl with another bundle of lettuce before setting it alongside the others. He always had a flask of wine beside the door of the shop, wrapped in cabbage-leaves when the sun was on it, which he offered to the men going by and to the old women, who waved it away. He would drink, wipe his mouth with the back of his hand and tell us how his great belly had saved him from the war, since they hadn't been able to come up with a uniform his size. He had got himself diagnosed as dropsical. And he laughingly claimed that it wasn't water swelling his belly but wine. He hid bottles of olive-oil under the vegetables on the cart to sell

---

aided entry into the land of the living. Some skin from a pig, and where possible even a bit of meat, is set to simmer in salted water. When the skin is almost cooked the vegetables are added: chicory, various kinds of broccoli, cabbage, etc., and the essential ingredient, borage, which is rare in city markets because it grows wild and since it is prickly, children, whose allotted task it is to collect such things avoid it as they do thistles.

When skin or meat are not included the soup is simple and no longer 'married'.

★ Althenopis dialect: purslane, lit. maiden's vulva. Infusions of parsley are a well-known abortive agent.

on the black market, and when he went about at night he was more afraid of the customs and excise than he was of bandits.

One evening the carter came dancing up to the tobacconist's entirely drunk, shaking a bundle of newspapers like a tambourine. 'The war's over!' – he clamoured – 'The war's over!' It was true. The war was over. His loud summons at the edge of the village boomed through the piazza and everybody came to windows and out on to the street in wonder. We stopped our playing and crowded round the tobacconist's in mute expectation. He had heard it that morning in Althenopis. And he waved the newspapers he had got from the opponents of Fascism, the people who pretended to sell lemons, until the tobacconist snatched them from him and set about reading them. And while people were running up he went down towards the piazza with the cart; and we, our first surprise over, skipped round him while the tobacconist brought up the procession spelling out the headlines. All the village gathered in the piazza, and from window to window and door to door the word ran: 'The war's over!' Everybody began hugging everyone else; the women were crying; Don Candido was called to open the church. Criato, Donn'Antima's son, went to ring the bells. Don Candido wept on the steps of the church and said: 'Thanks be to God, the war is over!' Our mother had heard it on the radio two hours earlier but hadn't said a word, either because she didn't think the news of any great importance, or because, distrustful and hard to convince she had thought it a lie. She didn't believe in the radio or the newspapers, but only in books. And then, whom should she have told? She wasn't like the others. She didn't even tell Granny. Only when she saw the crowd in the piazza and heard the word going round from door to door, from window to window, did she pull herself together, get out of bed, and lean on the window-sill with her hair damp from vinegar. Grandmother ran down the stairs, her hair in a mess and covered in the dust of the attic she was tidying.

With tears in her eyes, careless of the conventions of her rank, she knelt on the steps of the church to thank God and beseech him to bring back soon from the Indies her prisoner grandson.

When Criato finished ringing the bells and came down into the piazza red and panting, radiant with joy and self-importance, the carter took his hand, and with a gesture half burlesque and half serious, bent and kissed it. Criato burst into tears and in his blurry voice stuttered out a sound which seemed to want to mean 'The war's over!' 'ar's . . . ar's . . .', he went on saying. We gazed in silence and nobody mimicked him.

The women carried chairs out into the piazza, the men began to arrive with the *cacciate*,* some bringing out fennel, some cheese, or wine, walnuts, hazelnuts. Somebody brought out good bread, not the everyday bread that tasted of diesel. And all evening long people stayed up drinking, dancing, chatting, and with an extension from the church the radio was set up to address the piazza. From the window Mother called us in, but to no point; then, as if ashamed, she withdrew into the shadow.

Some days later we were playing on the New Road. Two jeeps arrived with the Americans. They seemed like royal swans. The moment they saw us lined up on the road, as if in church or school, they came to a stop. Out of a truck they dug wrapped white loaves cut in slices, and we devoured those heavenly slices with our eyes half-closed. They also took out packets of sweets, round with a hole, yellow, green and red and strawberry flavoured, blocks of chocolate, little tubes with strange pastes, light and dark brown, which we couldn't even guess at. They also gave us pamphlets and we all wanted one, and we went down to the village waving them, with our pockets and aprons crammed; the boys had taken off their shirts to hold their goodies. The soldiers followed us, they hadn't known that the fork off the New Road led to a village. Santa Maria del Mare wasn't marked on the map. Everybody came to the window to look at them and they waved back.

* Althenopis dialect: offerings of coffee, cakes, liqueurs and ice-cream on holiday occasions or when visitors come. Though the offering can also be of olives, cheese, salami, wine.

They began to take photographs, picking out children, myself and my sister and brother among them, and posing us against the wall. They handed out money to everyone, hundred-lire pieces the like of which we had never seen, and in a waving of arms and smiles they disappeared in an azure cloud, like gods.

3
The cottage

The windows of our house looked out on the piazza. You could tell immediately that it was a makeshift house. The small finishing touches that you give to a house where you have lived a long time and love, were lacking. The surround of the window, for example, always painted in vivid colours, was missing, the pots for flowers and succulents lacked their iron stands, the very flowers were lacking; no one bothered to pull out the wallflowers and the toadflax from the cracks in the stonework or from the tiles edging the roof. The windows were dusty; looking at them you would have thought the inhabitants long gone or just moved in. For all those years Mother considered the place provisional, in effect, and never wanted to leave a mark that hinted at definite settlement.

The sticks of furniture were few and poor: some iron bed-frames, a few stools with straw seats, a couple of tables, some pots and pans, a sewing-machine, a wardrobe. Not once did she try to make it more home-like with a cretonne bedspread, a vase of flowers, an ornament, a rug. It always had to look like an emergency arrangement, a house for evacuees where people had been forced to take shelter because of some drastic turn of events. We children had our beds in one room and in the other there was the wardrobe, our mother's bed, a folding bed which could be rigged up beside it when our father came, and the sewing-machine; then there was Grandmother's room, which became the dining-room for our father's visits; a cane armchair with a yellow cushion fringed in purple which our mother had brought with her from the sold-off villa, the only superfluous thing in the room and in the house. Granny would sit in the chair to tell us fairytales and the lace of her dress and the swirls of the woven cane were echoed in her voice; there Mother would solemnly sit with a photograph album on her knees and tell us about our past and warn us not to let the piazza children make barbarians of us. A hallway remote from the bedrooms was the only place we were free to play and invite our friends. In one corner Grandmother had built the little shrine to St Antony. From the hallway you went upstairs to a large room which was the scullery; here were hung the sorb-apples, sprigs of bay, strings of garlic and onion; laid out on straw there were apples – St Agathas, biffins, rennets, pippins – and potatoes; a locked cupboard held the sugar, the bottles of oil, some jars of lard and the candles; here the ironing board was kept. Here Grandmother came to cry in secret when a letter arrived from her prisoner grandson and here she came in secret to pray. She feared the scorn of our mother, to whom praying and weeping were shameful, an outrage to reason.

Different members of the family called the house different things. Mother contemptuously called it 'the hole', 'the shelter'; our father, trying to be ironic, called it 'the nest'; Grandmother instead called it 'the cottage', as in the lyrics of the songs she sang to me from the cane chair, songs in which there was always a little house the colour of red comfits, complete with grape arbour.

When we came to Santa Maria del Mare everything, you might say, was already over between myself and my parents. Mother had a remorseless sense of reality. When the warship took us away from Porto Quì, the beautiful island where we had lived happily, she did not shed a single tear; with me, the eldest, alongside her, she leant over the bulwark of the ship, dug the house-key out of her bag and threw it into the sea, saying: 'We shan't ever be happy again as we were here.'

I had never understood whether my father was to be taken seriously or whether he was acting a part. Even my mother was always telling him to stop playing the clown. At one moment he seemed a comedian and the next, a tragic actor.

The enigma: is he acting, does he mean it? is he play-acting, is he serious? was fascinating to me. But on his return from the prison camp in Tangiers, whenever he joined us at Santa Maria del Mare, the cabaret act had been transformed into a walk-on part. Perhaps it had been the repeated blows of those years: the fall of Fascism; his own personal fall; the squalor of his lowly job at the Ministry and of the bedsit he inhabited in the capital; the death of his mother, to whom he had been very deeply attached.

Everything was over between me and them because they denied me the only two consolations that life held: fairytales and theatre.

I used to dream in that period that I wasn't really the daughter of my mother and father, that there had been a mix-up over babies and that my real mother was a gypsy. In the dream the gypsy had the features of Dida, my wet-nurse on Porto Quì. 'Nonsense!' my mother said when I told her my obsessive dream. But for days I continued to compare the whiteness of her skin with the darkness of mine. I told the dream to Grandmother. 'Me too, me too!' said Grandmother. 'When I was a girl I thought the same thing.' In some of my rows with my mother I would accuse her of not loving me as a daughter; and to back my suspicions I would tell her that Granny had thought the same thing herself. Mother would become very bitter at that: 'Grandmother would do better not to encourage your fantasies. I could well credit the same thing myself from the way she treated me compared to my sister!'

Throughout her immensely long girlhood Mother had spent six months each year with her mother in a remote villa in the country. In that solitude, broken only by reading and the rare visit of a friend or relation, she had become a companion of nature: the shifting skies – in our part of the world the skies are very changeable, as if the Creator had wished to enclose in a perfect microcosm, tempering their harsh extremes, all the possibilities of nature – the cliffs, the sea and the exuberant Mediterranean vegetation, which in the hills overlooking the villas intermingles with Nordic plants, almost as if hinting at a possible community of peoples, and not just of plant species. And up there Mother had taken pleasure in reading *The Duino Elegies*. She climbed rocks, contemplated sunsets, showed curiosity or reverence for the lives of the insects; she sampled the beauty of grass stalks or the bark of tree trunks, went out to greet the dawn without needing an alarm-clock; she didn't quicken her pace during storms but plunged herself into them, her clothes and face drenched, her eyes dazzled by the lightning; and she would stretch out for long, long periods under clouded skies through which the sun plunges in straight white spokes; or under skies scrubbed blank, like an unwritten page, a future to fulfil, the ninth life to live.

And then, poor woman, a virgin bride of thirty-six, she had her ninth life; and from that mineral and vegetable nature she passed into the bloody, moist, sweaty nature of the marital embrace, of childbirth, of milk and of rhagades. So that she whose forebears were vegetable – to whose ear the maidenhair would bend, whose legs were reeds, in whose eyes the blue of flowers, the delicate grey of moss, and at times the icy emerald of the sea would be reflected – had tumbled into the third realm: the zoological kingdom. On with the blood, the milk, the humours, the sweat. And looming over everything, the 'things on her mind'. Her inwardness with the two natures had in part preserved her from the rituals and manners of her class; or perhaps her being the last of the children, the least attractive, the least gifted and the most neglected; or perhaps those years of penny-pinching; or the memory of her generous and ever heroic grandfathers; and even that piety of her mother which she mocked.

In those post-war years, alone with us children, almost entombed in yet another rustic exile, short of money and lacking even the distraction of her youthful beauty by then, she nevertheless gave the best of herself; those two natures, the vegetable and the animal, came together far from the realm of duties and *bienséances*. Or so it appeared to us children at least.

At school one year I learnt the use of parentheses; it seemed to me that Mother, who knows when, perhaps when we left the beautiful island, or perhaps even long before I was born, had put herself in parentheses. Even the walls of that house enclosed her like parentheses seemingly made of time: on one side there was the wall of the day we came, and on the other the wall of the day we would leave. But on occasion she would come out.

When they brought her a walnut, or a fresh-plucked almond, or a bunch of violets or narcissi, or a clump of tiny tormentil leaves, or the first spring beans, or a handful of rocket gathered below the Annunziata, or just a potato with a weird shape, or a pine-cone which opened to disclose its pine-nuts on the fire – her gaze, her nostrils, her smile would quiver; and her hands would fly to the freshness of those things as they never had to some novelty of fashion; then we would see revealed a child-mother, a playmate, so far removed from that other one of the Swiss manuals, the rows with Grandmother, and the perennial migraines.

In autumn or spring we would go to the wood of Schiazzano to gather chestnuts, pick violets or cyclamens, fish for tadpoles. They also sent us to collect snails, but we handled those unwillingly because we didn't like them. The boys would go into the stream in their underpants, splash about and swim. The girls weren't supposed to do so, and if one of the little ones started undressing, the bigger ones would stop her and put her clothes back on. Then we would lie on the grass. The sun above would burn our legs and the grass beneath would cool them. There were flowers whose stems had bitter, strident juices, which we sucked like a dewy lemonade; leaves of catmint, of mint and tormentil to chew; cyclamens with an earthy smell and cool petals which we placed on the tips of our tongues; bitter chestnuts that made our mouths go wry. Chatter and laughter broke into that continual chewing. Or handsprings or cartwheels. It was an abandonment of bodies, a lapping in the light and grass.

We went there at Christmas-time also, to dig the clay for

moulding the shepherds and to pluck mistletoe for the crib; the star-shaped mistletoe grew in the meadows, the kind with long fronds lay up the mountain, adapting to the bleakness of its habitat. There was little to be found on the ground in that season, a few dry leaves; the trees were bare, immobile in the windless air, filtering the tepid and insubstantial sun. All that side of the village was Nordic and in winter we avoided it. The rest of the land around was vivid with citrus fruit instead, mostly orange and lemon trees, which shone under the straw matting almost as if the sun had abandoned the circle of the heavens to hide beneath, there to grow and ripen; and in February the scent of mimosa wafted on the air; and eagerly everywhere the geraniums. Even on the Annunziata the rocks, though still moist from recent rain and apparently stunned by the thunder and the lightning, gleamed in the noon light. And everywhere around, in all the fields, the close-packed terraces and the paths, behind every field wall, the blossoming of birdsong, of the voices of labourers, of children, colourful with their woollies and burdens. And on the frames of windows hung pots of trefoil.

Our mother preferred the wood in winter. Perhaps because in summer, given incipient arteriosclerosis, it frightened her. Or because the sun in flush brought on the flushes of her climacteric. In summer she stayed behind the shutters, stretched out on the bed with a vinegar-soaked rag on her forehead, waiting for the evening. Or perhaps because the summer reminded her of sunbathing when she was young – now she no longer dared expose her body to the public gaze; or perhaps only because, so foreign to the village, she loved that foreign landscape.

But in winter, or preferably when autumn had set in, or at the start of spring, she responded as it were to the call of her youthful walks. Then on certain Sundays she would lead us to the wood. On Sundays it was not until the late afternoon that the band of children congregated in the piazza; they were all busy washing, getting dressed up for Mass or a visit to relations; and then came the grand lunch with macaroni and meat.

46

In our house though, there were no Sunday rituals, lunch was the same as every day. We sat by the stream and she dispensed bread and hard-boiled eggs or bread and salami or bread and cheese or slices of baked-up macaroni, or potato *gatto*★; and when the great hunger of the war was over, all this food together. During the war, in the absence of the owners, every inhabitant of the village had claimed a strip of the wood where they would gather chestnuts, the staple food of those years. We, the last-comers, and gentry as well, had no strip of wood and had to buy our chestnuts. But Agnese let me gather them secretly with her, and Totore did the same thing for our brother.

After lunch Mother sat reading or mending by the stream, while we wandered around with baskets. Mother always read books in French, because French for her was the only culture. Thus the close family community was recreated in the woods, brought back together by the memory of past cosmopolitan splendours, by the use of Italian, by being cut off from the dialect and, above all, from the friends of the piazza. Fresh from study – it was autumn and at the start of the year the schoolmistress had dictated the fable of St Francis and the wolf – we asked whether wolves roamed the woods; Mother mocked us with a 'Whatever next!' – as if we were speaking of fables – in the tone she used to repulse our attentions whenever she was stricken with a slight illness and we enquired after her health. Forced to defend her life with a daily punctilio, she had become so prosaic that she no longer believed in fables nor in death nor in love.

Her skin was white, with blue furrows on wrists and legs; her thin body softened at the stomach and breasts; and if it hadn't been for that whiteness of wrist, her hands might have passed for those of a young artisan: working hands but delicate, with large luminous nails. But already in those years you glimpsed the cruel purity of the skeleton, and the harsh blue that furrowed the back of her hands spoke of fatigue and the

★ Althenopis dialect: *gatto*, potato purée baked in the oven.

secret travail of the blood. I did not see her face steady and whole, it was made up of fleeting expressions, grimaces, looks pinned on. But there was surely something in it that contradicted her body. How in fact could that body, soft, though lean and hardworking, go with the ridiculous little brown hat she dug out at the end of the war, and wore as if out of some stubborn whim whenever she went into town? Or the lipstick that stiffened her lips, that rendered her untouchable, made her look in the half-dark like a wax seal or an outrage in the light, and held her back from our faces, forced her to turn away from our goodnight kisses on the rare occasions she went out visiting? And we, who wanted everything and everybody in brotherhood, looked on that lipstick as a piece of arrogance, a setting herself apart from the other women of the village.

Yet in the last years of our stay, American love-films reached even there, and the daughters of the villas came back in summer and hid in their bikinis behind the rocks; with the result that some of the village girls put on lipstick too when they went on saints' days to villages around. And the orange, purple or carmine heart-shapes seemed silly and transitory playthings, rare butterflies, poised on those country faces. Once out of the village the girls put on their lipstick as they walked along, elbowing each other and giggling. When anyone passed they hid behind their hands or large white handkerchiefs embroidered on one side only; their game was like the one we children played when we stuck geranium petals over our nails or made ourselves hairdos out of straw. Whereas what Mother did was not a game, it was a rite.

Nor was the red flush that rose up her cheeks as far as the temples, and spread over her neck when angry or during the lengthy migraines, in harmony with that diaphanous white body; nor the fragile fear that made a child of her whenever a butterfly or some other insect hovered round her and a palpitation of eyelashes, of gestures, of voice, even of chin and cheeks would invincibly take hold of her.

Her eyes, though, were in tune with that body; wide green

eyes, vague from myopia or from the passive and puzzled way the world mirrored itself in them. But of the other two shades to be found there, light blue and grey, it was the grey that became ever more dominant with the passage of years. Though on occasion still bluish, they were more often solely and inexorably grey. The vicissitudes of life had transformed her from Diana tender and strong, first into a mother and a lady, then into just a poor woman.

In that wood I would be overcome with pity for her. It stunned me that in the harshest period of the war she was barred from gathering chestnuts; she couldn't because of her position, join the other women combing through the wood – the wood that belonged to her cousin – and later when the worst of the famine was over, it made me pity her again that she had to collect them in company with the poorest women in the village, the wives of the day-labourers or bricklayers, or with the cobbler's wife whose children had tuberculosis.

What bound us together in that wood was less the splendours of the past than our present state of need. Compared with the other children's families, we had less to eat because we didn't produce anything. This, and the fact that Mother was a non-believer, was the reason we didn't get presents on feasts and name-days. Nor did we have the rustling summer dresses of our playmates which made them clumsy at parties, nor the expensive presents, bought less, it seemed, for the children's pleasure than to proclaim their parents' status. But we did have the perennial richness of the Italian language, which had still not freed itself from the awkwardnesses of a foreign language – a hangover from our exotic past. The supreme bond, though, was that basket from which the food was dispensed, and our great childish hunger, which was Mother's joy.

In our home, and in other homes in the village, there were various portents which enabled us to foresee that the group of children would one day be disbanded. The aspirations and designs of our parents cast over each of us a light that was sometimes reassuring, sometimes sinister. The elder sister of my friend Agnese was destined to become a schoolmistress. Since the family couldn't afford to educate more than one, when Agnese was eight it had been decided she was to be a seamstress and marry her cousin, a factory-worker in New Zealand. Maruzzella's elder brother was going to make mozzarella; and the baker's eldest son, even though he loved the guitar – they engaged him for weddings as far away as Metamunno – would have to go on with the baking. And the housekeeper's young daughter was destined to become the priest's mistress – at least that was the gossip. Everything was decided for us in the same way. The male would become heir to the name and carry on the family splendours; whereas I was to be the vestal virgin, tending my father's frustrated love of incunabula and history, and later, his ageing body. My little sister, the darling dumpling, the pretty one, the blonde, was to be married to a rich and refined man, preferably rich, because riches can refine, but refinement can never produce riches.

So in the woods under Mother's eye we each played out our appointed role. My little sister skipped about the grass, bracken and maidenhair; our brother, forced to take an interest in the sciences which would then shed lustre on his duties as head of the family, collected insects. And I sat beside Mother, chattering away about her past doings and sillinesses and every now and again, feigning interest, I would get her to translate a line or two of *La rotisserie de la reine Pedauque*, without understanding much. But in various ways we soon slipped through the mesh: the parlour game came to an end. I rolled in the grass or lay on my belly to inspect the earth and grass stains on the back of my knickers making Mother complain I was graceless, clumsy and common. My sister, tired of flowers, followed our brother around in his search for insects and even took over from him when boredom led him to play something else. We watched him as he pissed in an arc, trying to reach the far bank of the stream.

When dusk came on Mother made us pick up the egg-shells piece by piece, the golden brown scraps of omelette, the

50

orange peel, and put them back in the basket, or dig a hole to bury them. It wasn't only respect for unpolluted nature that drove her to make us clean up; she also seemed in a hurry to erase any trace of food around her, as if those remains concealed some presage of decadence, a mysterious and disquieting warning. She would then warn us not to adopt the dirty and untidy habits of low people.

And her words closed once more the circle of family unity to exclude others, from whom we were different.

Mother was very thrifty. So on the morning of the Epiphany all we would find were black exercise books with red borders, pencils and a few sweets. For Christmas, though, we got more impressive presents, brought by our father from the capital in shiny wrapping. While I struggled to fall asleep in my small bed, the ribbons and the wrappings strewn around the house fragmented into the bright coloured stars and spangles which formed behind my eyelids when I screwed up my eyes, but then I would hear Mother scolding Father for being spendthrift: 'We'll be forced to sell the painting if you go on like this.'

The Epiphany was entirely Mother's feast. A feast of women in general. It might also have been a feast for Grandmother but she went to her other daughter in Althenopis for feast-days.

Our first year in Santa Maria del Mare, a few days before the Epiphany, we happened to go along the path behind the village which bordered Uncle Alceste's lemon grove. Just level with the lemon grove, in a small embrasure in the stone wall, there was a well. A woman was drawing water. She was thin, tall, with her hair in a bun and a very old, cheerful, almost impudent face. The path was narrow and there wasn't room for two people. The woman stood in profile. She had an enormous high belly. Warily, so as not to attract her notice, we turned back.

When I told Mother of the old woman with the belly she blushed. 'She's got a cushion stuffed under her dress,' she said, and buried her nose in the overcoat she was turning.

51

I knew there was a baby in that belly but Mother's refusal prevented me believing it.

So perhaps for that reason as well, on the morning of the Sixth, I swore to everybody at home and in the piazza that I had seen the Witch of the Epiphany the previous night. I said that she looked like a grey stork, and wore a suit like Mother's, and that her sack was round as a belly.

Our father's rare appearances in those years always brought us face to face with the duties of our social class. The dialect expressions tolerated in our mother's presence stuck in our throats when he was there, like meatballs stolen from the kitchen.

When he was at home we all had to eat together in the dining-room, a room that, given the war, we only used as such on the occasion of visits or festivities. Some days before, after repeated urging by Mother, Grandmother would tidy up its scraps of damask, the sorbs, apples, strings of garlic and onions, and the figs that were stored there at night away from the damp which came down on the loggia. And the days when the dining-room was restored to its proper use, Granny would take the figs to her bedroom, where they invaded the marble top of the commode, the chair – on which boards were laid, covered with figs – the top of the wardrobe; and there she would sleep in the acid sweet effluvium.

When Father was away, Mother or Grandmother would make chips, and our eagerness to eat them equalled Mother's in frying them. Since chips were made only when she was in good humour, almost as if it were a way of playing with us, all four of us would be happily crammed together in the vapour rising from the fat. We would throw ourselves avidly on the crisp banquet, and our joy in Mother's cheerful mood, in that burning sensation mixed in the mouth with salt, would little by little fuse with a graver and more certain feeling of well-being as the inside of the chips melted in the mouth, the stomach felt full and satisfied and the grasping hands went out more tentatively, until she drove us away with playful threats to ensure that the whole pile didn't disappear from the dish before dinner. During Father's visits we were forbidden the kitchen and the chips lying in the *sperlonga*★ next to the boiled broccoli were no longer crisp but limp with oil, as if they too were tired of the wait, were no longer the feast in themselves but went along, abstractly, as a side dish.

When our mother was on her own and one of us reached for a piece of fruit from the dish between meals, she would warn us: 'Don't eat it all, otherwise there won't be anything for the others', or 'It's for this evening.' Whereas for our father, helping yourself to fruit was a theft: 'Don't steal the fruit,' he would say. And if we were caught in the act we had to adopt a contrite air, lower our eyes, suffer the rebuke and leave the room in silence. It was a ritualistic humiliation.

During his absence we might glance through the *Travaso* left around since his last visit, or the maid's *Grand Hotel* or a *Tarzan* I had bought on the sly. To read these papers in front of our father was to commit a misdemeanour – unworthy rather than illicit behaviour. He would stare and stare at us with grim disapproval to make us fully realize our abject state.

Once the gipsy children from the camp on the Annunziata induced us to steal some money from our mother. They dazzled us with magic objects and sweets which immediately disappeared back into their bags if we didn't produce the wherewithal: little necklaces, coloured stones, medals showing the Madonna Schiava, cardboard cylinders which you shook to make your destiny appear at the bottom, and extremely hard biscuits threaded on a string and covered in white or pink fondant. They also offered a lotion to drive away flies and wasps, but that didn't really tempt us. They were expert in our amusements, though, and enticed us with an ointment which served to make giant turds: all it required, they said, was to smear your arse before a crap. They didn't deal with us as a group but took each of us aside and whispered

★ An oval platter used for fish.

the virtues of their wares in our ears. In our band Agnese was the one who could make the biggest turds, and she laughed, smug and sure of herself, tossing her heavy blonde plaits like St Geneviève native of the woods. Her turds were spangled with the husks of beans and chickpeas because her family lived almost solely on those, or on potato, tomato and onion salads in summer. But I once got my revenge, for in one of my turds I discovered a segment of tapeworm and everybody ran up to look at it uncoiling in the still smoking element, rising up like an angelic ghost, questing, made lustrous by the air. And I felt an unspeakable happiness that I, I alone, had brought into the world that pale and mobile essence.

Any who could went off to rob their parents so as to buy those marvels. The thing was complicated for us by the fact that our father was home at the time.

Within a week he discovered that the thief wasn't the maid, but us. With charming condescension he persuaded our younger sister to tell the truth – to sneak on us, that is – because in dividing up our marvellous acquisitions we had neglected to give her her share. The smiling face became intimidating, and the caressing voice fell sternly silent. When my brother and I were within reach – he never deigned to chase after us – he grabbed us, stripped us, and spanked us in a calm and detached way, ten slaps each, not eleven and not nine, ten precisely, in homage perhaps to God the Father's discipline. We couldn't work out whether he was more wounded by the theft or by our exclusion of our sister from a share in the spoils, though the latter may just have been a fantasy of ours since the injustice to her did seem to us a graver misdemeanour than the theft. Then, and not in remembrance of the chastisements of his own youth but of the lessons he imagined the gentry's children received – he always remained the parvenu – he thundered: 'And you'll go without fruit for ten days!' unaware, poor man, that we stole fruit out in the fields and that the only real punishment would have been to deprive us of the first course or, when there was one, of the second. But Mother was to blame for that, for on the days our father was there, at who knows what cost, she tried to recreate the gentleman's lunch (first course, second, vegetable and fruit), which each and every day was regularly crippled by the wartime shortages (and sometimes she would ask me in a shamefaced whisper to bring her back an apple, or a walnut, or an orange from our raids, almost as if it weren't hunger that prompted the request but an irrational craving, a whim of memory, a residual childish gluttony). And still for three days of marital and paternal bliss she strove to recreate the proper sequence of courses!

The ridiculous humiliation of those spankings helped me understand that we children were outsiders in the common-wealth of the piazza. I didn't dare tell my friends of the punishment simply because it was ridiculous, grotesque. Those slaps in fact weren't slaps, they were a ritual of good manners. When the other children were beaten they were really beaten and would come up to us all swollen, covered in bruises, their eyes stricken, yet straightaway ready to laugh and play; and after pulling up their sleeves or opening their shirts to show us red or purple welts they would pull marbles out of a tattered pocket and say: 'Want a game?'

The fathers of the others also had sharper contours distinguishing them from the women; they were force and domination, abundance at times also since they alone might hand out the left-overs. At table those fathers always helped themselves first, taking the best and the largest portion, while the women and children waited on them. They would beat the male children and at table laughed with greasy mouths and put a tidbit into the hands of the youngest or thrust it into their mother's toothless mouth, or into their wife's, who would cover her face with shame.

But over and above every social requirement inculcated by our father stood the commandment that we come to know the difference between ourselves and others. In those years Mother tempered the harshness of this commandment and of others. And the severe paternal lessons could well be left as indications rather than rules because his long absences made it impossible for him to set down, as he would have liked, a *Book of Hours*. The book was already written and the best he could do was to go over the commentary.

When Father came to Santa Maria del Mare he would sometimes take us for a walk.

Murat's villa was his favourite destination. In those years it was a spectral place, always closed; bougainvillaea had overgrown doors and windows. A marble slab recollected heroes and the sighting of ships. The gracious eighteenth-century villa rose out of that absolute wilderness. Father would read the slab aloud or insist that our brother stumble his way through.

Standing in front of the slab, my father would exhort me to become a librarian when I grew up and to study history, and revulsion at a future as guardian of stones and spectres rooted itself in me more stubbornly. How was it possible – I asked myself – to reconcile my father's high, extremely white forehead, the silvery-black wave of his hair, the shape of his slightly aquiline nose, with the fatuous irony of his gaze, in particular with his swollen, almost flaccid belly, and the thing I had glimpsed him doing, his pissing into a small chamber-pot with nothing on except a pyjama-top, a woollen vest hanging down beneath.

And when he talked to me about Murat in the fire and smoke of battle, or about the splendour of the royal palace in Althenopis, the image of a half-naked man awkwardly pissing would overlay what he was saying. When our mother pissed it didn't upset me, on the contrary it made me feel tender towards her, remembering the way she took care of me and the hot childish jet of urine between her legs. In the toilet, when our father had been – though it happened with the other men in the family as well – drops of urine would be left on the bowl; the smell of cigarettes mingled with that of shit; damp, stained newspapers lay on the floor. At table our father would talk of Charles V or of the great Charles III of Bourbon, later king of Spain; but he was continually interrupting his evocations with mean little outbursts of impatience when the pasta wasn't quite cooked as it should be, there was too much oil on the peppers, or the fish had too many bones.

Once, after a visit more prolonged and tedious than the rest,★ during which he had inflicted on us his historical anecdotes and his plans for his children's future, I led an expedition to Murat's villa. We set off with bits and pieces of charcoal to scribble on walls or road in our games. We climbed the wall, scratched and pricked ourselves on the spiky bougainvillaea, and gorged on the unripe apples. In our urge to profane the place we slashed the leaves of prickly pears with bamboo knives to make the sap flow; we trampled on the wild strawberries and didn't even spare the capers in our eagerness to destroy. We toured the outside of the house and stopped in astonishment before a window with open shutters. Only the glass remained to protect the house. We stood there a long while in puzzlement. We set to shouting: 'Muratte, Muratiello!' No one appeared. Cautiously we approached the window. Photographs of a man on a horse hung on the white walls. The man looked like our mother's first love whom I had seen in the family album. He had riding boots, a white shirt slightly blouson, and his hair was parted in the centre. We didn't dare break the window. Mariarosa said that the pictures in her mother's bedroom were better, with gold frames and cherubs and pink Madonnas. The frozen splendours of the villa disappointed us; there was even a glimpse of an art nouveau console which looked like a dragonfly. We set off running round the villa again, brandishing our sticks. To the left of the portal, under the slab, we drew our battle-sign in charcoal: an obscene symbol which we then thought was a war sign. One boy, heedless of the sacrilege, drew his dog. But someone else added testicles below. We scuttled away, afraid of being seen by Augusto or Uncle Alceste.

Augusto was a young man who lived in a private wing of the seminary building with his old mother and a retinue of old

★ Our father's arrivals were the pleasure, not his visits; and his departures were sad. The space of time between the joy of his arrival and the sadness of departure was one long tedium.

relatives. He came from a rich family fallen on hard times. They had once owned the whole palace but more than fifty years ago had sold to the priests the part now occupied by the seminary. The part given over to the hospice had been expropriated in Garibaldi's day because held in mortmain, but the municipality later restored it to the nuns for a peppercorn rent.

Augusto was one of the few young men who hadn't gone off to war, because he had had meningitis as a child, or so they said. It was also said that he had been a student in Althenopis for interminable years – he was thirty-five by then – but had broken off his studies because of the war. He was a frequent visitor to Murat's villa and would arrive with a book and a folding stool, sit himself down in the sun and begin to read. We couldn't understand why he didn't sit on a boulder or a wall. Once he left the stool behind and we saw to it that he found somebody had crapped on it.

Uncle Alceste also went to Murat's villa. But that was only after the war because, like all the landowners and gentry of the area, he had fled the village. In fact they had feared a landing, and since the gentry couldn't live all that time cut off like hermits, they had all got together in cosmopolitan Corento. All those years, then, the villas were closed up. The gentry were also afraid that the turmoil of the war would increase social unrest and that the local poor egged on by the factors, would rob or kill them. Indeed at various times thieves broke into Uncle's house in those years, and stole the year's oil, disdaining the precious trinkets, the paintings, the silver, whose value they either didn't suspect or feared might betray them. Uncle then would go and watch the sunset from an eighteenth-century belvedere at the villa. Before leaving the house he would inform his mother who, fragile and terrible, would lean out of a high window waving and saying goodbye. We spied on him from behind the bushes as he contemplated the sunset, a contemplation that seemed very queer to us; how could such small eyes as ours see and not be seen by an eye as immense as that of the sun, lost and fixed in the water and the sky.

Our irreverence showed itself not just in our hostile silence but also in acts of grossness. It would happen for example that as Uncle left the village and made slowly for the Belvedere, we were ahead of him like lightning, leaping from one terrace to another, scrambling up the rocks to get there before him and make the gracious eighteenth-century parapet filthy with our shit, so that quite disgusted, turning his helpless gaze this way and that, he had no alternative but to retrace his steps.

4

The paths

The piazza was not a closed universe to us; each day we took a road, a path, a stair leading out of it. The old path which began with the steps for Metamunno; the Castle lane; the path for the Annunziata; the shortcut which went from rock to rock along the mountain also to Metamunno; the steep lane for Marciano, which led out of the piazza under an archway; the New Road, which going down led again to Metamunno, but going up, instead, to Le Tore, to Santa Maria della Neve, fabulous above the Bays, to Le Tre Sante, to Termini finally, and to Ieros;★ the woodland path towards Schiazzano, and beyond, by another little lane, to Monticchio; but it was by leaping down from terrace to terrace, avoiding roads and paths, that we reached the sea.

Roads and paths in fact we only took to fulfil social obligations; we took the road, for example, to go to school; we took the path to go and visit old Signora Galapaga who lived in a villa on the way to Marciano; and the path again to go to the cemetery or to other villages on feast-days. But always when going to the sea we leapt down from terrace to terrace as if drawn by an irresistible call; or when we were out playing, or

★ The 'finally' should, according to the rules, have preceded Ieros: 'to Termini, and finally, to Ieros'. But Ieros was a place extremely far away where you might have gone but didn't. More than the distance, it was the numinous quality of the name that held us back. At one bound of our world therefore, beyond Termini, there was Ieros; and at the other, under the mountain that separated it from the city, were the model stables of Don Aniello. But while we once got to the stables of Don Aniello, we never got to Ieros.

looking for chestnuts, or cyclamens, or salad, or to make dreams or flight from the world come true. Sometimes we would go for a holiday along a path – it was always in spring. We didn't play truant, instead we left the house earlier, driven forth by some fervour in the air. There was no hurry then. Or coming home we let ourselves be drawn by that ferment of sun and weeds in flower, which grew thicker in the early hours of the afternoon.

Often the path led us into new realms, of the horrible or the marvellous.

Santa Maria Annunziata was dominated by the horrible, not so much because the path led to the cemetery with its flowers and silence, but because it went through the place where the poor lived. No piazza had arisen there courtesy of the eighteenth-century gentry. In times past a fortress had stood on the rock as a bastion against the Saracens; then a church had been built on it and a convent, which housed the derelict old in one wing and the young seminarists in the other. And around them, almost as if to underline the enlightened eighteenth century architectural mercy for the needy, the houses of the poor had clustered. It was, so to speak, the slums of Santa Maria del Mare, where those who were not the heirs of long-established farmers, those who were not in business nor had a trade, those who owned no land, nor even rented it, might find refuge. The miseries, trials and mishaps of life and the world seemed to have arranged a rendezvous. There lived the sailor who had travelled the globe to return not rich in tales and savings, but maimed in body and soul; and every day on the doorstep of the house his eldest daughter would delouse her brothers and sisters; beautiful children the ex-sailor had, very pale, with great dark eyes and long unkempt hair which every now and again would disappear, lopped by the razor when the lice crowded too thick for other remedy or the scabs were too numerous on their scalps; then their shining skulls would be covered with the yellow gleam of a sulphur ointment. There lived the farm-hand who had been struck by lightning and lost

61

an arm, with the blind wife who had given him no children. And there lived two old lags who had done a great many years in prison, one of them a Sicilian shepherd exiled for sheep-stealing, who had finished up there, Lord knows how, far from his native soil. All around lay the houses of poor farm-hands, day-labourers and even beggars; a swarm of women, old men and thieving boys who hit us and sneered whenever we went by. And we had to pass through their very midst, as kings pass through the storms of revolution.

It was there, also, that the gypsies could rely on complicity and a helping hand and only there did they manage to camp; and not only the gypsies but others fleeing the rout of war.

Young single women from distant provinces landed up in a neat little room let out by the convent. For two years a schoolmistress stayed there, for another two a post office employee. The schoolmistress was tall, slim, with long blonde hair gathered up in a bun. She said she was Venetian. For us Venetian meant of royal stock. The poor woman always wore the same dress of white cotton with a small blue check, slightly open at the neck, with short sleeves that exposed her bony arms with their freckles and slack skin. At moments, when she raised them in effort or a gesture you caught a glimpse of tangled, tawny hair which we took for a nest of red ants, believing the freckles on her body to be the eggs. The schoolmistress did it with her dog, so people said. She shared the little room, in fact, with an alsatian which seemed to understand everything she said and her every smallest gesture. We often went into her room. She had shifted the chamberpot from the dresser and put it under the bed; in its place she always kept two or three bottles of wine. Once a parcel came from the Veneto and for some days there was also a bottle containing a transparent white liquor in which swayed a beautiful plant; she called it grappa. And her eyes would sparkle when she got it out and said: 'Behold the water of life!' She had some small trinkets: a gondola with a ballerina, a shell with Piazza San Marco painted inside. In one corner there was a basket full of crusts for the dog, but we noticed that she nibbled some of them herself. She also had a tin painted all over, with an ugly man in a broad straw hat on the lid and the word 'Habana', though all it held was home-grown shred which she would sniff from time to time and stuff up her nostrils. Signorina Luisa, as she was called, had hairy legs and wore white socks. This struck us as odd, because the village women went bare-legged in summer, and in winter wore long stockings kept up by a garter above the knee.

Signorina Luisa liked going for walks. She wore a large blue handkerchief tied round her head and walked with a rapid masculine stride, the dog at her heels. She would make a halt on a rock among the clumps of broom and we all sat round her while she taught us history. She never told Bible stories, only stories of Amazons, gods and Roman matrons. Pallas Athene was so called because she held two great balls, the ball of the world and the ball of the sky, and she always walked straight-backed because she had to balance an ivory tower on her head. She had been born from her father's head in a burst of thunder. She also told us about the fierce Sabine women, scratching the necks of their abductors as they were snatched up kicking and screaming on to horses; some were flung from the horses but their veils snagged in the riders' belts and so they were dragged along the ground. But especially she told us about Diana who roamed the woods with one breast bared, alone with her pack of dogs.

In the area of the Annunziata, in what year I don't remember, a shepherdess appeared with a crook and three sheep following. She was extremely young, thin, with a blonde plait of wiry hair that hung all the way down her back. She was straight and proud, with a white and brown check skirt, a white blouse, very dirty, and various pieces of knitting knotted round her chest. Her face was bright and freckled, her eyes pale blue and she looked straight at us from under her brows. Her gaze was strange, remote, like that of certain fish; it seemed that those eyes had not penetrated the world, but that the world and history had penetrated them and left them, as it were, on one side. The shepherdess was dumb, though at

63

times she seemed to want to speak to us, the tendons of her neck would grow taut and her mouth would gape, and she strained and strained before giving up the effort; to call up her small flock she made noises in her throat. The women of the village said she had lost her voice in terror of the fires and the Germans at her home far away. In the evening she led her flock to drink at the stream in the wood of Schiazzano; she sat down by the water and took out of her bundle a loaf the baker had given her. She ate the loaf and filled a ladle from the stream to drink. She chewed over and over with great slowness; a ruminant. We children knew the urge to eat, good food and bad, but never felt any duty to nourish ourselves. The way the girl ate was like a ritual; she ate slowly, thoughtfully, absorbed in the task; and you were aware of the saliva at work, of the opening of the stomach, of the guts getting ready, the well-being of the blood as it flowed to her cheeks; she slowly rolled her eyes, as if to say: ah, that's the way. At times the wind snatched at her clothes, at times a light rain wet her, or the clement sun poured down on her, but she was always slow and even in that motion of chewing, salivating, swallowing, with those gratified eyes. None of us dared disturb her.

She and the sheep went to the cool wood of Schiazzano only to eat and drink; at other times she wandered the stones of the Annunziata because it was not yet private property, or no one had claimed ownership of its barren rocks. One day the shepherdess vanished. We asked the women of the village about her, but they wouldn't say. In the end one of them told us the truth. She'd been found some way off in rougher ground, dead and covered in blood. She'd been raped – the women said – by drunken Americans.

We talked about it at length among ourselves. And for many days the boys in our gang did ugly things: they took a kitten, tied a rock round its neck and drowned it in the stream. I watched in horror, hiding behind a bush with the other girls: we had refused to join in and my brother, whom I had dragged away, looked on trembling and indignant.

The cemetery stood among rocks, as if not to encroach on

more fertile ground. There was an area inside called the old cemetery, old tombs which no one looked after any more, mostly the tombs of emigrant families who had never come back; but there were also the tombs of families of note who had been swallowed up by the fleshpots and occupations of the city and had forgotten their origins. Don Eugenio Gargiulo, University Professor of History, was the last survivor of a rich Schiazzano family which had moved to the city more than a century ago, but had held on to some property near the village, almost forgotten about till then. And lo, in '42, Don Eugenio Gargiulo enamoured, perhaps, more of family heraldry than of history, set himself to restoring the family tombs. He had come to the village in pursuit of his historical research, they said, or because of the air-raids, and drifted idly from village to village finding here a coat-of-arms, there a plaque or some such trace of his ancestors. He had been struck by the dilapidated state of the tombs in the Annunziata cemetery and armed with the permits required by the town-hall and the diocese, he had got down to work with the grave-digger. They passed August in this way: the grave-digger, his nephew and young son digging and moving loads, and Don Eugenio standing by or sitting like the site foreman. They dug up a heap of bones and laid them out neatly on a slab, where they waited to be rehoused in the mausoleum that was to be built. But when the work was well under way even Don Eugenio was called up, and despite the influence of a relation, a general, he still had to go and immediately. So the work was left only half completed, because the Gargiulo family had its own skin to look out for and its property, rather than the remains of its ancestors. Thus all the Gargiulo bones were left lying around and we often went to play with them.

Our games were always inspired by school, perhaps because the bones reminded us of History, the fossils of Science, the Human Body, Geographical Exploration – the bones of Captain Cook – Geometry: not simply because some of us didn't know the hypotenuse from the tibia but because we had been taught that the perfect forms of Geometry derived from the imperfect forms of things, they were perfect forms purged of life, just like these bones. On the ground or on a marble slab we tried to reconstruct bodies with the bones and named them after our relatives, or people from the village, or even ourselves. We put a wisp of straw between the teeth of a skull and lit it if we had matches and pretended it was smoking. When comic books began to arrive, *Tarzan* and *The Iron Mask*, we set fire to straw inside a skull and in the smoke ballooning from its mouth imagined we could see words – one of us imitated the voice of Tarzan and somebody else did the elephant. When broad-beans were in season, Totore, the carter's son, put large pods between the legs of the reconstituted dead; all the boys laughed in a dirty silly way, and we girls moved away in shame. Though when the boys weren't there, laughing to ourselves, we girls took round stones and arranged them as breasts. Round about '47 the bones disappeared and decency returned to the cemetery. Two medical students came back from prison camp and carted them away to study; though the sacristan, who was also the cemetery keeper, said they had sold them in Althenopis.

In a ditch beyond where the crowns of the furthermost olives descended in parallel towards Metamunno, under the rock of the Annunziata, lay the cow graveyard. It was there that the bones of the butchered animals were dumped. But we didn't play with those. We only looked at them from the top of the ditch because we were afraid to go near. And we never went there deliberately, it was always as if we had been led there by chance. Whereas the bones of the dead had been scoured by time, oblivious of blood, grey and familiar as our schoolbooks, the bones of the cows, though the seasons had washed them and the ants and mice had gnawed away the last traces of the corruptible, still bulged with life. Their primordial shapes were frightsome.

The old men's hospice gave on to the piazza of the Annunziata. You reached it by a small side door in the colourless and silent façade of the church. This stood at the far end of a dusty piazza, empty of children and animals, where it made a gesture at baroque grace, though its decaying plaster gave the impression that its volutes and scrolls were merely stuck on, like the hairpieces of certain old ladies. Entry by the main door, the fine stone portal crowned with toadflax which tapped against the worm-eaten wood in the wind was possible only at Easter when an impetuous glory seemed to conquer all doors and sweep away the cobwebs with a fine highhandedness; then the bells responded one to another over the countryside and opened the gates of heaven.

But we almost always got into the hospice from the kitchen side, which we could easily reach without being seen by climbing over fences and jumping from terrace to terrace. The old men were allowed out on that side to breathe a freer air than in the interior courtyard. There they would sit in the dusty twilight on wobbly chairs with broken seats, next to heaps of garbage.

The hospice merged into the seminary and they had a common scullery. When stuff arrived it was divided into two skips, the good tomatoes went into the seminary skip and the overripe, almost rotten ones, into the other. So pasta with *pappici*★ in the hospice and wholesome pasta in the seminary. And the same with beans. This arrangement caused us no surprise: there seemed to be a secret correspondence between the superior food, the clear skin and deep luminous eyes of the seminarists, and between the deformed bodies of the old men and their sickening food.

In front of the hospice kitchen there was always a bin full of rotten or wormy potatoes for the pigs; occasionally one of the old men would take one, choosing it carefully and then slowly sucking it. The moment the nuns had gone into the kitchen we would take a few as well. In the evening sometimes we got them to sing and a foolish, raucous, tremulous singing it was, followed by the harsh scolding of some nun; and on some of the old men's window-sills in the last light of the day geraniums would blaze or sometimes whimsical freesias,

★ Althenopis dialect: the worms and grubs in pasta and vegetables.

grown in old blue saucepans where the soil was held by a mere crumbling lattice of rust that came away in pieces. In mockery we would drown out the singing by drumming with stones, bits of iron, dried gourds. Then a nun would appear, wielding a broom, and we would flee making the sign of the horns.

Our relations with the seminary were not so familiar. We managed to get in only a couple of times when the son of Ciccillo the farm-hand became a seminarist. He knew us and at first would let us in, but as the fine colour gradually waned in his cheeks and he became pale and slender, he became snooty and no longer invited us and wouldn't even speak to us – ashamed of us, perhaps, or because he wanted to rid himself of the temptations of the world, or perhaps it was just that he didn't want to remember it continually. When he bumped into us, he would shoo us away with an imperious and mannered flap of his wide sleeve.

We searched about the countryside for an element vital to our games: the coloured shards of plates, cups, tiles. The most likely places were near the outlying houses, in the ditches where they threw garbage, or on land freshly ploughed. The shards were not really supposed to be recent but old, scoured by soil or water; they had to look as if they weren't fragments of objects used by grown-ups but something of our own, and whole. And above all they had to be a lucky find, like a gift of fate. Some of them were white with a gold border, like the hems of princely garments, with flowers or with blue geometric patterns; some were more precious, fragments of porcelain cups or teapots, fragile and opalescent; sometimes they had a gold thread like the sighs of the villa children; others, instead, the parti-coloured mosaic of a kimono, but these were carefully wrapped in newspaper, treasured at the bottom of a pocket, shown only in secret to close friends.

Once, on Ciccillo's holding, we laid out with large stones the plan of a house; we played kitchen with the shards, and with the brighter colours we made a blanket, from under which a small pomegranate stuck out to stand for a baby's head. Two of Ciccillo's sons came to watch our game, which for them was strange, childish, almost saccharine. They were the same age as us but they looked at us as a boy of nine looks at his baby brother of four: tenderly, indulgently, they now and then pretended to be playing with us; and at a certain moment, drawn in by their own pretence, they really did play, but immediately drew back in shame. They stood up then, straightening their backs, and took out their catapults in a deliberate and self-conscious way and fired at a tree in the hope of hitting a sparrow. But in our presence they hardly ever hit one. And it seemed to me that we were of the magical company which deprives giants of their strength.

Their sisters, though, we almost never met; they never moved away from the house. Passing in front of the farm buildings we would see them feeding the chickens or hanging out the clothes, often with a baby brother or sister clinging round their neck. Barefoot, they would withdraw at our approach with great slow smiles, awkward with shyness or already perhaps with pudeur.

There was, finally, a way of roaming far from the usual tracks; the most unpredictable way, the most adventurous, the most beautiful. On rocky slopes exposed to the sun, at times along the walls of precipices, the men of old had built terraces with soil they had carried up by hand. Edged by dry-stone walls, the terraces went down to the sea. And because Santa Maria was at the centre of a peninsula we could leap down from terrace to terrace in all directions as far as the rocks, taking care not to trample the tender pea-flowers, the beds of broad-beans, potatoes, tomatoes, wheat. So that in leaps made daunting by the height we had to be as wary as divers among rocks. When the drop was too deep or the terrace too thickly grown, we climbed barefoot down the wall. The girls were often forced to choose between the fear of jumping and a wanton exhibitionism. I always chose the latter and flew from field to field with miraculous rapture and a sense of balance beyond the reach of the others, even the boys, as if on the swing of a benign destiny which had rendered me invulnerable. The same constraints or set of false alternatives, forced us either not to climb trees at all, or to reach the very tops, careless of the fragility of the branches or the difficulty of coming down once we were up.

Considerate of the crops to the point of hurting ourselves, dropping awkwardly so as not to come down on them, we nevertheless picked what we liked since we believed they belonged to everybody. So sitting at the edge of a field we would eat the smallest peas, the smallest beans, knowing that we were breaching a law of the countryside which says the largest should be picked first.

Sometimes the patches of land were interrupted by a grove of citrus fruit, and we would run like mice along the poles that held the straw matting. There was every type of citrus fruit and we knew the most intimate flavour of the flesh and of the peel, even of their flowers, of their seeds and of the tender burgeoning leaves. Sometimes we would find the tree of the bread lemon,* at others the blood orange, the mandarin, more rarely that of the lime or the bergamot. And we would peel them in heaps, digging eagerly into the rind with nails that became encrusted with green and sourness which we then gnawed away with our teeth, and the thicker the rind the greater the pleasure in peeling it, even if the flesh inside were dried up, so that we went on to another with a thinner rind promising a juicy flesh, and another scrawled with red, and another twisted and deformed, and another perfectly round which we tossed in the air like a ball. Sitting in a circle, one after another, we gave our views on the flavour of the oranges, the various gradations of sweet and sour, of juicy and dry, of red and yellow, the coarseness or fineness of the grain – there was one with a grain so large it seemed like pomegranate seeds. During these explanations, eulogies, descriptions,

* A variety of lemon common in the Corento peninsula, having a thick mesocarp but little endocarp and that not very juicy. It is neither a lime nor a limette, the flesh of which is very bitter. The teeth sink into the yielding white pith, a sign of the pleasure to come. Bread lemon, as 'bread melon', as the bread-fruit tree in Salgari's novels; for country people and children bread was once upon a time a recurrent metaphor.

commentaries we all swapped segments of orange; great the wonderment of the smaller children when the oranges had babies squeezed in at the top and deforming the rind, or in cradles scooped in the fleshy centre. And in eating them we seemed to feel a forbidden and cannibalistic pleasure, almost as if we were eating human babies. After feasting we went on sitting, so pleasant did we find the cool shade fretted by the lacework of the sun.

Occasionally someone had their own secret plot of land where we were taken to be initiated. Thus Agnese once took us to her uncle's land where there was an orchard of yellow plums. Many of us had never eaten them before. Another time we went to a plot that was surrounded by a wall of living rock. The rocks were full of holes and covered in moss. Two or three children could fit into the various holes and we imagined that we had our own house at last, or rather a castle. We once played convent there too, and imagined ourselves cloistered nuns let out for the first time in thirty years to vote. And little by little we brought some furniture for every hole, a tin spoon, a little clay dish, some coloured shards, a rag or two. One evening we left a live cricket shut up in a box to symbolize all us inhabitants of the castle. And we made plans to go there one June night to cage fistfuls of fireflies in the holes behind wire mesh and invite our friends to festivities in the illuminated castle.

5

The villas

Sometimes we visited the terraces overlooking a villa. The villas were almost always closed-up and uninhabited and had the same fascination as the ladies in the family album, who seemed to be waiting for better times before emerging to take on life. From a distance the villas were distinguishable by a lush surround of rare ornamental plants, sometimes by the pink or yellow plaster of their boundary walls, or marble benches, or wooden gazebos, belvederes, graceful wells. Every villa showed a different whim in its colour and stonework. One was rectangular, stuccoed in bourbon red, weighed down with bougainvillaea like those thick manes of hair which cause migraines; another huge, white, spectral, with stepped terraces descending either side, with arches and columns supporting wistaria or vines; another with volutes of stone that looked like shells from the Marina, pink, eighteenth-century: two staircases curved at the sides, then coming together like a garland; yet another simple, square, dazzling like a sheet drying in the sun, but surmounted by terracotta dogs as a reminder that it was a gentleman's residence. And all of them had wrought-iron grilles bellying over the windows of the ground floor and solid double-doors with iron knockers in strange shapes, a hand, a lion's head, a sphinx, a snake. Each villa was linked to the oddities of its owner. The proprietor of this one gave parties with fairy lights, another one sunbathed nude on the terrace. Lower down, another, the richest of them, had a motor yacht and not so much a guest-house as an entire second villa, white and inaccessible down on the rocks; and a widow came to that one there who had had her daughters' bedrooms decorated in the Florentine style.

That was the way of the gentry. And we spied on those realms from behind the bushes; only when we were sure that a villa gave no sign of life did we enter the forbidden enclosures; we wandered among the rare plants, whose names we did not know, and the multitude of flowers which nevertheless someone seemed to look after from time to time; then lying under the eucalyptuses, the pines or the rare weeping willow, we recounted the histories of the villas. And with the histories of the villas we mixed in fragments of fairytales.

When the Americans came, the villas took on life; sheets, blankets, underwear, checked tablecloths appeared at the windows. The doors were opened: by order of the absent owners the caretakers had to pretend to live there to prevent their being requisitioned. And the villas became even more spectral with all those clothes hanging out, behind which one expected the animation of great families and instead silence responded to our calls. 'It's the ghosts' washing!' we cried as we fled. But sometimes the farm people who were supposed to be caretaking exceeded their offices and actually lived there; they would send a young couple whose home wasn't ready, or an old couple, or a nursing mother who couldn't yet face the labour of the fields, or a convalescent son just released from TB clinic. And then we heard from behind the washing familiar voices, which sometimes drove us away and sometimes, recognizing a relative amongst us, would invite us in.

Only towards '47 or '48 did the owners of the villas begin to return and we no longer dared go near because they brought dogs with them, the caretakers could no longer fraternize with us, and we felt intimidated and ashamed.

Our mother had entrée to some of these villas and she would take us to visit. For the occasion she would dress up in the pre-war clothes she had kept in mothballs in a chest, almost as if the war and the village piazza had been unworthy to see her sporting them. She wore either a blue dress with a linen jacket or a heavy cotton dress printed with an exotic fantasia of palms, monkeys, bananas and other tropical fruit on a white background, which reminded me of our return by sea from the warm sunlit island. This dress was completely cut away to the armpits at the back and front but it went with a long-sleeved bolero which hid everything; nevertheless it cheered me to imagine that one day all that nudity might be exposed, because Mother was always complaining about being old and what we wanted was a young mother. And I would say playfully: 'Take your bolero off', but only when we were already in the grounds of a villa and then she became as bashful as a young girl with her boyfriend.

Or she would wear a suit of raw silk with red seahorses glowing on it. And when we asked her what sort of thing silk was, she would say, 'This is nothing!', and go on about the clothes stored in trunks in the Althenopis air-raid shelter, about those finer, swirling silks she couldn't wear in Santa Maria, even in the re-opened villas, since they were outfits for gala evenings and for the city; or perhaps only because of a splendour of the flesh which would never be hers again.

We walked beside her, careful not to get our footwear dirty because on these occasions we exchanged our clogs for freshly whitened leather sandals, bought at great sacrifice precisely in view of the re-opening of the villas; careful also not to brush against the field-walls with our white piqué clothes, so as to arrive unsullied; and we tossed our heads nervously like colts unused to the bridle because we had been decked with large white hats tied under our chins with ribbons. Once through the shame, the awkwardness and the circle of chattering women who complimented us (in the villas we didn't know how to behave when greeting people, or eating, or sitting down, and we felt like delinquents disguised as gentlefolk), we quickly joined the band of children.

Being together there was not, as it was in the piazza, as natural as breathing and play was not born spontaneously out of imagination or the prompting of the moment,* or, to put it

* The opposite of this kind of play is going to a fun-fair.

another way, from the course of things themselves. Instead we systematically played one game after another, almost as if performing a duty: Blindman's Buff, Pussy-Four-Corners, Hide-and-Seek, Cops-and-Robbers, Treasure-Hunt, and a great many other games with complicated rules that I can't remember and which were often a combination of the simpler ones. Some of these games were the same as those in the piazza but they had different names and the rules were more rigid; in the same way, the women in the rooms played with packs of French cards and not with the Neapolitan kind. At times, when there were fewer of us, or when we were the only ones to have dared the rain, we played *Monopoly*: this was how we learned the names of the streets of Milan, linked to rents, capital, shares, maturing interests. Cousin Achille was the one who gave the best explanation of the rules of that game.

On those rainy days it might also come about that one of the bigger girls or her governess would dig out the game of Mah-jong from a leather-lined box. I would find a pretext for not playing, spellbound by the strange markings, more message than sign, and the beautiful colours of the ivory pieces; the room, as if cut off from any link with the world, turned into a magic pavilion drifting towards unexplored lands. Thus I voyaged and was much startled by the cook who came to call us for dinner.

Certain particulars to which I gave no attention in the piazza became important in the villas; for example, whether a girl was blonde or not. I wasn't. Thus she was beautiful and already walked in a different way from the others, stately, with her shoulders back, with her long hair lovingly combed and set in ringlets. If a male child had long hands and feet it was considered an auspicious sign: it meant that he would grow up tall. These in fact were signs of belonging to the gentry.

The interiors of the villas struck us for two different reasons. Either because certain aspects were too neglected or homely, and made us look at each other in astonishment and scorn, whispering: 'But they're just like us, then!' If, for

75

example, you pushed open the door of a darkened room you came upon an old aunt in bed groaning, and the gleam of a chamberpot on the floor; if you went in the aunt wailed more insistently; and if you peered into the chamberpot, it really was full of brown urine. Or again, the chickens scratching in front of the kitchen door and the dogs snuffling in the rubbish bins. Or yet again, creeping up on a row about money between the mistress of the house and the maid; or finding a toothless comb, greasy and tangled with hairs on the rim of a bathtub; or surprising one of the men of the house, later to appear all shining in a linen suit, sitting on the edge of the bed, absorbed in having the pimples on his back squeezed by his wife.

Other particulars, though, rendered the inhabitants of the villas extravagant and grandiose. How could the small daughter of the house sleep on her own in the big room, in the great Florentine bed? From behind the grille of the cupboard where she kept her books and toys, we expected the Masked Man to appear at any second. Or again, how was it possible to walk, play, eat, in those blouses and starched frocks we saw drying in the attic? And whatever could be the purpose of certain large, stolid rooms you passed through, furnished only with consoles and mirrors leaning like sentries against the walls?

And there were vast incongruities: huge bathtubs with complicated brass art-deco taps of English manufacture, from which no drop of water ever came. And what could be the use of certain tables lavishly set with silver and crystal and two forks each, two knives, two spoons and two glasses? At times some of us might remain to dinner; meanwhile in the drawing-room or under the pergola the ladies played bridge. But why were those tables set out like that, if what was served was only noodles with butter, a slice of cheese and an apple? I regretted on those occasions the large coloured terracotta bowl out of which the village families ate bean soup with hunks of bread floating in it or potato salad with onions, tomatoes, courgettes, sprinkled with origano, everyone dipping in with a spoon or a fork, with what would have been

76

greedy lunges – for fear of its coming to an end – if it hadn't been for the threatening glare of the head of the family. But we felt a secret correspondence between the pale, blonde, slender girls of the villas and that diaphanous food from which we got up hungrier than ever. Into a second glass at the end of the meal milk was poured. And we hesitated at length in front of that milk, unusual for us at that time of day, because we didn't like it cold and without sugar and barley as it was; we tossed it down in one gulp, like medicine, so as not to attract notice. There was skin on the milk, and dreading that we had mistaken their purpose, we used the silver spoons to skim it aside.

And yet all that crystal and those milky foods, the delicate noodles barely yellow with butter at the rim of the plate, the thin slices of mozzarella almost dissolved in the whey, the milk in the wine glasses, had for us a particular spell: they gave us a glimpse of a refinement of manners that would always be beyond our reach. And these feelings were similar to others we experienced in our acquaintance with those children. We knew, for instance, all the plants and the flowers but often we did not know what to call them, or we gave them imprecise and collective names that grouped whole families: there were for example more than ten species of flower that we called bells, and we confused the toadflax and the dandelion; and the marguerites were innumerable. Those children knew the names of dozens of plants and flowers, but could hardly ever identify them in their garden. When we played the alphabet game they always won. Give the names of ten flowers begin-ning with F for example. And straightaway they said: fuchsia. It took us a long time to understand that the difficult fuchsia was no other than a variety of bell we knew extremely well. A girl smaller than me, whose curly head sprouted from a fluffed-out yellow dress embroidered with honeycomb stitch, wrinkled up her nose and gave jonquil for J, and I imagined the sound in the air forming a whimsical, refined flower, wreathed in tendrils, which leant back slightly on its stalk to look at me with condescension. They never said 'right, then', nor 'cor', nor 'nar', but emitted as if with effort a 'now' with a tight well-behaved 'o', which greatly resembled their closed mouths as they chewed and their little smothered laughs.

When it happened that we were with the gang from the piazza and we met these children on the beach, the three of us would feel ashamed: of the company we were in for sure, but also, in regard to the kids from the piazza, of being on speaking terms with the villa kids. All we had with us were the clothes we wore over our bathing suits. No change of underwear nor a towel, just a paper bag with our lunch. And there on the rocks we slipped out of our clothes, wrapping them round our lunch to keep it out of the sun and away from the dogs. Then without a moment's hesitation we plunged into the water. The children from the villas, on the other hand, arrived with a retinue of women, umbrellas, beach-robes and towels, camp-stools, hats, two or three costumes which got changed every time they came out of the water. The women dried them, concerned to see they didn't get a chill on their stomachs or their backs, counted the hours and the half-hours after they'd eaten their lunch to make sure the cold water didn't interfere with their digestion. The fairer ones had sunglasses, and the women smeared their faces and shoulders with oil. I felt as if I had been deprived of those well-bred maternal rituals. I would sit on the beach by myself, midway between the beach gang and the circle of villa dwellers, until I made up my mind to join my friends on the rock, and there, in the headlong races along the breakwater, in the diving, I forgot my envy for Diana, the blonde, the beautiful, who was already a 'signorina'*, though she was only my age, sitting placidly beneath the umbrella beside the women mindful of her every little wish, worried about her eyes, her skin, and even her feet, which were well protected in rubber shoes.

* Girls became 'signorinas' on menstruation.

6
The Marina

During the long summer, which lasted the six months from
April to September, we went down to the sea. From April to
June only on Sundays, because of school. But of all the piazza
children we were the only ones to enjoy this long intimacy
with the sea, because the others went only for a month, in July
or August – the big sisters who accompanied them couldn't
stay away for too long from their chores, and in any case sea
bathing was looked on as medicinal. The villagers who gave
their children such liberty in the piazza, on the paths, in the
fields, were afraid of the sea and didn't want them going down
on their own. They also thought that too much of the sea
made them highly-strung.* During all those months therefore
we went on our own, but we were always joined by some boy
who trangressed the ban or whose family was going through
a difficult patch, with the result that the parents couldn't keep
an eye on what the children were up to.

Often, in spring or autumn, Mother came too, and then we
didn't go to the marina but to deserted bays and steep rocks
known for their particular beauty to Mother and her cousins
from their youth. But in latter years Mother no longer came.

When we went with the piazza children we were entrusted
to the big sisters. And these sisters walked slowly behind
while we ran ahead, going down by the path and not the
terraces on these occasions, because they were loaded with
baskets of fried-up macaroni and bottles of water or

* We always found ourselves in the middle, between riches and poverty,
town and country, sea and village, luck and mishap; or passing, rather, from
one to the other. This helped to give us knowledge of the world.

lemonade. They slowly lowered themselves into the sea, the skirts of their costumes billowing around them. Underneath they wore bras, and there was always some girl on the beach who would amuse herself by undoing another girl's bra all of a sudden, and large breasts would suddenly flop on to the wheel* of fried macaroni, and with her hands busy slicing the girl wouldn't be able to do it up for herself. But the sea I remember is the sea of us three together.† We went down with our lunch, jumping from terrace to terrace, hurrying to get to the great happening every day renewed and never a moment's boredom. The moment we woke we glimpsed through half-closed lids the light from the shutters, golden tongues from the piazza trying to lick us. Mother lay on her bed in the shaded room of summer, the small pan of water and vinegar beside her; before setting off we kissed her hand, so as not to hurt her head, changed the vinegar rag, she would smile and say: 'How cool it is!' And free, we ran for the dazzle of the piazza.

Once down at the Marina, heedless of maternal warnings, we plunged all sweaty into the water and we felt like fish back in their own element. The water stung the long slashes left on our legs by the grass and the cuts on our elbows and knees which in those months never healed. Then we would lie back on the wet sand or roll around in the dry sand which scorched too much for us to stay still; or like fakirs we competed to see who could stay motionless on the burning sand, as stiff as possible to reduce the area of friction, until the damp given off by the skin cooled the sand: the entire world seemed to converge in a burning spot in the centre of your stomach until the

---

* A baking-tray of copper or aluminium. It is a luminous and festive term that should be introduced into the Italian dictionary. The word baking-tray ('teglia') cheapens the food that comes out of the oven, though it should be kept for those baked tarts with a recondite flavour based on butter and bechamel; it is to be excluded altogether for baked macaroni, tomato pizza, stuffed aubergine, anchovies gratinée, lettuce and cream-cheese tarts.

† The siblings returned together to the immemorial realm whence they had sprung.

scorching became a living clot of life that you had to loose, shake off, release; so you got up and dived in again. Or stretched out on the seat of a boat to let the rocking breeze slacken the grip of the sun; or lay with your head hanging over the wooden jetty and became intoxicated with the movement of the sea under the planks; for ages you would lie there as if spellbound, and when a wave came in, there was a thud away to the right of the Marina, followed by other, nearer thuds, until the jetty was shaken, and you might be sprayed. It was not easy to shake off the rhythms of those colours and thuds and often one or other of us would be discovered on the jetty seemingly asleep when we were simply stupefied but pretending to sleep, so enchanting was the stupefaction.

We would set off, leaping sure-footed from rock to rock, to the far ends of the Marina; and our leaps were so sure, well-judged and serene – even if they appeared rash to others – and as though tuned to a secret rhythm, that we seemed like sleepwalkers; trouble would have come with a warning shout or a call; we would have fallen, toppling from the magic circle. We showed off our marine paces to the villa children, feet so hardened to sand and burning pebbles that they never hesitated even at certain sharp-pointed rocks hollowed by sea-lice; and in haughty revenge I matched my sureness of foot against the graceful charms, almost well-rounded by then, of Diana and her friends.

In those coves and grottoes, far from the eyes of sailors, we discovered the pleasure of freeing our arses from the damp of our costumes and exposing them to the fresh air – in the first instance the damp evaporated and ventilated the flesh – but immediately it became roasting and the sun seemed to concentrate all its ardour on that white flesh; and we changed position to wash off the grating sand; setting our arses to soak in the sea like floating butterflies. But we never took off our costumes completely, only dropped them down a little behind. Because, the front part of that zone was what was truly shameful, even with us three, though never the arse. So we all tranquilly gazed at each other's white arses exposed to the sun or soaking

81

in the water, and they seemed familiar to us, innocuous and stolid, domestic objects, recalling the shaded room where we were quarantined because of the usual infections, measles, scarlet fever, mumps, when all the mattresses lay on the floor, the door opening every now and then for Mother's or Granny's ministrations, the constant whispering when the fever was high; and the somersaults from mattress to mattress when it had gone down and the door was closed. Or further back in time, before we could walk, each sucking a bottle in the sunlit morning.

On the beach, or on the stony soil going down, we would find the skeletons of prickly pears looking like the remains of prehistoric animals; apart from the barbarous shapes, we discovered when we cleaned away the remains of the rind the delicate wonder of the woody white lace which severally laps its secret; for that almost animal plant had a lunar secret of its own and in the face of the evidence we liked to think that these were not the torn remains of fleshy prickly pears but those of a vegetable meteorite, falling from some planet on one of those summer nights when you gaze and seem to float skyward and wheel in the luminous dust of worlds. When you had delicately peeled back the various layers of lace, as carefully as possible so as not to destroy the web, you came on a white substance dotted with black seeds which had the consistency of cotton-wool and the extraordinary property of phosphorescence. We took it to the grottoes on the Marina, when the tide was out, and over the darkest depths we dusted our bodies with it, whereupon they gave out a celestial glow. And waving our arms we ran about the grotto covered in the magic substance; or slid in gently to explore the depths of the sea like sleepwalkers.

We knew the secrets of the sea floor and the rocks for miles along the coast; for hours we would help some fisherman's son collect winkles and crabs; seldom did we know these boys by name but it came naturally to pass the hours together. Sometimes one of them would take us home; the rooms would be painted blue, and on the dresser there would be little ships, large tropical shells and photos of drowned uncles. The piquant odour of fried garlic always hung in those rooms, or the impalpably greasy odour of steamed polyps burbling away to themselves in an earthenware pot; there were piles of nets everywhere, in the corners and under the beds, and there was always someone squatting on the floor to mend them.

The numerous inhabitants of the fishing village seemed more civilized and more savage at the same time. The houses ran down the wide steps to the sea, tightly packed as if jostling for elbow-room. All day long and in the evening people – slimmer and darker than those of the village – swarmed in and out of the houses. The women wore earrings, and gold and coral necklaces not just on feast-days but every day; often the smaller children went around naked, without even the traditional woollen vest to protect their shoulders. The women walked along the strand with baskets of fish or nets on their heads, their skirts bunched up around thighs which were sometimes massive, more often slim and tanned. Sitting on the doorsteps in the evening the girls combed each other's long black hair, and since they were always bent over, sorting fish or mending nets, they didn't wear their plaits loose but wound them several times around their heads. The men wore red headbands that faded to pink – red, because it combats the rays of the sun and keeps them from the brain. Even the patron saints of the shore village were strange, especially the Black Madonna, all decked in gold, whose image was enthroned above their beds or pasted up in a smaller version behind the doors.

It was in those houses that we first saw stuff which was later to spread to the houses of our own village: small calendars with a sickly odour of face-powder, showing a different nude woman on every page; cans of tomatoes, with labels showing a peasant girl in local costume surrounded by gold medals; we got them to give us these labels and flattened them in our schoolbooks to prevent them from rolling up like tubes; or newspaper cuttings of Hollywood actresses; or scented soap, pink, green or purple, that the men brought for the women from the ports where they sold their fish; and even sachets containing powdered orangeade.

The men did not smoke loose Nazionali, but had shiny coloured cardboard packets of cigarettes; wavy coils of scented smoke rose above their black curly heads when they stretched out on the beach to rest with legs spread. Even the plants were different, they grew smaller, but had more intense colours and scents, in plant-pots made out of cans – whereas we used only clay pots, worn-out pans, white chamberpots with a blue rim – and the basil was more pungent, the geraniums redder and more thickly clustered; and the carnation had a perfume so intense as to make us catch our breath. The sweetness of the rose was missing, as if their petals couldn't stand up to the sea wind; little, slightly hairy tomatoes grew on the small patches of land behind the houses where the soil was grey and mixed with sand and we would pick them furtively to taste the bitter concentrate that burst in our mouths; the capers were smaller and sweeter, and the figs less watery.

The walls of the houses, the doors and windows, were painted in vivid colours matching the various combinations on the boats. From the rocks all around the sweetish scent of wormwood drifted lazily down.

We waited for dusk; when the noise of the sea died down the boats swaying in the harbour went out to fish. They had carved and painted badges nailed to the foremast, one showing a fish, another a siren, a dolphin, the Madonna Turrita, many had the Black Madonna, while some had just a star. Lying on our bellies, with our elbows buried in the sand and our heads resting on our hands, motionless, we gazed in fascination at the coloured emblems swaying against the pink and violet sky; on the horizon an intenser blue indicated the islands. Listlessly, tired out by now, we watched a boy make a late dive from a boat or the more daring dive of a young man from above the grotto. In contrast with all the heat accumulated in our bodies and now rising to the skin, the twilight hour made us shiver.

84

We gathered up our clothes and very slowly took the steps and the upward paths; yet ready again once we got home, – after a hasty greeting to Mother and the rapid theft from the kitchen of a biting-on from dinner, a meatball, a boiled potato – to run out to the headlong evening in the piazza; and Mother's complaints would follow us down the stairs because we had left our wet costumes on the floor and not even combed our hair. In the evening, with the coolness, the games became wilder, the shouts louder, as if to blot out the calls that we knew would start coming from the windows before long; as if to ward off the nightly account of ourselves we would have to give at table, and especially the anguish of sleep.

And after all the evening rituals – washing our feet was the most unwelcome – we tucked ourselves under the sheets, which were none too clean since the laundry was done by hand in those days and they weren't changed often, with the result that we immersed ourselves in our own sedimented body odour; every time I recalled Granny's repeatedly telling me that good people don't smell; and I surely wasn't good. The saints even went so far as to give off a perfume.

For a long time I would lie quietly in the dark, trying to fall asleep. The noise of the sea still thundered in my ears and all the sun carelessly caught during the day woke up on my red legs and stomach; not the even-handed sun spread over everything in the day, but a malign, febrile, stinging sun, not yellow and luminous, but red and lowering, and now I shivered without the sheet, and now the sheet was unbearable to me; I tossed and turned, I felt creased like rustling greaseproof paper, and if I sniffed my wrist I seemed to catch the odour of putrid things burning and of sulphur. I would wail then for Mother, who took off the panties which were irritating my skin and went over my stomach and legs with slices of lemon, or cucumber when there wasn't a lemon in the house. Then she would close the door.

But the excitement of the day had been too much. So that when the noise of the sea dimmed in my ears and the febrile heat lessened on my skin, I seemed to plummet headlong into a bottomless darkness, broken by enormous coloured crabs which took shape behind my clenched eyelids, and then by myriads of stars which faded one by one into a voracious dark as I unclenched my lids; now I seemed to hear far off thunder and so opened my eyes and for an instant mistook the small light, which lit the village piazza and could be glimpsed beyond the shutters, for a flash of lightning. But immediately I realized that the quiet persistent light could not be the terrible and naked flash which furrowed the sky in cruel games. Seeking something to correspond to my ferocious anxiety, I let myself be chilled by the amorous quarrels of cats, or the long and pointless baying of a dog would lengthen out my anguish.*

Overwhelmed by that pitiless dark I took refuge beside Mother's little lamp in the other room. Mother had the habit of reading late in bed, perhaps because an anxiety more concrete than mine and no less strong prevented her from sleeping. In those days there were no sleeping pills. And if she lost her patience she would scold me and make a futile appeal to my pride, and in any case push me away, and I would spread out a blanket on the floor and lie down there, all hunched up so as to be invisible, almost not breathing so that she wouldn't notice my presence while she read. And there I would fall asleep, preferring that irritation and incumbent anger to the lonely and voracious dark.

But the days at the sea were not all like that. There were times when you set off with a clear sky but then sultry clouds came to cover it for the rest of the day. And you would hang about for hours in that sultry desolation, dragging yourself unwillingly into water that was more torpid than the air and furrowed by fish that jumped as if to escape that motionless heat; and no one bothered to explore the clouded depths, the

* I have since learnt that this state is known as 'pavor nocturnus' and generally goes along with slender and nervous constitutions. But no science of the doctors has ever really managed to convince me that those fears were unfounded, since it was later revealed that the things truly to be feared are a great deal more disquieting than what I was afraid of then.

86

rocks or the grottoes; no one wanted to buckle up to a dive, every now and again you simply let yourself drop in, feet first, as if dragged down by the weight of the day. The violence of the sun and of the sea allowed no scansion of time; not even the space of the morning seemed to have passed when one left in the evening; listless, one got home to find Mother almost buried under vinegar-soaked rags and the dark. The piazza was dusty and empty, the sultriness did not encourage play; just a child on a doorstep slowly sucking a plum. At moments, as when the lights go up on stage and the show is about to begin, a single last ray of sunset would fight its way through various curtaining layers to kindle the colours of the hanging washing. A night storm was rehearsing; already at the far end of the valley my fierce brothers, the lightning flashes, were battling.*

---

* At that time, in fact, I thought I was a cloud and had the lightning for brothers. I played continually at changing shape and they at light and war.

7
Uncle Alceste

At one end of the village – where the steps leading down to Metamunno began, where the cobbles and the blocks of tufa in the boundary walls became more slimy and mossy, where even the water-loving maidenhair grew along the track which was always damp from the water that ran off down that sloping part of the village whenever it rained – there stood the house of Grandmother's relations, in front of a dark, cool lemon-grove, cut off by a tall gate between gateposts of fluted marble which interrupted in graveyard fashion the whimsical wall of tufa which, bulging from the pressure of the lemon grove behind, eaten away by wallflowers and topped by toadflax of the palest pink, bleached by the shade, went hopping, as it were, down the steep steps. The relations' door was tall and heavy, always painted dark green, with a knocker in the shape of a lion's paw, flanked some years later by a shining electric bell in the shape of a rose set in the granite, like some emblem of the modern age vainly masquerading as a flower.

On the first occasions, I went into that house hiding behind Granny's black skirt but later, when I had grown used to its inmates, I skipped along beside her. You had to stand at the front door rapping and rapping because the house was vast and almost everyone inside was deaf. After repeated efforts we would move away from the door to stand in the middle of the drive facing the windows, waiting for someone to look out and recognize us. Sometimes Aunt Celeste, Grandmother's sister, looked out, sometimes it was her son, Uncle Alceste. And in saying: 'Ah, it's you! What a pleasure! What a nice surprise!' to us, and 'It's Chiara, it's Chiara!' to somebody inside, the old housekeeper, the mistress, the young master, even the housemaid, all had the same voice, strident and drawling, nor was it clear who was imitating who. And you would hear a clapping of hands from inside, one of the family calling the cook, who was busy in the kitchen on the ground floor, to go and let us in; and finally with cats and dogs at her heels she would peer through the chink in the door, still mistrustful, her face red and greasy from the stove, delighted to see me but almost disrespectful towards Grandmother. On the one hand because Granny was her rival in the kitchen, and on the other, having learned from her employers of Grandmother's oddities, she found in being disrespectful a kind of link with the world of her superiors, or perhaps only a way of getting her own back.

If that stretch of road was shady and cool, the hall of the house was even more so. To me it was like entering the crypt that I had crossed, candle in hand, before emerging into the light of the church the day of my First Communion. To the left stood a pot-bellied earthenware jar twice my height; in its narrow mouth a cactus writhed, refusing to grow in the shade that seemed to imprison it, in the same way that in the cemetery, the female faces sculpted in the marble struck me as prisoners, helpless to free themselves from their confines. To the right, like a luminous secret, the tall double-doors rose up blue, white and gold, giving on to the drawing-rooms which were always closed to us, except on cleaning days when, by chance, or lured by the turmoil, we came to the house. And directly in front of the main door, which was immediately closed behind us, rose the stone staircase, its banister ending in a sphinx's head polished with use, which I always avoided touching when going upstairs. The iron handrail on the right was fixed to the wall at intervals by little hands that clutched it like fists, and which strongly reminded me of Aunt Celeste's hands, always clutching something, the handrail itself to prevent herself falling, or the dog-headed knob of her stick, or her brown velvet bag, or the knob of the wireless as she made me free of the noisy planet spinning inside; and even when she leaned on my thin shoulder, it seemed that she had clutched hold and kept some part of my bones for herself.

Half-way up the stairs, in the middle of the wall, there was a granite tondo with a fresco of a madonna dressed in red and there Grandmother would pause in sighing prayer; and not, as was said, to take the chance of a rest as the other sisters did, because Granny was all go and urgency even climbing the stairs. The beautiful lady dressed in red and gold, and especially the plump baby, seemed to have grown gloomy in that perennial gloom and the only urge I felt was the impulse to take hold of the baby and run off with it up the shady cool street, up the steps, to the sunlit cobbles outside Agnese's, always rowdy with babies busy with large bowls of pasta and beans or, still unsteady on their legs gazing in laughter at the trickle of piss between their feet.

Leaving the madonna to the company of the roses set in front of her as if in consolation, you would climb the second flight to find Aunt Celeste waiting at the top, her hooked hand resting on another stone sphinx, or sometimes Uncle Alceste, curly-headed and clapping his hands. He was neither a child nor a boy, nor a youth, but a man of over fifty. After all that cool gloom, bred as it were by the granite of the staircase, in the upper drawing-room one entered a sky-blue luminosity. Cool light filtered in from the large window open on the lemon grove, but from the french window a sun multiplied by the white reverberation of the loggia dazzled me. The white and blue arabesques on the majolica floor-tiles introduced me to the alarming concept of infinity; but the swollen nineteenth-century furniture with its homely embonpoint reassured me; only to be alarmed again by the bas-reliefs of heraldic plants and animals on the ceramic stove, and the underground smell that came from its cast-iron door, an earthy metal for it had no lustre whatsoever. A sagging divan upholstered in flowery blue cretonne on which a worn fur rug was draped had the air of a monstrous pet, on which the numerous cats of the house lived in symbiosis. The two armchairs were also covered in blue cretonne and in winter one of them lodged Aunt Celeste, hunched in a blanket, with her parchment face in which a pair of grey eyes stood out, miserly, sharp and yet gentle in a remote way, as if fifty years of married life and widowhood had not erased the memory of the airy, almost eighteenth-century grace in which her life and that of her four sisters had passed in the paternal home in Via Casba.

The round curve of the central table made the room even more gracious, its shining surface always carefully waxed, on which specks of dust appeared like crystals; and it was in fact through a magnifying glass that I examined them. It was there that Uncle's work tools were laid out, always religiously in the same place: first of all the books, sometimes flaming red, sometimes sky-blue, or if they were more rare and arcane works, yellowish with the titles done in brown or bordeaux red; and it wasn't mere aesthetic frivolity that caused all the books to be one day red, another yellow, another blue, because the binder's art had a way of making the binding correspond to the book's contents, and where the binder's art was not enough it was supplemented by Uncle, who passed hours with the antique binders of Althenopis giving advice and making suggestions, explaining how that shade of red suited such and such a book of D'Annunzio, the sky-blue, the thoughts of Lao Tsu or Proust – he had two editions of the *Recherche*, one with the old Gallimard cover, kept in the library on the lower floor, and another edition so worn by handling that he had had it rebound – thus the colour of the books on the table corresponded to his passions and the curiosity of the moment. Between one book and another there were various trinkets: the magnifying glass, an ivory paper-knife, a glass sphere containing an oriental landscape, a brass paperweight in the shape of a hand that opened and closed like a spring clip and which made one of the series of anthropomorphic or zoomorphic objects which started with the door-knocker and continued in the Sicilian swastika or triskelion etched on the terracotta jar in the hall; in the clawed feet of the sphinxes at the ends of the banister; in the eyed sun painted on the ceiling; in a rock-crystal ashtray in the shape of a scallop; in a brass comfit-dish with bow legs that ended in dog paws.

Behind the divan there was a large closet, which on certain solemn or family feasts was opened up to become a chapel. I saw it open only on those occasions, or on certain mornings when the house was cleaned from top to bottom, generally before or after these feasts. The looming presence of that closet – after a few hours in the house had lulled me into forgetting the warnings coming from the strange objects – was enough to remind me that I wasn't at home there but in some sort of anteroom of a closed-up chapel, which I imagined as containing the secret of that family and of my own past splendours, but especially the secret of my future beyond the piazza. And the moment I was sure that the grown-ups were nowhere near, I was irresistibly tempted to open the door and stick my nose through the crack to sniff an odour of mould and incense that made me pale with desire and terror.

There was a year in which my uncle put his secretary, an ex-seminarist from Metamunno, at Mother's disposal to give me private lessons in Italian and Latin.

The time in fact was approaching when we were to leave Santa Maria del Mare for a more splendid destiny. And perhaps because our destiny had announced itself by then as splendid, Uncle dropped his reserve with regard to us, for from poor relations we were about to become his equals or perhaps only because we children were turning into young persons, almost on the threshold of adolescence.

I was a year ahead in school and steering most unskilfully between the rocks of the Odyssey. To these lessons at my uncle's I took my classmate, Maruzella, who would give me a hundred lira whenever I helped her with her homework, stealing her mother's money before my eyes from the drawer that smelled of sour milk, in the great cave of the dairy which was always awash underfoot with water and whey.

Kicking against the difficulties of the Gallic Wars, encouraged by the complicity of the tutor, by his sleepy round eyes, by his curls, by his fresh pink cheeks and many dimples, we would abandon the translation and begin chasing round the table; and he would chase after us in vain, we mocking him, until he would laugh as if suddenly come awake, laugh and chase harder with his arms stretched out to catch us; and we, more agile, would dodge him. Already almost adolescents, we played that chasing game in the shaded room, the shutters half-closed to soften the light of the early afternoon sun and encourage us in concentration and study. Every now and then the poor tutor would pause in the chase and turn towards the door, worried that some member of the household might come along. Then he would threaten to open the closet and let the devils out after us. But we had quite a different devil in us and went on with the game unperturbed, and seeing him hesitate we pretended to come within reach and then we were off again like eels, and the chase went on, until we stopped again slyly, and he, on the other side of the table, would also halt and laugh with the afternoon light filtering through the shutters behind him; and I would have liked that suspended moment to have gone on for ever, but already, in the pause of thought, the ending of the game was heralded, and shortly afterwards, out of some unexpected determination on his part or some almost deliberate clumsiness on ours, he would manage to grab us, catching Maruzella by a breast and me by the arm, or it stopped because he would slump down tiredly in front of the book, making a move towards getting down to study, or again – and then he seemed really annoyed – he would threaten to go and fetch help. And then we ran after him, pleading with him not to go, and he would pinch our cheeks.

On certain days the room lost its radiant celestial look; I wasn't allowed in and could only get glimpses from the terrace through the chink in the french window. Uncle and his secretary sat in there, buried under mountains of papers and under the words that took flight from them. I listened unseen to Uncle's querulous, drawling voice as he dictated and to the keys tapping away; and from time to time his voice changed and reached solemn sharps that I would never have suspected, or muted into a mumble broken by snorts of bitter mockery, or sighs – perhaps when his opponents' reasoning seemed altogether too base to him – or took on a sharp peremptory tone that snapped like a whiplash – his anger must have been great at such moments – and then he would hang suspended in a sequence of subordinate and incisive clauses so that I waited in vain for the end of the tranquil tangle, which never arrived for the voice took up again further on without pausing; perhaps the conclusive argument I waited for had already occurred, wrapped in a meaning I did not understand, without any echo of it appearing in the voice – in the way that definitive decisions often ripen in the mind with no external sign to betray them.

The poor young man signalled to Uncle to break off, since it was only by taking advantage of pauses in the outburst that he managed to catch up and wipe the copious sweat that stood out on his neck and under his fair curls. Uncle would stop dictating and begin debating, less with the young man than with an invisible audience, for in his intellectual solitude – he was an opponent of Croce's – he discussed philosophy sometimes even with the cats. His voice took on a biting, indignant tone and I wondered whom he was getting at; in the meantime the young man made the most of it to fan himself with his handkerchief and nod drowsy assent, his great round eyes staring wide as if kept open by invisible clamps. Uncle, I learnt many years later, in that period immediately after the war was putting the finishing touches to an essay attacking Croce, inspired by his reverence for Proust and intellectual esteem for Bergson; and even thirty years later he still attributed his isolation and the critical vacuum around him to mean-minded persecution by Croce's followers in Althenopis, whereas the Master himself, less mean-minded than his disciples, had shown his appreciation of the essay.

I went from my hiding place towards the dazzle of the loggia, my eyes half-closed against the unbearable light, and walked under the portico to the very end of the belvedere where it hung over empty space. I leant over the parapet, pressing hard against it because I liked to see my legs white with chalk. I opened my eyes, now used to the light. And opened all my senses to the landscape. Spread out below, golden, lay all our universe, as far as the sea, and beyond, as far as the vague outlines of the islands and the other side of the bay. And in the middle of the sky, the sun which loved me and to which for long moments I held out my face. Mild and most civilized, the landscape sloped down to the sea, no shape or colour was fierce or rough or too intense, no piece of land uncultivated; the long winding boundary walls stood out from the plain, the longest those of the mortmain lands, in the shadow of which we would walk as if afraid; Granny's stories had given us the idea that those walls would have kept on expanding endlessly, devouring little by little all the growing-land. Garibaldi had come on his horse and broken them down with his sword, restoring the soil to the round of the generations.

Metamunno, large and colourful, centred on the red tiles of the bishop's palace, while the pale houses of the other villages nestled round the domes of their churches cheaply covered in asphalt, seemingly waiting from Sunday to Sunday to gleam with majolica bought out of the offerings of the faithful. West, beyond the rock face, on the other side of which ran the road to the cities – Corento, Althenopis and far off Capitale where our father dwelt – the clear blue went on, then lost itself among mists, it seemed to me, instead of arching over the hills like a crystal sphere, enclosing our universe and protecting it from a future which frightened me, for all it was proclaimed as more splendid. And there below the rock face, as if to herald that other world, stood the model cowsheds of Don Aniello which, in the company of some farm-hands, we once walked three hours to see: wide passages and enormous sheds opening out of one another, all lined with white tiles, and every cow separated from the next in a little pen fenced with metal tubing; the milk was collected in great vats with brass covers and everywhere there was the sound of running water and the humming of electric motors.

I looked at the little houses scattered over the countryside, the convents, the bell-towers, the villas, of which we tireless explorers knew every secret. Nor had we drawn back from the shadow of the cypresses, or the high gates of the cemetery by the sea, or empty houses, or those sometimes taken over by poverty-stricken widows so that people said they were haunted; nor from the delightful bell-tower at Alisistri, soaring up pink from the tiny square like a doll's piazza with its concrete paving studded with coloured shards and shells, and earthenware jars in strange shapes scored all over with acanthus leaves; a white and spectral Madonna stood in a fountain in the middle and goldfish lapped her feet. A donation, all this whimsy, from an emigrant returned from Australia. Once a year only the bells of Alisistri pealed out holiday; on other Sundays the church stayed closed, because the little village perched on the steep slope had been almost emptied by emigration. Only the poorest folk had stayed, the ones who hadn't the money for the trip, no relative to invite them, and who hadn't even managed to get as far as Althenopis to sign on with an agency. And one would see them there at the feast-day, particularly lavish at the wish of the ocean-crossing benefactor, wandering stunned and barefoot around the stalls from which they couldn't buy; the inhabitants of the other villages called them brute beasts, deprived of those religious rites which alone lift creatures into the realm of the human.

Above the valley, right across from the terrace and at the same height, stood the ruined castle of Santa Maria del Mare, where the caverns of Maruzella's dairy spread through the rooms still standing; toadflax and wallflowers grew on the walls which we would sometimes explore when time was heavy on our hands, as if hoping for fresh life from the legends that had grown up around them since the Saracens arrived out of the sea and the people of the valley were besieged.

And everywhere I looked reminded me of some event, some tale. In that group of houses on the path leading from

Santa Maria to Metamunno, there where the cupa* widened out into an avenue of walnuts which kept the houses cool in summer, in a little room with a steep outside staircase, lived a woman who had a lover. The woman was brown, thin, with lank, greasy hair, and after the war – but only at home – she painted her heart-shaped lips a purplish red; and she had a daughter as old as us, one of our schoolmates. Every Saturday this faraway lover would turn up; as soon as he arrived he washed his face in a tin bowl, got into pyjamas and took out presents from his case; one never saw his naked feet – whereas the men of the village went barefoot in summer – because he always wore socks; as he struggled to undo the strap round the case the toes of his long feet would curl up inside thin laddered socks of a dubious white. When the presents had been handed out he would cross his legs and one could see his suspenders; with a mug of lemonade in front of him he would light up a cigarette; lemon leaves floated in the mug, according to the local recipe, so as to add the original concentration and freshness of the bud to the flavour of the ripe fruit. We would examine the presents: pieces of what looked like silk, coloured cottons for the girl, nylon stockings, and a music box or an inlaid case; and once, in his left hand, in a little cage, he brought a canary.

Farther on, where the valley sloped more gently, one could see the large estates, the Soria place, the Vozzaotras', the Gargiulos', the Persicos', the Di Sommas'. I thought of Old Signora Vozzaoatra, fat and pink, in white and black cotton, with white stockings and shoes, her white hair gathered in a bun, a heavy necklace of gold and garnets round her neck. At the grape harvest they would carry her out in an armchair to preside at the banquet set out on wooden boards in the open. And old Signora Soria, who drove her own trap to the grape harvest; whereas Signora Di Somma didn't go, was always closed up in the house with some part of her body giving her pain; what pained her most was her womanising husband,

---

* A narrow sunken path which carries water away after rain.

going round the village all suntanned, with a blue and white polka-dot cravat knotted at his throat and his moustache still golden and lustrous – useful, so they said, for tickling the necks of beautiful women.

Tired at last of gazing and telling myself stories, restless with the somnolence of the house which only the tapping of the typewriter disturbed, leaving door after door quietly ajar behind me, I glided towards a room wrapped in the cool and dark where Granny and her sister slumbered on a great double-bed. And I crept in on them where they lay rumpled in sleep and heat, their long nightdresses shamefully hitched up, their mouths wide and snoring; their white hair straggling loose from their buns; and they, who were said to have been great beauties in their youth, seemed so to me, in the sumptuous grace of their arms, their throats, their hair.

I slipped away across the waxed green floor of Uncle's room, next door to that of his mother, where there was nothing to remind me of the domestic squalor of my father and most of the men of the family. Every object in that room, though having in part a domestic form and function, managed to distance itself from the domestic by some magical property of taste.★ The bed had the austere imperial lines of the early nineteenth century and seemed ready to receive the brief rest of a high official, the statuesque repose of a woman concerned even in sleep to preserve her immovability, rather than the curled up sleep of the curly-haired uncle forever hovering between the ascetic and the voluptuary.

How different that bed was from that of Grandmother and

★ By the operation of a quite different law, similar objects achieve apotheosis and escape the context of domestic squalor in the furniture showrooms of large stores in cities or along motorways, in which entire rooms, the bedroom with the enormous double bed, the dining-room, the kitchen alcove, the sitting-room seem ready to welcome into a funereal eternity the stereotyped soul of the family, but not its sweaty, dripping , shrieking substance. But the law operating here is that governing commodities, while what governed my uncle's room were the laws of the Parnassians.

her sisters! From that of the cook of the house, Gelsomina, who had bed-springs with a torn, lumpy, horsehair mattress on which she threw herself only for an afternoon nap, because in those years she still had her own house where she was bringing up a young son, fathered by no one knew who. But after Aunt Celeste's death, which was a dreadful misfortune to that house, and since her bastard son* was by then launched on a career in the post office in the North, Gelsomina had a permanent bed of her own; for as the separation grew between her and her far-off son, now married and independent, so did her affection for the house and Uncle begin to grow and she became more and more part of the family, indeed seemed to replace for him the person of his mother. So that in the last years their relationship was no longer that of master and servant. And as the years passed that bed moved from the attic to the main floor, and from the store-room of the main floor to the guest-room, which was also Uncle's dressing-room, next door indeed to his bedroom; and instead of the horsehair she got a flock mattress, and then two flock mattresses and a feather one; and at the end of her time, her strength sapped by breast cancer, she was lovingly nursed by Uncle who had raised her to the highest heaven in the hierarchy of the house, that of love; and he wanted her to be served *caffelatte* in bed, but she still insisted on getting up at five and going down to the kitchen at that hour; perhaps life on the main floor did not seem life to her, away from the stove, the garden, the animals, the gossip of her young helpers.

Nevertheless she had to spend a lot of time in that high bed during her last months, so baskets were placed either side, one for the bitch and one for the cat and their frequent litters. And there she seemed to suffer less from her illness than from having to abandon the house to the care of others – or rather to their lack of care. Then she had to leave even that bed for one in the Fatebenefratelli Hospital in Althenopis, from which she

* The children of widows, especially if poor and without powerful friends, ended up considered as bastards.

was constantly asking for news of the house in which she had spent more than forty years, upset one instant because she heard the household was going badly, and upset the next because cousins from the Island told her that things were much better, a good housekeeper had come to take her place. Meanwhile Uncle wailed at her bedside that the house was upside-down – and not simply from delicacy of feeling; well he knew that the love Gelsomina had brought to her work in latter years, when she too had felt herself to be mistress of the house and almost a mother to him, could never be replaced and no money could buy it. So when at half past seven in the morning he went from his bedroom on to the loggia, his claps summoning the housekeeper seemed to be answered by an empty silence rather than by loving concern; and the voice that finally came up from below after repeated calling came not from a motherly breast, but merely from the damp little terrace outside the kitchen. Off he would go then, shaking his head in desolation, to the far end of the arched loggia, to his ablutions in the bathroom he had managed to get built many years before – with money dragged out of his mother – to replace the tiny privy that was all then to be found in a country villa.

The new bathroom was a jewel. The white walls were studded at irregular intervals with coloured tiles showing the signs of the zodiac, work commissioned from an Althenopis artist. Calmed perhaps by the cosmogony depicted on the tiles and purified by water, he would re-emerge smiling and re-born. In the middle of the room, above the bath, there was a larger tile showing a smiling sun framed by dancing beams. I used to look ruefully at the sign they said was proper to me, flatly similar to what I was and to the destiny augured by my father, for my sign was that of the Virgin; a boy might have been able to fantasize seeing his sign in the image of a girl. I would have preferred Pisces instead, voyaging through water, or the submerged Crab, or the bizarre Scorpio even though it disturbed me; but most of all, the blonde and effulgent Twins. And certainly not Libra. Nor Aries. Nor the Bull. I had then an unspeakable aversion to Libra, it reminded me of that right balance in everything that was always being preached at my extravagances; and of Mother weighing out the ingredients before making pastry, so that everything came out balanced in quantities and flavours, whereas I loved Granny's losing herself in the eggs and flour and flames, I loved her reckless cakes swimming in cream, smothered in fondant and burnt sugar, large slices of which always remained after our eager onslaught, so there was always something left for our friends and their smaller brothers and sisters; even for the following day, when we again had the appetite for them.

But I would really have liked the Twins for my sign. Not to be me, at least, and always to be accompanied by someone else!

When it rained one went to that bathroom with a large blue and green umbrella, which stood in an earthenware amphora at the end of the porch. The umbrella was a present from a Jewish friend whom Uncle had hidden during the war; he had brought it back from London, remembering one of the small inconveniences of his stay in the house.

There was often no running water in that bathroom because the pressure was too low, and hence a faint smell of excrement hung about, held in check by the scent of rare soaps, ambergris or sandalwood, that Uncle ordered from London once the war was over. These soaps didn't make much lather, yet their scent was so intensely penetrating and lasting that their lingering acidulous alchemy fixed the vapours from over-heated fecal rot and the smoking staleness of urine which in other privys took me by the throat and stomach; and they reminded me of the vague and sweetish nausea I felt when I was sick with acetonaemia and which has left in my memory a trace as it were of weariness and disgust with life and the world.

There were two dressers in Uncle's bedroom, one topped with a mirror, the other without, and they seemed less the holders of underwear and other clothes that I knew them to be than the proud supports of the trinkets and precious objects that stood on top. There was the original of the well-known statue by the great mad sculptor of Althenopis,* which showed an urchin pulling a thorn out of his foot, and a portrait in pastel of Uncle as an adolescent, the work of Aunt Callista, our mother's sister, who had been a pupil of the great sculptor; there were two lions in blue crystal, as if keeping fierce watch on that portrait and on that youthfulness; a crystal ball holding coloured stone chippings which Uncle used to shake in the mornings to descry portents in the pattern of colours; a Chinese box that held his cuff–links; strange little pill boxes; pomanders; and phials of a bluish medicine, the taking of which perhaps explained the recurrent presence on the dresser, next to a book with an expensive binding – always the same book because Uncle never read in bed – of a balloon glass holding a curved glass spoon.

And one never saw slippers or dressing-gowns in that room, not because they weren't there, but because they didn't appear as such; draped on a beautifully polished bentwood chair of delicate workmanship, a white or blue string vest suggested the sea, for in summer Uncle disdained shirts and would step out in his vest to the rocks of Queen Costanza where von Platen had gone bathing, from which Goethe had merely taken views, and on which, after the liberation of Italy, Salvemini strolled arm in arm with a left-wing priest and his young charges. The habit of wearing vests in summer came from the three islands; in the village only the carter, farm-hands on their way home, and the Annunziata bricklayers were to be seen wearing them; the farm-hands in any case worked stripped to the waist and only put their vests on to sit back under a tree with a glass of watered wine or a jug of lemonade. But Uncle's vests were something else again, tightly-knitted and shiny, in dazzling white, or sky-blue, or pastel green, or bordeaux red, and, on certain daredevil mornings or at the high points of the social season, even pink.

If I leant on the bed, violating the perfectly squared-off

---

* 'The real life of Gemito' as described by Savinio in *Racontate, uomini, la vostra storia.*

bedcover of red damask or green and white striped satin, it felt very hard indeed; Uncle slept on a wooden board, not because he suffered from arthritis but because he was a health fanatic. If I wiped a finger across the marble top of the dresser, not a speck of dust or a spot of lotion came away on my finger, but the cold of the contact would penetrate me and I would wait in vain for waves of warmth to emanate from the auroral pink running through the veins of marble. If, in search of some homely sign, I sniffed the armpits of the vest lying on the chair, no odour of sweat came to comfort and disgust me, but only the subtle and penetrating scent of sandalwood and ambergris that belonged in the bathroom, but here was free of the mingling of body odours.

Sometimes I slept over in the house to keep Grandmother company – it was the custom in our family that the children's limbs should warm those of the old, and that their fragile shoulders should serve as crutches – either because Grandmother was involved in the huge preparations for Easter lunch, or because she had to nurse her sister who was sick; indeed Aunt Celeste often fell ill. Grandmother would wake me at dawn and tie my plaits with a blue bow; trembling with cold I would lean on the parapet of the terrace to watch the daily awakening of landscape and house. It gave me pleasure, as it did Grandmother, to be up before the rest and for an hour at least be mistress of the sleeping world. At half past seven I saw the white door of Uncle's room open little by little, and he would come out; not rumpled and dishevelled, but like a small child rising from its cot still wrapped in the marvels of sleep; and because of some decorative hemstitch or some subdued warmth of raw silk, like that of the tea rose, or their oriental cut, or their delicate shade of purple, his pyjamas then made him seem like a fairytale wizard, and not one of the squalid fathers of families.

So intense was his lifted face, as if his eyes were being rubbed by the light, so radiant after those stunned moments of opening his eyes on a new-found world, happened on by surprise, so exultant and festive his exclamation at what the new day promised that he seemed closer to the world of us children than to that of the grown-ups; and less to the world of children than to that of infants at the breast, who seem not to communicate with single individuals and single things but rather with their own aura which blends everything together into a coloured medley, makes no distinctions, is everywhere diffused and cannot be grasped by anyone past that stage.

Every act of Uncle's day appeared to be officiated at rather than performed, and not by some thoughtless, hasty, vulgar or bombastic priest but as a wizard might officiate in his castle.

The rite began, after that wide-eyed awakening, when he took up from the little marble table in the loggia the bottle – mineral water before the arrival of the Americans, and then coca-cola – he drank on waking to stimulate his digestion; with little hand movements in the direction of his face, to keep off the flies and the blinding light, but which also seemed like applause for the new day; he then went off to the bathroom where he locked himself in for some time. The smell of toasting bread rose from the kitchen to herald the breakfast feast on the terrace; Granny had already eaten her bread soup in the kitchen and, red in the face, her black dress covered in flour and her sleeves rolled up her white arms, vigorous still though blue arteries stood out in furrows on them, she was busy kneading and rolling the pastry into strips for the lasagne, for the rice *sartu*, for the cheese or lettuce flans, for the puff pastries.

And the poor cook, Gelsomina, went round muttering, having to wash an endless pile of ladles and pans, stoke continuous fires under boiling cauldrons, stir thick sauces or mushroom or chocolate bechamels; or she was made to dice up candied fruit on a corner of the marble table-top, or cut cheese and salami into little bits. She, the mistress of the kitchen, demoted to scullion! On those occasions, in the opulence of her sister's house, Grandmother rediscovered the splendours of the house she had lost, with its crowd of poor relations, children, hangers-on, some drawn by the open-handedness of the house, but most by the exuberance of the life that reigned there.

Since I was too young to be allowed at Uncle's table, I would go down to the kitchen to eat buttered toast; but, that done, I would spy on him from the blue shadow of the spiral staircase leading to the terrace, where he took his breakfast under the portico and asperged the four corners of the landscape with his morning joy, his exclamations of satisfaction at the toast done to a turn, the freshness of the butter, the aroma of the tea. Never once as I spied on Uncle at table did I witness any of those painful domestic scenes in which a man reproves a woman for the imperfection of the food, nor that greedy haste when the food instead is to his taste. For it wasn't so much that Uncle found relish in everything, but rather that he discovered secrets and hidden quintessences and correspondences between the perfection of the food and that of the universe.

And he covered with praise the serving and the cooking women, all the women who took care of him, from the humblest little maid to his mother, to his Island cousin; for every single thing, even the most simple, he came up with a particular plaudit, a grace of speech or smile; he never showed impatience at any lapse of perfection in the food, but rather a sorrow, not at the small contrariety but at the perturbation in the order of the world that it signalled; a wail would come from him, an indistinct muttering, and what he bewailed was not the fact that his senses remained unsatisfied but the failure to reach the peak of art. And when something gave him particular pleasure he tasted it with religious slowness, his fork or spoon suspended in the air, interrupting the gesture with frequent exclamations of praise; or he might smack his lips – he was deaf and perhaps could not hear himself – as ill-bred children do. Almost always when he drank he made a loud slurp, as if every common drink was transformed in his presence into nectar or the elixir of life. Whereas I when I ate felt only a satisfied animal fullness.

And whereas I thought I noticed in my father's belly – and in those of many other men, generally flaccid bellies, bulging, covered in hair, white – a gurgling and a warring, in my uncle's belly – flat, muscular and tanned – I felt instead the sedimenting of a pleasure that went on beyond his mouth, so that the honey, butter, toasted bread, the transparent filaments of orange marmalade fused slowly together, lapped and melting in the aroma of tea, to spread then throughout his whole body where they became the sparks of intelligence and joy in his eyes, the concentration in his mouth and forehead, the tight little curls at the corners of his ears. There seemed to be no part of that body that wasn't wrought upon and civilized, not only by daily massage and gymnastics – which at a certain moment in those years turned into yoga – by a moderate exposure to wind and air and the sun in summer, but also by the humble and silent services of a superbly fit digestion in conformity with the precept of the School of Salerno, 'Mens sana in corpore sano'; all of which was philosophically supported and sustained by an epicurean leavening of certain oriental practices which he nevertheless knew from an initiate – and it certainly must have been a dramatic recognition – must aim at higher things, things he was to find difficulty in attaining given the drag of his frivolous self-indulgence.

In those years the house was customarily out of bounds for us children, crammed as it was with precious trinkets; our every gesture was a bomb plot and we found the constraints on our talking and movement difficult. Uncle had not then fallen into the loneliness of his latter years, when he was grateful even for the company of children, having to communicate his every thought, from the simplest to the most philosophically rarefied, to any creature at hand, dog, farm-hand or child. And in the last years, after the death of Gelsomina, he would read out his writings and recite his poetry to the farmer's son whom he paid to sleep in the room next to his and guard the house against burglars, and discuss Balbec and Tunisia in a familiar way as if the lad had barely arrived back the previous day.

But at great festivities – Uncle's name-day or Great-Aunt Celeste's, Easter, the grape harvest – when all the relatives were invited, we children too might enter the house and especially the forbidden rooms. At those times I didn't arrive as Granny's shadow, as her crutch or bedwarmer, but all decked out in the glorious community of brothers and sisters. Only then did Uncle seem to notice me and say, 'Hasn't she grown!', and not to me but to the relations. Nor did he even notice my little sister, though with connoisseur's eyes, full of curiosity in the early years and then full of love, he turned his attention on our brother standing stiffly in white, impatient to get back to his playing till lunch should arrive. Then the boy would come back very embarrassed, trying with strange, contorted, affected gestures to hide some stain on his clothes; the aunts would scold him affectionately, but for Uncle, whose childhood had not been so free, those stains made the boy more attractive. 'Leave him be!' he would say, 'Stop tormenting him!'

On these occasions Grandmother's other sisters would come, with their children and other relations. The women of the family dominated; almost all of them had been widowed young. The five sisters would sit on the large divan and the armchairs, while the bentwood chairs went to the daughters, our mother among them, the sons, and then the other guests.

Grandmother, never entirely relaxing against the back-rest, in black, with a lace blouse for the occasion barely open at the neck, and the wide velvet band round it adorned with a piece of costume jewellery, holding in check her palpitating vein, sitting on the edge of her chair as if ready to rise at any moment in response to a call, red in the face, gesticulating, with her white hair piled up, suddenly leapt to her feet in indignation because someone had perhaps passed on a piece of unpleasant gossip (it was murmured in the family that Granny suffered from persecution mania): her great dark eyes became suddenly vivid, flashing; it was indignation more than anything else that brought back Granny's youth.

Meanwhile Great-Aunt Celeste, the second of the sisters, who not much later became the source of authority when the first-born died, sat all hunched up in a corner of the divan with

107

her blue-grey eyes smiling vaguely, wrapped in a grey or blue wool dress with a gauzy lilac scarf around her neck, or in colourful Turkish shawls given by her son, her feet resting on a red silk stool which had short curved legs ending in dog paws. Her feet, encased in beige wool stockings and shoes of velvet or of canvas with the laces undone, were swollen, while Granny's shoes were narrow with a low heel, her foot still trim and slender, her long shapely legs restless and quick so that she seemed ever ready to leap to her feet, to run up and down stairs, to fly from the room and from the world if need be.

Great-Aunt Ada, the fourth of the sisters, sat opulent and statuesque, her white shoulders still plumply rounded; this was the great-aunt aunt I admired in undress beside her sister during their afternoon nap; it was impossible to decide whether the majestic calm of her face was grander and more resplendent that its insipid indifference was abysmal. She had always obeyed her mother, her husband, her children – the very opulence of her flesh would have been a hindrance, so to speak, to disobedience; next to her sat the son who had inherited her vacuous dethroned majesty. I remember his opening the door to me with stiff courtesy while his plump little wife bustled about for hours in the kitchen making a mock-ragout, without meat that is; he, back from the lowly job Granny's influence had found for him, waited on lunchtime, rigid in an armchair reading a newspaper, and every now and then lifted his eyes to the vista of drawing-rooms through doors propped open with pyramidal marble doorstops; the smell of the mock-ragout seemed not to reach him and the obstinate, hovering flies seemed to tug at his sleeve in vain.

A great lover of the sun, herself still radiant, Great-Aunt Egle, the last of the sisters, sat in one of his beams; Great-Aunt Egle of the violet eyes, whose colour had been much romanced about in the family and in Althenopis; her hair still quite blonde, her tiny, perfect face rising like a rare flower from her florid body; who always wore striped or pastel suits and always lifted the veil of her little hat to free her gaze the moment she was inside. Our father would kiss her hand with gallantry and then sit on a stool at her feet. Of all those women she was the one he liked, for her elegance, her steadiness, her openminded composure, her secret knowledge of the world. Aunt Egle had been only twenty when she lost her much-loved, extremely handsome, but consumptive husband; for ten years, until she married again, she had been able to enjoy a freedom from which nubile girls and married women were then excluded.

Of the fifth sister, Anita,* the first-born, I only have faint memories. I almost never saw her in that house because she was gravely ill, with the result that her image is overlaid by that of her two daughters, the Island cousins, or the Cousins par excellence,† because not having married they had never left the family and had not acquired an identity of their own. When over the course of the years the five sisters began to disappear, the Cousins came to represent the unity and continuity of the family.

Both of them were small and energetic, though very different: the elder blonde and bony, the younger minute and brunette. The hierarchy established in their childhood remained with them; the elder was the one in charge, who took decisions, who could permit herself more aches and pains and even imagined illnesses because the other sister nursed and looked after her, and more bad temper because the other always replied submissively and sweetly. The management of their small family income, relations with the men of the family, the cultural slant to give to their reading, the plays

---

* Before giving her the name, Great-Grandmother had made certain that Anita was actually the wife of Garibaldi, and not his mistress, as her confessor claimed.

† The spinsters of that generation were always caught between their own lives and their families'. In the case of the Island Cousins this uncertainty was doubled by the fact that there were two of them and they lived together. They had the chance after the war of acquiring a personality distinct from that of their family, when they went to work for the Americans. But once the Americans left, they reverted to their uncertain position. The chance was lost.

to see together, their social life, family correspondence, important decisions like moving house or repairing a roof, were dealt with by the elder, while the younger did the shopping, the cooking, kept things tidy, looked after the children and sick relations, and listened patiently to the grumblings of the elder.

The elder sat with her legs crossed and, being a bit deaf, spoke in a high chirping voice – one of the reasons, Mother said, why she had never found a husband, because women must have, if not a melodious voice, at least a low one – while the other sat with her legs hidden under her skirt, listened a great deal, spoke in a soft and slightly anxious voice, and if some guest new to the house offered her a cigarette, she would point out that she did not smoke in the tone of a child begging forgiveness.

They had never married, according to Mother and the aunts, mainly because they were not possessed of any great beauty or wealth, whereas they had pretensions to spare. Their mother, the eldest of the five sisters, was the only one who had studied and had inculcated intellectual mania in the two daughters. It was said in the family, that in 1878 there were only five women in Italy who had taken a middle school diploma, among them Aunt Anita.* Somehow linked with this, they gave me to understand, was the fact that her beauty was less splendid than her sisters', for she had spent too much time bent over books and as a result her shoulders had become narrow and curved, her gaze too sharp, her fingers inkstained and she had ended by marrying her physics tutor. While away on a business trip he had been killed by a malcontent† who mistook him for the mayor, and left his wife pregnant with the second daughter.‡ After a family conference, the sisters

* This was an item in the family collection of glories, like descent (through a cadet branch, naturally) from Clare of Assisi; or from Giambattista Vico, or from an ancestor who had taken part in the expedition of the Thousand.
† An anarchist, a socialist, someone envious or someone mad?
‡ So that her womb seemed like a grave from which someone was expected to resurrect.

decided to entrust to their elder sister, widowed and with no means of support, the administration of their revenues so that she might receive a factor's stipend; and this practice of entrusting financial administration to unfortunate relatives* then continued in the family. The male role of the eldest sister thus took on ever firmer outlines. She wanted her daughters educated in the modern way: she sent them to study German in Leipzig, English in London – French was already spoken in the family.

Only defeated men could provide stable elements in that congress of women, reuniting so amicably in the months of *villeggiatura* and at times of festivity, men who in their presence might heal from wounds suffered battling with the world: Uncle Giobatta, for example, the husband of Aunt Callista, who had gone headlong into some dodgy engineering ventures and had designed a bridge which collapsed, thanks to a partner's skulduggery, and since that date, like the women of the family, had to live off his rents and avoid the world of business like the devil; or like devil-may-care Uncle Nini, only there when he had been cleaned out gambling; or like Uncle Ubaldo who, unable to keep up with the dizzying whirl of Uncle Chinchino's business affairs, sought refuge in a small job; or like our father when he fell into disgrace with the Ministry.

At these times of truce with the world, the men devoted themselves to managing what was left of their fortunes after what they had wasted on rash business deals, the folly of gambling or of women; or after public calamities, like wars or changes of regime, which made inroads into their substance.

With the passage of decades these revenues became smaller and smaller, though still sufficient to ensure the women a dignified existence. But lack of means, though veiled, showed in the clothing of some of them. Grandmother's lace blouse,

* Unfortunate meant fallen on hard times. The distress in fact was softened more by comfort than by time.

for instance, had holes in more than one place. She had no fondness for mending, and the niece from the Island hadn't yet seen to repairing it, for domestic gaiety seem to shed a light of luxury over the women's garments and on that day of merry-making it had skipped her notice. Nor was Aunt Egle's elegant suit quite in fashion, refurbished some years later with trimming à la Chanel; and in this instance it wasn't merely a question of lack of means but of her conception of elegance, for she didn't think it done to follow the latest fashion and held that clothes must never, never, look new; this was true for *princesses*, and for boleros but above all for suits. And then only two or three styles really suited any particular woman, so it was a mistake to change. It had been her way, at the time of the frequent train journeys of her first widowhood, to set off in an immaculate travelling suit of white piqué; on arriving she would take an identical one from her trunk and change in the toilet before leaving the train; and her travelling companions could only contrast their creased and grubby clothes with that miracle, altogether spotless and untouched. It was only to a very few that Great-Aunt Egle confessed this secret.

Even the strings of pearls they all wore had fakes interspersed with the real things, in the coils closest to the neck.

And in the evening, so as not to be a burden on the house-keeping, but also for health reasons, the aunts ate bread soup together, and only infrequently did the mistress of the house, Great-Aunt Celeste, garnish the table with a mozzarella cheese; but she always saw to it that there was a handful of dried figs or sultanas, hazel and walnuts.

Social upheaval, often such a boon for business, dealt crippling blows to income derived from the land. Should some member of the family make money – it could only be a relative by marriage – slight scorn went into any mention of his name, even though the aunts condescendingly pretended to justly appreciate the efforts made by such men to enrich themselves and come up to the standard of the family. But if misfortune struck one of these entrepreneurs, the nobility conferred by the misfortune gave full membership of the family and the veiled scorn and condescension gave way to a growing esteem for his manner of dealing with difficulties; for it was facing up to an adverse fate, rather than gaining money, honours and glory, that was considered a title to merit. Achievement and success in the world were looked on with suspicion, for what counted was being born into the family, and not becoming someone. This was not aristocratic arrogance: a system of values, both civic and religious, and known as gentlemanliness, was considered a rightful property of the family and was set against the world of the vulgar and the useful. Only by going beyond, in an intellectual, spiritual or religious flight, was it possible to rise above the family. This attitude without doubt was based on landed income but it also derived from a sense of civic duty inherited from their father; or mainly perhaps from the fact that it was a family of women. The men died early and, in effect, didn't count.

The wives of the few males born to the family, however, entered it with full rights, becoming even closer kin, so to speak, than their husbands. The exception was Aunt José, the wife of Uncle Nini, who never managed to like that world. This Aunt José used to behave in a slightly different way from the other women; for example, she borrowed a friend's fur in order to show off at a wedding; the great-aunts saw this as social-climbing. Or she made her daughter's dresses at home and said they came from the dressmaker; and the aunts also deplored the fact that the dresses, so charming and in such good taste, were poorly finished, with the result that the hems immediately came down. And then they thought it most eccentric of José that her drawing room should have low, wide ottomans, where she lounged to receive her women and men friends – the most secluded nooks of her handsome body, the places where thighs and arms joined, outlined not just by her dress but by her pose. And then she was a knowledgeable judge of the way nieces and young daughters were coming along physically, and discussed it as if they were mares for the sale ring, altogether indifferent to their qualities, should they

113

have any, of mind and spirit; and that knowingness did not go down well with the aunts.

The only male who had not been struck by misfortune and yet was admitted to full membership was Uncle Alceste, whose daily ritual was so closely intertwined with that of his mother.

The married daughters of the five sisters, married in general to men considered of lower rank, were imperceptibly excluded from the family by reason of their misalliances, but were fully reinstated once they were widowed or when struck by misfortune. Their husbands tried, at least in the early days of marriage, to loosen the ties with all these women, perhaps because they couldn't manage to sort out the features of the loved one from all the rest and felt as if they were being sucked into that broth. But it was in vain, for they couldn't keep their wives or children away.

Nevertheless, following the principle of divide and rule, each of them chose a favourite and confidante from among the women in an attempt to cut her off from the others, fomenting small incompatibilities and resentments. Our father, for example, who was a man of the world, picked out Great-Aunt Egle; Granny was the passion of a banker uncle, a man of deep feeling and humble origin who had remained simple-hearted: loving his wife as he did, he was grateful to Grandmother for having heaped her with gifts, caresses and compliments when she had been a girl and poor. Great-Aunt Celeste, naturally, was the confidante of Uncle Alceste and Uncle Francesco found in the lucid spirit of Great-Aunt Anita that capacity to see reason which was, in his opinion, so lacking in his wife and the rest of those women.

But the case of Uncle Giobatta, kinsman by marriage, will best exemplify the complex relation between men and the women of the family. After thirty years of marriage, he was abandoned by his wife. He had previously been ill thought of by the women, perhaps because they regretted having agreed to his marrying Callista, then so young and innocent of the world; or because he was of a sullen character; or perhaps

114

because he came from an old Piedmontese military family (so found it difficult to put up with their *dolce far niente* and the slight barely discernible, disorder resulting from their lazy way of life), and then he had the provoking habit of speaking of Garibaldi as if he had been a useful idiot.

From the moment his wife left him, however, until the moment of his death, he found himself surrounded by the loving attention of all of them; this one inviting him to dinner, that one to tea,* yet another to lunch, telephoning to invite him to a wedding, to the birthday party of a nephew, to a funeral, or simply to enquire after his health; and he let himself be lapped in those tender and assiduous attentions. Perhaps he saw shining through details of each face the wife he had once found so winning. And it seemed that in adopting him all the great-aunts wanted to be forgiven for the hurt one of them had done; but the more they deplored her behaviour, insisting that never in the memory of man had such a thing happened in their family, the gloomier he became at the injustice of that bare exception. Then for days he was not to be seen, though he came back soon enough, to find again in the yielding southern folly of her kin the memory of his young wife before her folly in his regard, against him, or perhaps for him, had not yet turned into cruel extravagance.

The room in which the family gathered, the adjacent room, which was Great-Aunt Celeste's, and likewise the vast kitchen on the floor below, were the only rooms which had not been changed since the time the five widowed sisters used to come in summer with their children and camp on mattresses strewn about the rooms. For half the summer season the sisters used to gather at Great-Aunt Celeste's and for the rest in Granny's house at Quisisana, the house from which our mother when young had set out for her walks.

Managing little by little to loosen his mother's purse strings,

* Being less troublesome and expensive than invitations to dinner, invitations to tea were more frequent. To newcomers it was also possible to say, particularly if tea was on a Thursday, that it was the maid's time off. The same couldn't be said at lunch or dinner.

often by unconsciously exploiting psychosomatic distur-
bances that worried her, like his aerophagy, Uncle Alceste
had restored the house and one by one re-opened the drawing-
rooms; so that where once the comfortable shabby country
rooms had resounded till late at night with shouts and the
smothered laughter of children, while upstairs the sisters were
in company with men and women friends from the villas (nor
was the odd rejected suitor lacking), there now stretched a
vista of drawing-rooms, doors thrown wide, opening like
jewel caskets, each in its own colour, in its precious particular-
ity. First came the green, perfumed with attar of roses; then
came the red, perfumed with amber; the yellow closed the
sequence, and was a library rather than a drawing-room.
Here, protected by glass and a delicate grille, stood the Gallimard editions, the *Recherche*★ most venerated of them all; the
signed and dedicated *L'Immoraliste* prominently displayed;
two notes from Romain Rolland as if by accident, were
propped in front of *Jean-Christophe*; the works of Céline and
Barbusse were the occasion for Uncle to recall his part in the
drôle de guerre, when he had gone off to the front an eighteen-
year-old, accompanied by three big cases in Russian leather.
And there was a photo of Uncle during his trip to North
Africa, in the steps of the *maître*, who knows. But he never
used this room, always preferring to work in the sunlit upper
room, close to his mother who brooded over him in loving
dominion.

These three drawing-rooms were dark, since they were on
the ground floor and their windows, protected by bellying
baroque wrought-iron, looked out on to the damp and shady
lane which separated the house from the lemon grove. The
serried trinkets and the various other ornaments and trophies

★ Uncle had a great veneration for Proust, who had withdrawn from the
drawing-room to his cork-lined bedroom, while Uncle not only frequented
the drawing-rooms of others but was opening his own, one after another.
Then, as opposed to Charlus who had sold the family furniture to a brothel,
Uncle was constantly adding new furniture. He venerated D'Annunzio, of
course, as well as Proust.

seemed to block out light and air, and when, to escape my overseers, I dawdled there, I felt a sense of constriction, an anxiety would take hold of me and a fear that the sky had turned to glass, that all the air in the street smelled of amber, so that I would part the heavy curtains, green, red or yellow as the case might be, to see whether there was, as I remembered, a world outside.

Beyond the drawing-rooms lay a well-lit corridor; old prints of fleets, Vesuvius in eruption, battles. When no one could see me and no sound of voices reached me from the first and farthest drawing-room, I used to take long slides along the shiny waxed floor. And as I slid it seemed to me that all the luxury of the house served no other purpose than to make possible a game that could happen nowhere else. The ends of the corridor were closed off by two great doors which were never, in those circumstances, to be opened, for one gave on to the great kitchen and the other on to the celestial spiral staircase – which didn't lead to heaven, as it suggested, but only to the terrace – in whose walls were set the small doors of larders where dried grapes, almonds, sweet wine, convent biscuits and jams were kept. Those two ends of the corridor embraced the family rooms and beyond them began the servants' quarters which were to remain out of sight.

Across the corridor one finally came upon the dining-room, three sides of which opened on to the same Mediterranean landscape as the terrace above. The roundness of the table seemed to reproduce the circle of the horizon, and its shine, whether it was laid or not, fused with the dazzle of the sea. The handsome face of the young Alexander of Macedon, the work of the great Althenopis master, was set on a plinth in front of a balcony and his soft, fleshy, half-open lips seemed both envious and scornful of the table when it was laid. I was always taken aback by the eyes, which close up seemed empty, but from a distance seemed to stare at you with a stern and detached kindness. A large canvas showed 'The Multiplication of the Loaves and Fishes', and we children, who were guests at Uncle's table only on great occasions, watched anxiously as the food grew less and less on its way to us at the bottom of the table. All the aunts and uncles were good eaters and we feared that a similar miracle of multiplication might not occur for us. But from the kitchen appeared a second round of dishes, for if the everyday housekeeping of the place was sober enough, there was no cheeseparing on feast days. The canvas also seemed to offer reassurance to the diners that Christ had taken care of the destitute by way of miracles: one might eat without qualms.

And the macaroni arrived, the rice *sartu*, the vegetables covered with parmesan, grated and grilled; then came the roast chickens lying on beds of peas or new potatoes; satisfied by then, almost overfed, we watched indifferently as fish gave way to Russian salads, to cream cheese and mozzarellas, served up on beds of lemon or mulberry leaves, salads of luscious colour and arrangement which the older aunts liked so much, while we hung on for the dessert; and at last the tall babas arrived – the memory of their soft deliciousness made one delirious for months after – or crêpes flambées, the marvel of whose bluish flames sweetened our greedy waiting. As alternate dessert there were Grandmother's sweets, the puff pastries full of various shades of custard, or Sicilian snaps. They came announced as a second dessert: people were never sure in her latter years whether her sweets would turn out well, and fearing to create a scene, they made the feast a pretext for having two desserts. The aunts meanwhile, lest Granny's ready susceptibility lead her to suspect, whispered in her ear that Alceste was incapable of doing without his French dessert, though they, of course, preferred the traditional kind. Thanks to this show of tact towards Grandmother, we were able to stuff ourselves with custard, only regretting that we had to use fork and spoon, for our pleasure would have been multiplied had we been able to use hands and mouth and feel ourselves fuse with the sweet into a single substance. Thus, for example, mozzarella, which gave us such pleasure when we ate it in dripping mouthfuls in Maruzzella's cave or at home, when our father was away, lost its flavour when one had to eat it at table with knife and fork. All the milk was lost in the cutting, while the sharp pointed fork ill-matched its elastic softness, with the upshot that I claimed not to like mozzarella. But at my Uncle's table the gleaming glassware and the richness of the food softened the rigours of etiquette.

The best feast of all in that house was Easter, while the celebrations that took place for Uncle's name-day started out least pleasantly for us children. They began at eight in the morning when the priest came with two altar boys to say mass in front of the massive closet, transformed into a chapel with flowers and candles. (Every year on that day Great-Aunt Celeste paid for two masses to be said in church, in thanksgiving to Our Lady for safeguarding her son during the Great War.) The mass was over quickly, since the priest had many more to say elsewhere, and then he was aware that Uncle was an unbeliever and didn't want to expose himself to ridicule.

Once the priest was gone, the chapel was hurriedly closed up lest the candelabra and other sacred ornaments be stolen in the confusion of the feast, the divans and the armchairs were pushed back against the wall, straw-bottomed chairs were brought from other rooms and the farm people were let in to offer their good wishes and their gifts of produce. They remained standing, waiting for the signal, with baskets on their arms or at their feet, heaped with dozens of eggs, or flasks of sweet wine, trussed-up chickens, cherries or plums. Aunt Celeste would say, 'Make yourselves at home', and the straw-bottomed chairs would be pushed towards them, for they were not to sit on the upholstered chairs in case they soiled them. At that point we children didn't know where we were supposed to sit, and remained standing uncomfortably, staring at the men and women we were so much at home with in our daily comings and goings, off whose plates we often ate, suddenly turned into Christmas shepherds. The few words they came out with were in thick dialect (and we had the impression they were deliberately speaking more thickly

119

so as not to be understood, for we had often heard them speaking correct Italian), and they complained about the rise in the price of fertilizer, animal feeds, seed corn; the hailstorm at the end of spring, the rain that hadn't come. The cordial they were served came in ordinary glass beakers, not crystal.

When the farm people had left, Uncle would burst out with exclamations at the sun-ripe plums, the shine on the cherries; and Grandmother would happily recall the house at Quisisana, where her farm people also came, bringing their produce into the kitchen or the larders, and she ordered the killing of the chickens. Meanwhile Aunt Celeste and the other aunts complained of the insolence and growing demands of farm people, and an aunt by marriage who came from Apulia spoke angrily about the land troubles of the past. And the Island cousins spoke of the sufferings of certain distant relatives of theirs in Hungary. Grandmother, who happened to come back into the room at that moment, flew up in indignation at the torments inflicted on the nuns in Barcelona. But in no time the smiling calm of Aunt Egle – the only one to read the political page of the newspaper – re-established the more pacific and less disturbing truth. Living in the capital with her banker son-in-law, she knew how far from taking power the common people were, and since she also had democratic leanings, she was able to reassure her sisters and their children on the one hand by appealing to their humane and religious sentiments with her description of the injustices suffered by the people and by setting out the need for reforms, and on the other by extolling the harmony reigning between her banker son-in-law and his employees, respect for whose union rights was indispensable if agreement were to be reached.

And there and then the recriminations of the aunts against the common people turned into voluble sympathy and benevolence, one of them listing the misfortunes of a certain farmer, another those of a maid, or the family carpenter, and Grandmother recalled in apology the occasions when she had prayed *coram populo* with bombed-out people in the Caporetto and Fuoriporta tunnels; only the aunt by marriage from

Apulia remained shut in fierce and stubborn silence, because, I think, having seen the power of people in revolt, she was no longer able to cherish any illusions; and for this reason among others, leaving aside her arrogance, she was not suffered gladly by the rest. The aunts, in general so generous in their judgement of others, descended to vicious gossip in her case, hinting, for example, that she had never made use of the trousseau she had brought with her from Apulia as a bride, with the intention of passing it on to her daughters as she had received it, which explained why her home was short on sheets and embroidered towels.

Soon forgetting their complaints against the insolence of the common people and their pity for its sufferings, they helped themselves heartily to the fruit in the baskets, and when they could eat no more, set to arranging it artistically on stands.

Then Grandmother would call me to go down to the kitchen with her, because the steps made her giddy and she needed me to lean on; or the younger of the Island aunts would guess at my boredom and get me to accompany her because Great-Aunt Celeste and Uncle Alceste didn't want us wandering around the house on our own: we were surrounded by a constant suspicion that we might break something or even steal, for in their eyes we children belonged more to the species of underlings than of peers.

Once in the kitchen I would stay till lunchtime, my curiosity about the newly arrived aunts and the various strange objects cramming the state rooms by then satisfied.

When she had checked the consistency of the galantines, the proper coldness of the custards, the baking temperature of the pastries, Granny would go off, and when the younger of the Island aunts, bundle of keys in hand, had brought the required ingredients out of the larder, she too would go off.

I would sit on a stool in the fragrance of the kindling under cauldrons of water, and all morning long I could observe the house and its inhabitants from a point of view different from that of upstairs.

Uncle's hand-clap, which from up on the terrace seemed a gay summons, was received down there with irritated condescension, and in no hurry, with dragging feet and an ironic smile, Gelsomina would set off to answer or send a grinning young helper, who, instead of responding promptly, merely seemed to ape response. Down there Uncle was called 'the young master', and I always had difficulty in grasping quite how irreverently it was intended.

In a small cupboard painted the blue of the Marina houses, which, though they guessed its contents, none of the aunts ever dare open for reasons of tact, Gelsomina set aside large platefuls of titbits for her son's lunch and dinner. Though she personally scorned certain kinds of food, especially galantines, mayonnaise, bechamels, she would set aside large portions for her son; in the same fashion she devoted all her savings to paying his school fees, despite her claim that it was better to learn a trade and that school made children proud and only taught them to be better than their parents. Once in a while, when she was out in the courtyard, I would open the cupboard and help myself to the dried figs and almonds of which I was specially fond. And so did all the kitchen helpers; we were all shouted at, but tolerated because Gelsomina seemed to see it as a moral principle that the weak rob the stronger in a chain of tolerant complicity without which it would be impossible for human beings to live together.

When women or boys came into the courtyard to sell fish, meat or vegetables, Gelsomina would beat down the price mercilessly, and what she managed to save she put aside for her son. And when the time came round to tease up the mattresses, she even found a way each year to make off with a handful of feathers or flocks that would go towards a mattress or pillow.

I was glad to see all these little thefts and wished I were capable of doing the same for our mother.

The little lads who succeeded one another as helpers in the kitchen didn't manage to steal from the house – that was Gelsomina's exclusive privilege – but they did rob her; they spent their time mimicking the various inmates of the house and I often joined in, because once in the kitchen I took sides with its inhabitants and despised the people upstairs.

I would curl up drowsily in the dog's basket and watch the chickens as now and then they entered the square of sunlight which at that hour lay like a carpet over part of the damp terrace; plucking up courage they advanced into the shadow of the kitchen and pecked about under the tables. I would come awake only at the crackle of frying fat, and sneak fried potatoes or cabbage and aubergine fritters; the brain fritters unfortunately were numbered and not to be stolen.

Sometimes, lured by the unusual goings-on in the house, friends from the piazza would come to the doorway to say hello, but Gelsomina immediately drove them away; on occasion she might give them something tasty to nibble or a custard pan to lick; we divided it into sections and everyone licked his own.

I would get sudden cravings while I was there and beg Gelsomina for a slice of bread and suet, or bread and dripping with salt, or get her to pour some oil into a saucer for me to dip bread and fresh garlic stalks.

Often I went to sleep on the dog's cushions until I was shaken by Grandmother or the cousin from the Island. And then they would make me go home to change, because my morning party dress would be all covered in kitchen stains. So I would put on a clean but ordinary frock, and Granny would put a fresh ribbon in my hair. And contrite, I followed the procession of relatives as it set off through the state rooms to lunch.

It was decided one year to make the most of the presence of a young housekeeper and tidy up the attics, which no one had seen the inside of for decades. And we gaily went along on the pretext of helping. During the entire fifteen days it took to tidy up the attics, we were able to go up and down from roof to roof by pulling a wooden ladder after us and there in the mornings, carefree and sly, we could look down on the little terrace where Uncle took the sun for an hour in the nude; and

123

see for ourselves that what they said in the village wasn't just idle gossip.

We watched for some time, waiting for something scandalous to happen, but nothing did, except that every now and then Uncle took a sponge from a bowl and dowsed himself with water, quite deaf to our smothered laughter, which we in any case grew tired of as the minutes passed, since between the harmless nudity and the sun, there was nothing to laugh about. We were tempted to drop pebbles or a small piece of plaster, but we held back for fear of being discovered and thereafter excluded from the non-existent scandal, for which we continued to wait in vain.

Gelsomina scolded us one minute for our curiosity and the next grumbled that her clumsy stoutness prevented her from climbing up with us on roofs and ladders, and with sparkling, humorous eyes, egged us on; the housekeeper instead played the innocent – being involved in certain things doesn't befit a young lady and a housekeeper to boot.

Various small canvases painted by Aunt Celeste and her husband – according to family gossip they had been much in love and painted and even washed together – were found and put in a chest; and into another went hundreds of holy pictures with prayers on the back that, Aunt Celeste sent to inform us, had to be arranged according to saint; so into one box went all the St Teresas, into another the St Anthonys, in another the St Francises and then we were blamed for not distinguishing between the three Francises; into another the Madonnas, which after being blamed for the Francises, we separated into Our Lady of Sorrows, Immaculate Conceptions, Madonnas and Child, Black Madonnas, Assumptions; into another the crucifixions; we had fun then calculating the days of indulgence, box by box, and tried to say the prayers for the remission of sins but slipped very quickly into imitating the priest's voice, so it ended with everybody laughing; and yet the dusty smell of those holy pictures has remained with me tenaciously, like a hope of forgiveness.

Nothing was to be thrown out of the attics, neither the

hatbox from the honeymoon or from the happy couple's other trips, nor the rusty three-legged wash-stands from before the bathrooms were built in the house, nor the tyres and unattached wheels of a strange bicycle from Argentina; only the droppings of mice and doves had to be swept up, the cobwebs cleaned away, the place dusted, articles arranged by category, with the result that when the job was done everything seemed to have died by classification, like the beautiful flowers in the botanical pages of the dictionary; every now and then Uncle came up, not so much to give orders as to fall into a trance in front of something that had turned up; then down he would go to his mother, whose leg was in plaster after the trap taking her to the grape harvest had tipped over, and together they would summon up the family history.

One day – and this is the last image I have of that house before our departure, and it was certainly a revealing one – while Gelsomina was below stairs preparing dinner and the pretty housekeeper, my Uncle, brother and sister were dawdling in the attic where I was on my way up from the kitchen, I came upon Great-Aunt Celeste. She had managed to reach the landing with her stick and the further aid of a chair dragged behind her, and there she stuck, calling out her son's name, her head lifted towards the door to the attic which was as gaping and dark as her howling mouth. No one heard. So I was sent up to call them, nor could she bid me do so by word, so hoarse was she, but only by gestures.

That evening with tender solicitude but with firmness, she informed her son that the housekeeper would have to go; her pretext was the financial burden, and she fingered her chequebook while her son looked at her in alarm, burying his gaze in his mother's blue eyes, vainly seeking entrance to the abyss which he had seen gaping some hours before, when dashing down the stairs he had found her as I had, speechless from shouting, the strangled voice in her throat seeking outlet through the eyes, as she leant as if paralysed against the banister – the chair she had leant on had slipped to the ground – and when he got to her she toppled on him dumb and rigid as a statue.

And pouring tea into his cup he shook his frowning head, till, as he dunked a Donnammare biscuit★ in his cup, a mischievous smile banished the gloom, and the only sound heard was the discreet salivating click as he nipped the tip of the biscuit. Grace had re-entered the room.

Thus was revealed to me the intimate secret of the house, and since that time, behind every loving outpouring between two beings, I cannot help hearing the tragedy lurking; and behind the loving voices, I lie in wait for the howl.

★ Those Donnammare biscuits, which were one of the sweet things of his table and our childhood, were hymned by Uncle Alceste in the following lines: 'When the Achaeans came forth under sky/and steady the world turned round/your seed buried in the ground/gave strength to man and gods on high// Grave modulation or gracile,/ a whimsy of butter, of sweet a dare,/ the beguilement of that Tchaikovsky air/ recalls in its closure your style.// About you now at my table, ceremoniary/ cats circle their way,/ round biscuits of Donnammare!// Far-off childhood: it is June in the grand day,/ stately the sun on the table/ fragrant the bread on the oven-tray.'

8
The roofs

The airy world of the roofs offered us refuge when the company of adults became insupportable or when we wanted not adventures, races, violent games, but dreams, reflection, story-telling and talk.

The roofs were flat or domed, dazzling white so as to reflect the sun and keep the bedrooms cool. One felt lighter up there; it was as if the air were rarefied, free of smells and noise. We would look about, making the round of the terrace, or balance on the rim of the dome, hanging over the drop while making three tours.

The soft landscape was always there, unchanging and always itself, whereas in the piazza, and in us, time and circumstance pressed on. Now and then, with the same slow rhythm as the clouds, the scent of wistaria or jasmine or orange-flower drifted by, or that of a cess-pit suddenly uncovered, but also, as the wind blew, the smell of bread fresh from the oven and of wet earth after rain; and certain ample African winds brought the smell of the sea, making us clap our hands. The sea was the grandest of our feasts.

Towards five the women came up to take in the washing; they would tell us to go down from the roof, but as if it were automatic or eased their conscience; they didn't insist. We remained lying there, or sat up in silence to watch them, our daydreaming hardly disturbed. We saw them down below, mopping the little terraces like oriental carpets, or somewhat later setting off for church, where sometimes their husbands went looking for them when they had got home early and wanted to eat. And we heard the bigger children complaining at home, but not daring to fetch them from church as their fathers did. Sometimes we saw our mother, ever so small, crossing the piazza, and I felt like flying down to give her a hug but was paralysed by the height, and when I saw her go into the tobacconist's I imagined her frowning, annoyed because as usual she hadn't found any of us to fetch her cigarettes; but when she came out on the street to cross the piazza, she seemed small again and defenceless, as if in a world far removed from me, unreachable, as after some irreparable happening one dreams of the dead, and I wanted to run, to fly from the terrace to make sure of her solidity and bring her back from a world of shadow.

We amused ourselves on certain roofs by throwing pebbles at the chickens and watching the poor creatures run to peck at them; from others we liked to aim for the well or for water-barrels and in that great silence hear the plop. And I remember the irresistible urge to throw something of ourselves down, a hair-ribbon or a shoe, a favourite coloured pebble, a holy medal; and the sense of oafish guilt afterwards, like pulling the scab off a sore or when playing hairdressers we cut great hanks of each other's hair.

In the evening seven of us★ would sit in the cool on the roof, the asphalt still warm from the sun, and everyone had to tell a story. And we used stately, incongruous subjunctives to give dignity to our tales: 'In Metamunno there lived a king,' we would begin, 'and he were very old . . .'; and Totore's dialect bent and twisted into an Italian progressively more pedantic as he went through elementary school and the dramatic parts of his tale. Our kings and queens often interrupted their regal functions to go for a shit, and then the laughter would burst out and we almost had to lie down to laugh more easily. There were bugs in the beds of our princesses; our Snow-White had

---

★ Seven like the seven dwarfs, the seven deadly sins, the seven plagues of Egypt, the seven hills, the seven kings of Rome, the sciences in the Trivium plus those in the Quadrivium, the seven sages, the seven wonders of the world, etc. If there weren't seven of us, the stories didn't come out right.

lice and it wasn't in puzzlement that she scratched her head. Often in our tales there was a young trickster who managed to put horns on the devil. From Monte San Costanzo one could see a group of rocks out at sea. Mother had told us the story of Ulysses and the Sirens, but we went on with our old legend of how some devils had to build a harbour before cock-crow, but the cock crew and they fled with the job unfinished.

One of us might go off, clambering from roof to roof, from terrace to terrace, to where we knew some women had forgotten to take in the fruit set out to dry, and would come back with handfuls of figs or apricots which we shared out in strict fairness, beginning with the youngest.

When we managed to get hold of a torn sheet, we anchored it with stones in the angle between two roofs or pegged it between one washing-line and another, and so we had a hut to keep off the vast sky, to protect us against falling stars. In the daytime two or three of us would go inside to talk and whisper secrets. How would it be possible to remember those interminable conversations, shining and shooting as stars, whose only syntax was the pleasure of being together? In that tent we were in our own home, we took things to eat and a bottle of water from which we drank conscientiously even when we weren't thirsty. We offered each other bits of what we had brought, and every mouthful seemed to have a rare, exquisite flavour. We took out small presents to swop, scraps of ribbon, holy medals, stubs of pencils carefully sharpened, or little notebooks made by folding pages of exercise books into eight. Round our wrists we tied threads of the same colour to signify the indissolvable bonds between us and we were sorry when our hands and feet turned out to be of different sizes.

When one of these friendships went on too long or was too intense, the others would play tricks, making the tent collapse, for instance, or filling the bottle with mud or piss; sometimes they even broke the bottle and there were splinters of glass everywhere and you had to be careful where you put your feet. And then if it was a boy and a girl who went off – though that happened rarely, and only with the smallest – the others would immediately appear rubbing their index fingers together, meaning 'They're having it off', and make other rude gestures, whereupon the objects of mockery furiously retorted with the sign of the horns, but then went down to the piazza to play with the others, and then other friendships could be born.

In the domain of air on the roofs we performed dangerous feats, had contests to see who could walk round the terrace on the parapet or who could crawl to the edge of the roof and spit down into the road; or who was quickest at going round the village leaping from roof to roof; or who dared go round the dome of a house overhanging the valley. Often the getting back was more arduous than the going, there were long moments of hesitation and you didn't dare – it was a point of honour – to ask the owner of a roof to let you use the stairs. We believed ourselves invulnerable. The most daring were the poorer children; and myself among the girls; perhaps we hoped to make up for what we lacked with a fierce sense of pride. But it was also true that neither I nor the poorer children had ever been taught to take care of ourselves; when Mariarosa scraped a knee she looked on the blood as an insult, an outrage, whereas we felt we finally had something to ourselves, we were somebody at last.

Sometimes after a row with our mother, Granny would go and march up and down on the roof, her black skirt flapping like a mad bird, beating the air time and again with her hand as if listing unpardonable offences, and threatening to throw herself off. At other times, at sunset, Mother would go up with a book, but it was soon laid down on the wall; the breeze idly turned the pages, gently ruffled her hair as if wanting to make her acquaintance, while her eyes, decidedly blue at such moments, stared into emptiness. Since she had told me – to me, the eldest, she had the habit of confiding her disappointments – that Uncle Alceste wouldn't lend her books on the grounds that children would ruin them, I imagined that she broke off reading to save the book and make it last longer. Feeling closer because of her deprivation, I would approach and yearn to turn into a book for her to read, and would start chattering busily, hopping from one subject to another; to my distress I knew I couldn't be a book, only a thin little booklet, and my chattering died away.

On certain evenings a maid whom we often had with us would go up on the roof before preparing dinner. Up there, with only us children to see her, she would hoist up her skirt and give her legs a lengthy inspection, while asking me if they were as good as those at the cinema. All I could see were two legs like so many others, brutally pink, more helped than harmed by the odd bruises like precious stones; and I couldn't grasp the meaning of those thighs cut off from walking and the rest of her body. At other times, instead of examining her legs, she would mould a head out of a lump of wax and put a spell on it with pins – for a friend, she said, who had been ditched by her boyfriend. Then she would inspect herself in a bit of broken mirror, straighten her hair, and stroke it while talking to someone called Oscar. 'Do you love me, Oscar?' she would ask. Then she would remember us and burst into a great laugh. I would laugh too and throw myself on her and we would roll round the terrace tickling each other.

When our father came he never went up to the roof because it annoyed him to come across the hens that lived on the stairs or bump into Grandmother. When he came he would unwrap all the presents he had brought, eat, smoke a cigarette, sleep, and then go down to Metamunno to play cards with his friends. But one evening, from the kitchen window, I saw Mother and Father standing on the terrace; she had her arm through his, they chatted for a while and then came down. That scene struck me as strange, like something out of the photograph album which she occasionally showed us, or out of some film; we never saw Mother and Father arm-in-arm, nor the men and women of the village.

Sometimes Mother would lock me out on the loggia. After shouting at me and slapping me she would shove me out violently and slam the door behind me. I howled till I was out of breath, till my desolation finally found comfort in the hens stolidly pecking up and down the stairs at grains of maize or crusts of bread. Granny would come to let me out, shooing the hens away so they wouldn't follow me into the kitchen, but doing it quietly so as not to be heard by Mother. I came in unwillingly and began sobbing again because I had found comfort among the hens, lying down on a stair with them walking over me, clucking quietly. In the feather-strewn dark and in the warm smell of dung I felt myself mingle with something as vast and obtuse as my pain, while when Granny let me out, I had to distinguish between myself and it and cut myself off from it; and my misery then became mean and small and compelled me to renew my complaints about the cause of the quarrel and the rights and the wrongs of it.

9

The feasts

At dawn, on certain days from three in the morning, the bells began to peal joyously. Father tossed and turned in his sleep; while at five Grandmother began to roam the house. It was the feast of one of the village saints or of one of the neighbouring villages. Throughout the summer, feast followed feast every Sunday, now in Schiazzano, now in Monticchio, in Marciano, in Alisistri, at the Marina, in Metamunno.

The children from the piazza set off for the feast hours early, with the girls; later would come the elderly, the old, the young men. Our mother never came; the feasts seemed barbarous to her. The girls, not allowed to go off with the young men and impatient to get out of the house, came along with us so that we could serve to keep an eye on one another: they had to see we children didn't hurt ourselves and we had to watch that they didn't go off with their boyfriends. We were their tormentors and confidantes at the same time. But they could never entirely count on our complicity, for it took nothing at all to bring us round to betraying them. They, on the other hand, never let us down, but at times their boyfriends mistreated us. If we needed soothing when the dark came down, or had suffered some wrong, or came begging a coin or a handkerchief, or if – when we had no reason at all to whine – we approached our minder and her boyfriend and interrupted some moment of bliss, the young man would turn on us and give us a pinch, a kick, a shove, or might even stick a finger up one's arse with a lascivious jeer.

Insensible to the expansiveness and tendernesses that take place between lovers (we in fact never felt upset when disturbed during our tender moments), we caught only the grotesque and sinful aspects. The girls and their friends bought our complicity with little gifts and particular permissiveness. We were allowed to leave the path and walk along the top of the high field-walls, to climb trees and pluck fruit and raid birds' nests, to leave the path for a stretch and scramble down from terrace to terrace, dirtying our clothes; and even to steal – a rag ball or some peanuts – from a stall; or to make the sign of the horns when we passed Christ and the Host, because we'd been told that Christ would shed tears of blood at the sign and the Host would drop all bloody to the ground, and we wanted to see if it was true. The girls pretended not to know us and not to have seen and moved away from us, but we needed their ample flowered skirts to hide us from the old women. They also bought us off with long embraces against breasts smelling of sweat and scented soap, with recherché tickles, with kisses; they even allowed us to put ants down their blouses.

At these feasts the poor girls found themselves all sweaty and laughing, hemmed in by our tactless and annoying demands and the insistence of their boyfriends, confused between our spittle and theirs, our digging elbows and theirs, between our joint pinching and tickling; and tenderness and transports of love had a hard time extricating themselves from this tangle of mischief. Fun-loving girls who, after conceding their favours, often had no alternative but to swallow *varichina** in some lonely corner of the countryside where they were found all twisted and agonised from the torment in their bellies: Bianchina, Teresa, Nannina, these names were whispered round the villages; and unbeknown to the grown-ups, we went with ribbons and bright bits of cloth to the places where they had killed themselves and hung them on the bushes.

On our way to the feasts we often hopped from terrace to

* In Italian, bleach. It is the most frequent form of suicide for seduced and abandoned girls in Althenopis and its environs.

terrace down as far as the last bend in the road, to sit and wait for the girls. Panting from the race, already in our minds we saw the village banging its bells and swarming with people, the fairy lights already switched on. We were too hot to feel the breeze on our skin and were surprised to see the olives stirring in the motionless silence: the leaves gleamed in the last intense sweet rays of the sunset and the swaying brightness of the foliage seemed to herald the feast, but in the quiet bliss of that annunciation there was something yearning, a muted expectation that would be lacking in the feast itself. And I almost dreaded leaving the field-wall for the noisy, colourful mêlée of the piazza.

The old women from the outlying houses went by in shot–silk dresses of brown or bottle green or black, women whom we always saw either bundled up or half unbuttoned, their legs knotted with varicose veins and with misshapen feet hoisted on a stone to rest. They went by, dressed up from top to toe, shining and stiff as ancient statues, repositories of wisdom, tutelary watchers over the earth, over childbirth and rearing, over the sick and the mad, and guardians of the basic rules of society and religion.

They went by so dignified, stately and awesome that we jerked out of our slouching and sat up straight and penitent on the edge of the field. Their husbands had gone ahead long since, called to be stewards at the feast.

Once in the piazza, the band of village children melted away, one lured aside by some marvel, another bumping into a relative, or being summoned by his grandad to hold a cord of the saint's banner; and others, the elect, went into church to dress up as monks and Children of Mary. The big girls immediately disappeared, some into church, others off with their boyfriends.

The fairy lights weren't yet lit up, or if they were, flickered in the sunset which still outshone them.

Avid for marvels, we ran for the stalls. We were the ones with least money, as Mother was very thrifty and then she didn't celebrate feasts, or at least not these. This in itself was

135

always a reason for feeling cut off from the others. Neverthe-less she couldn't get away without giving us a little, or my brother and I would steal some for fear she would refuse. Or I would still be helping Maruzzella do her homework which meant a hundred lire. The money thus earned I spent on my brother and sister as well. I was the big sister and if my role very often had its disadvantages, for example, that of coming in for the worst scolding, it also had its advantages, and I dispensed sugared almonds and nut-brittle like a saint. And if it hadn't been for the fear of suspicious questioning, I would have bought something for Mother as well.

When the procession set off – and to see it one had to be in the front of the crowd on either side, before everyone tagged on at the end of the official cortege – we felt awe and a blasphemous itch simultaneously. The priests of the various villages, about all of whom there was wicked gossip going the rounds – though the effect was that of bringing them closer to other men – suddenly seemed to stand above that whole human gathering. They processed along in their robes, elevat-ing the monstrance, waving incense, asperging holy water, reciting the litany in Latin, when with us they spoke in dialect. It was only by looking at their feet – their shoes hadn't been polished, unlike those of the villagers – that I could keep a hold on what each of them was in his own village and in our daily lives.

Following them came the dignitaries, all stiff in black suits, holding candles: the mayor, the municipal officers, the police sergeant, the landowners – people we always badmouthed among ourselves – without their usual ambiguous and know-ing expression of complicity and double-dealing, but with a cold and solemn fixity impervious to mockery and curses; and the furrows on their cheeks and foreheads, which *bonhomie* masked on normal days, shone like an indecipherable enigma. And all around, keeping back the crowd or ordering the illuminations to be switched on or the fireworks to be set off at the right moment, went the stewards of the feast, the old farm-hands in their good clothes who suddenly, and only for the day, took on dignity in our eyes, though a moment's familiarity could still break through the solemnity. And there was always the steward of stewards, who had held the office at every feast from time immemorial, and who always wore a starched white dickey under his black jacket instead of a shirt, and a top hat which he swapped for a cocked one when the procession was over and the religious functions finished and the stewards might sit down under a grape arbour to eat and drink with their wives.

When the Children of Mary paraded by in their white and blue, the young children in order of height followed by the older girls, it put an end to our awe and the catcalls and the comments began: who was the prettiest; which ones had done a novena and why; and whether that one had been put in the front row because of the embroidery donated to the church or because she taught Sunday School. Then came the boys in their Communion clothes, holding candles with lilies twined round them like white ribbons and this was the least solemn, most entertaining section of the procession. One would pull a face, or stick out his tongue, or aim a kick at the boy next to him, or play a trick for our benefit on the boy in front and hope to escape the eye of the steward.

On certain feast-days just after the war, ex-soldiers appeared who had made solemn vows in moments of danger. There was one who walked barefoot on crowns of thorns, another who went into church and began licking the floor; and from the horror of that self-sacrifice we formed an impression of how horrific the war had been.

When the solemn part of the procession had gone by – the statues of the saints, the priests, the dignitaries, the school-teachers, the Children of Mary, the communicants, the old women of the congregations, the band – we all tagged on behind, and although the old women and the wives sang hymns, we finally felt free to laugh, joke, skip, shove. The women's foolish singing and our yelling seemed to drive the procession onwards, hurrying it into church to shut within the flower- and incense-scented walls the solemnity and compunction which had been forced upon us, and our remorse for being silly and guilty. When all that was sacred in the feast had been swallowed up by the church and only the occasional waft of perfume and sound came out, the piazza was shaken by the din of exploding firecrackers, the crowd lining the street broke up, the band burst into Puccini and we swarmed towards the stalls.

There was one selling water-ices, mint, lemon, or myrtleberry – red, voluptuous, intensely thick, the myrtle cordial soaked through the crushed ice. The women took their time in choosing the colour of the cordial and hardly one of them chose lemon or orange. Then there was the nut stall, various native varieties plus peanuts, and again we hesitated about the choice because though we loved the nutty intensity of the hazels, it seemed too everyday to us and often we preferred peanuts, which evoked the monkeys we had never seen or the dates that some people had let us try at the Marina; also because we could poke curious fingers in the light hollow of the shell which left shreds in our mouths when we cracked them between our teeth. And then our fingers, providentially shod, could tapdance on the bandstand where we went to lean.

Sugared almonds and nut-brittle scented the air. We would get one piece wrapped and each take a bite in turn, but the nut-brittle didn't have the delicacy of the nuts and we were soon fed up with it; it coated our mouths too thickly, leaving a cloying taste when we were eager to move on to another, with the result that there was always a bit left in a pocket, and on the way home the sticky sweet that had hampered us in the piazza was welcome as a foretaste of maternal warmth and bed. Then there were the stalls with knobbly comfits and others tasting of cinnamon, candy floss, crumbly pastries, fondant or aniseed biscuits, and all those people making and selling sugary things seemed magicians to us. They had black moustaches stiff and shiny as toffee, their eyes smiled inviting as cherries, but if we hung around too long without buying they chased us off with kicks.

We could hardly buy anything at the toy stalls. We saw our

138

friends' fathers buying them toys, and Mariarosa's father walking by with a doll in a big cellophane box under his arm. All Mariarosa wanted was dolls, and at night I dreamt of her in front of a mirror with all her dolls in a row that seemed to multiply her to infinity in a glossy coloured universe. We would buy a rag ball or a whistle of red waxed paper. Once I bought my little sister a small zinc colander, and she was so happy I cried with joy and then felt ashamed of my tears.

There were people going around selling canaries and dwarf parrots, and boyfriends would buy them for their girls, and sometimes husbands for their wives, and Mariarosa's father would buy one for his daughter though she already had four in a great gilded cage. When the money ran out and the little bags of nuts were empty in our hands and a thick darkness surrounded the piazza like the night sky round a star, we would begin to look about us and feel lonely and companionless. The others were with their relatives, the girls to whom we had been entrusted had gone off to dark corners, and even my faithful friend Agnese was standing with a baby in her arms, surrounded by relatives in ecstasy over her plaits. We looked around us like orphans. My brother had forgotten his woollen jumper of course; his narrow tanned shoulders shivered and the shoulder bones looked like the wings of a plucked chicken. I was happy to take off my jumper and wrap it round him. Then Mariarosa's father, who aspired to become Uncle Alceste's factor, called us over and dealt out comfits from his round benevolent hand, invited us to a table under a grape arbour which seemed to be the hub of the feast and forced us to drink a finger of wine. Then all of a sweat he forgot us, and went back to administering his own private feast. Mariarosa, tired of preening among relatives and acquaintances, joined us to play hide-and-seek. But when it was her turn to hide an edge of her billowing blue organdy dress always betrayed her, she gave up petulantly and began stroking the cellophane wrapping of her doll.

Forgotten once more, on the edge of the circle of light, we wanted to be gone. My brother gave a special whistle to call

139

Ciccillo's son, or some other boy who had come without friends or relations and whose money had run out, and we would set off into the night, shivering, in no need of lights given our old acquaintance with every ditch along the way. Now and then we stopped to unwrap the nut brittle and pass it round. Our footsteps and voices would fall quiet and straightaway the chirping of the crickets seemed to increase in volume. We were so tired that we seemed to float on the sound as it carried us towards the village where, assured that it had brought us safe home, it stopped as the houses began.

The biggest feast was at Metamunno and lasted three days. The band there no longer played Puccini but *Zaza* and *Lili Marlene*.★ At Metamunno the firecrackers went on for ever. I hated them because they reminded me of the war. Or I felt I was caught in the thunder of the sudden storms that fell on us on the road to Sant'Agata where we went in autumn to gather apples for the winter; or the storm that caught us on the bare top of San Costanzo on our way back from a visit to the hermitage.† So I would cling to a tree. And I felt that the tree I clung to was my big brother, that non-existent big brother who appeared in dreams to me, confident and radiant and who remained smiling and unmoved when I embraced him; and I pleaded with him in vain until he disappeared into the

★ At a time when almost no one sang it any longer in the city – the Germans had left and it was the Americans one had to please – the song arrived in our part of the country, where it became very popular, on its own and in a mishmash with Zaza, lipstick and Hollywood films. History always reached us late; even the war had cut off our little peninsula at the height of the hills where it joined the mainland.

† The hermit wove osier baskets which he bartered for food. Mother, unable to imagine that men might choose to live according to vegetable principles, tried to persuade him to go to the hospice. But he turned away with his toothless smile.

The mountain was bare and white as his life. One day we went there on our own and as we were coming back the lightning began striking around us like the arrows of a savage and malign God. We were too frightened ever to go back. I had a sudden insight then: in Catechism, Don Candido had told us that God made man in his own image and likeness; matching the lightning and the air raids together I understood what he'd been trying to say.

darkness of sleep as if I had irritated him. I felt the tree should shake its crown and drive away the distress and reawake the luminous intelligence of the sprays and fountains of light in the seemingly stultified men who were lighting the fireworks. And when the bangs ended and a spray appeared in the sky the crown of the tree seemed to spin round for joy. Calm again I moved away from the tree and gazed up at the sky with dangling arms. But I couldn't give myself up to the delight of those silent colours because there was always the impending threat of the bangs. So I would end up crouching at the foot of the tree with my eyes closed and my fingers in my ears, vowing never again to fall for the devious tricks of the lighters of fireworks. Sometimes, instead of the tree, I might find a girl without a boyfriend and cling to her.

As one left the sea behind and the civilization of the towns and their trade, commerce, and crafts, and the fine houses full of priests, arch-priests, government employees, landowners, abbesses, policemen, and climbed towards the remote hill fields, the nature of the feasts changed. Our Lady of the Snow, for example, who was on a mountain peak between the two bays, was patron of convicts and after the amnesty ex-convicts came from all the villages around, even from Corento and Althenopis, to thank the Madonna and ask her protection against the Law. And we went secretly to this feast, without telling anyone and without the girls.

The ex-convicts seemed like foreigners, like emigrants returned from America or ocean-going sailors. They had hands tattooed with the signs of the Camorra; tight checked suits and often a tie; a jerky, wooden way of moving, like marionettes. Some of them limped. They took large, neatly folded handkerchiefs from their pockets to spread on the benches in front of the church, and opened them out with snappy little gestures before sitting down. Others elongated their necks in an exaggerated way when they looked at things, others had tics and rolled their heads round all the time, or winked with dull eyes; others stared at their toecaps, some cursed others, some fell into sudden embraces. And they were

141

always taking papers and documents from pockets or bags to show each other, or bottles of alcohol which they handed round; out would come sheets of music, sometimes handwritten, and away they went into old songs in dialect or songs in Italian or the dialects of the North, or arias from operas. We spied on them from behind a wall until we felt it was safe, then we would stroll nonchalantly to the stalls and mingle with children we didn't know – their children or grandchildren perhaps.

We went to other feasts of the Madonna by way of rough paths we hardly knew and often we went wrong. In the neighbourhood of the feast we would come upon groups of country people dancing. Only the men and the old women danced, ringed by the girls and the children, and they danced with ungainly movements of their hips but the movements of their hands were full of grace. The good dancers among the old women were pushed into the circle, egged on by the girls who were not allowed to take part. At that time of year it hardly rained, the earth was dry and a great cloud arose and the leafy sprays hung between the trees as bunting were grey with dust; the old women's wrinkles shone out more clearly in the sweat of their dirty faces. Hesitant and shy we approached the dance circle, then seeing that everyone ignored us we hung on to each other and pushed through. Wide-mouthed with laughter, the girls elbowed us accidentally as they pushed the women into the circle. The mother of one of them, younger and prettier than the rest, held back fiercely, dodged behind her daughter and even slapped the girls who were trying to force her into the circle. The young men dancing with the old women smiled at the girls and sometimes in passing would tug at a plait or pinch a cheek, then forget them altogether as the dance took hold of them and their faces became still and unmoving as masks.

I thought how terrible it would have been if our mother had been there and had had to dance in the ring; it would have filled me with shame.

10

Cousin Achille

It was about '47 that cousin Achille came back from the prison camp in the Indies. He was tall, extremely thin, burnt by the sun, slightly balding and wore steel-rimmed spectacles over his myopic blue eyes. His smile was constantly shifting between the sardonic and the tender and back again, with an ambiguity that seemed to me then irresolvable.

We went with Granny to meet him off the bus. For two days she had done nothing but cook puff pizza and pullets and clean the house. She had even re-stuffed the mattress that was to be his, and the feathers slowly drifting over the terrace parapet seemed like kisses and words of love addressed to the arriving grandson. Our mother had made her change her dress at the last moment so that it wasn't stained or white with flour or feathers; and she had also made her take off the Franciscan girdle she had been wearing underneath for some time. At that point Granny had even powdered her nose. Mother was in a cheerful mood that day and suggested she wear her small diamond, but Granny wouldn't. She laughed and said that what it needed was the ruby she had sold the year before to pay the bills. She even refused a garnet brooch that Mother wanted to lend her. 'It doesn't shine, it doesn't shine!' she said. 'I shan't wear anything so Achille can see the shine in my heart, only the shine in my heart!' She seemed to fly down the road, not leaning on her stick but simply giving it the occasional twirl. Standing on the verge during the long wait – we had arrived very early and the bus was always late – she wept and prayed, not believing he was back, despite the letters and the telegram, until she saw him. In the meantime we picked narcissi to offer him. It was spring.

He leapt down boldly from the bus, with a small tartan suitcase in his hand. They flew into each other's arms; the rest of the world might have ceased to exist. Grandmother hugged him and sobbed, and he chucked her under the chin and smiled like a lover. Arm-in-arm they set off, and we skipped round them; now and then he poked us with the stick and asked one of the solitary questions children get asked: 'How old are you?' 'What class are you in?'

When we got to the tobacconist's we ran ahead to tell Mother, who was standing on the doorstep screwing up her short-sighted eyes behind her glasses. She was trembling and palpitating from emotion in a way I'd never seen before. She looked like a baby in his arms, and I remembered a photo she had shown us of herself as a young woman with him in her arms; in effect she'd been almost a mother to him.

Earlier that morning Granny had laid out on his bed all the things she had embroidered for him in those seven years. And he smiled his tender sardonic smile as with awkward delicacy he fingered the velvets and the damasks embroidered with gold and silver thread and put them away carefully in his appointed drawer, along with his checked handkerchiefs, two shirts and a razor. Early in the morning Granny took him a zabaione – prison had worn him down, she said – and made him drink half a litre of milk; at eleven in the morning, behind everyone's back, she even cooked him a steak.

The cousin got us to sit on his knee and stroked our legs. It seemed that prison had made him hungry for caresses. He told us unending stories about his experiences in Africa and the Indies that became entangled with memories of Salgari and Verne. Fascinated by the story but disturbed by the stroking, which seemed improper to me, I felt like an insect in a spider's web, in an intricate and false situation, because when I asked him for another story it seemed I was asking for more of his caresses and when I wanted to get away from them it seemed I was bored with the tale. These tales, inflated and exaggerated at certain points and abbreviated at others, we told in turn to our friends in the piazza, so that when Cousin Achille passed through the streets they gazed at him with curiosity and admiration, seeing him imprisoned in a cage, swimming rivers as wide as from the Marina to the Vervece rock, his fights with tigers and the English, with boa constrictors and with Indians who keep small daggers hidden in their turbans. They called him 'Captain Glorious' and offered us catapults and whistles to pass on to him, but we refused without consulting him, boasting that he already had everything, that he was rich and wanted for nothing.

Even when talking about everyday life in the prison camp, Cousin Achille didn't fail to highlight his capacities for enterprise: as when he taught his companions how to grow things so that they could have more to eat; or when he got together a 'little capital' by trading with the sentries – but it then got stolen by an officer; or when he begun studying English grammar, because, he said, to know a foreign language is 'a little capital' (he often used the expression 'get together a little capital') and he regretted not having it available for this or that investment.

He had a practical spirit, lucid and inquisitive, and in no time at all he found out about the small sums of money I got hold of, though they had escaped the attention of Mother, Grandmother and my father. With an amused, implacable air, he asked me where they came from. Crimson with shame, I had to tell him I took money for doing my schoolmates' homework; but to my great astonishment, instead of upbraiding: he congratulated me. And gave me a comradely pat on the shoulder. The unexpected backing of Cousin Achille didn't, however, alleviate my guilt. It was as if he had said that it was right to cheat, that it was one of the rules to be learnt in life. And he demonstrated with arguments and examples that it was the way of the world, that work was to be paid for, that one didn't work for nothing, nor for love, but for money. I didn't know how to refute him but inside myself I stubbornly held to my old conviction and vainly struggled to find arguments to back it.

145

Once Cousin Achille took us to visit Don Aniello's cow-sheds. He had a vague idea himself of setting up a farm or a model cowshed. He always found it amusing to scare or scandalize Mother, so he told her that he was taking us for a lesson in animal husbandry and the facts of life. And he did in fact take us to the stall where the cows from the neighbouring countryside were brought to be covered. And with the bull mounting an unruly cow that had had to be dragged there and immobilized, he smiled a different smile from the sickly ones we usually got from teachers and said: 'Learn: that's what love is!' Out of *amour propre* I was forced to look, and blushed. The lesson was meant more for me than for the others who were younger, and even though I feigned indifference, I seethed with resentment, not for what I was looking at – living in the country I was used to that – but for his language and the desecrating smile, and for the feeling of constraint, like at school or the doctor's.

Cousin Achille wounded me in everything: for instance, my friend Maruzzella who looked almost grown-up came to see me; he looked her over shamelessly and when she'd gone he said: 'Pity she's short and fat; the face isn't bad.' Or after lunch, while Mother was out of the room getting the coffee, he joked with my father about the maid's bandy legs, though in recompense she had 'skin like a peach.' Sometimes my father would have liked to talk politics, but Cousin Achille said that he'd been taken in enough already by politics and that he wanted to concentrate on making money. He would look at me knowingly and make me frightened he was going to tell my father about my money; I blushed and sat fast, caught as in a spider's web.

One evening Mother was away in Althenopis. I was feverish and delirious. One moment it seemed I was on a ship in a storm at sea, then in a beautiful garden so hot I wanted to take my clothes off and bathe in the central fountain, but the maid wouldn't let me take them off, and when I said: 'Look at the beautiful water!' she laughed as if I'd made a joke, for she was too young to have had any experience of delirium. Before

146

leaving she asked me what I wanted for dinner and I got a sudden craving for pizza. In vain she tried to convince me that it couldn't be done because there was no raised dough in the house and no yeast. Sitting up in the bed with burning cheeks, I kept insisting, first in an imperious tone, then begging and playful. My brother and sister ran in from the other room and climbed on to the bed where the maid was pulled as well to join the game, and then won over by the rowdy fun she dashed off to the kitchen to improvise a pizza.

Meanwhile, my cheeks more aflame than ever, I egged on my brother and sister as if possessed, ordering them to dress up as kings or as pirates in Granny's and Mother's clothes. When the pizza arrived, unrisen and not even well cooked, the aroma that spread through the room seemed heavenly; though the effort of getting it into my mouth was too much for me and I felt satiated with just the smell and the sight of tomato soaking into the pastry and the flavour of origano I could anticipate. And I even imagined I would eat the cloves of garlic they were putting on one side because they didn't like it cooked and always left it for me.

But the moment I tasted it I fell back on the pillow and hazily saw my brother and sister doing honour to the pizza and the maid pulling away angrily because they wanted to stuff a piece in her mouth at all costs and she didn't like it unleavened. Little by little the haze gave way to silence and then darkness, and I was aware of two separate darknesses, that inside me and that in the room, and I made unspeakable efforts to keep them apart but they flowed into one. Perhaps I dozed. Something, like a slimy beast, lay in my hand and I didn't have the strength to lift it; from my hand the beast climbed up my body, my shoulders, my neck, my forehead; and from small beast it became large and oppressive. With a terrible effort I hauled myself out of what seemed like a deep pit and opened my eyes; I thought I saw Cousin Achille bending over me, indeed I was almost certain; yet I couldn't disentangle his image from that of the beast, rather they seemed closely intertwined. My eyes, Cousin Achille said afterwards, were staring and gleaming in my burning face and I seemed unconscious. He had to give me a long shaking before I came out of the torpor. He put an ice bag on my forehead, but I went on trying to refuse, signalling him to go away. Later, when I was calmer, he asked me to tell him my nightmare. But I didn't dare and told a lie instead. Since he was always mentioning the goddess Kali in his stories, I told him I had seen her standing before me. He spent part of the night at my bedside. That was the first time I ever disguised the truth about a dream.

11

Departure

In the year of departure there were premonitions of separation and change, not written in the stars, in apparitions, or in the shapes taken by melted lead – which was our method of reading the future – but everyday events.

The group of children going down to school each day thinned out; and though it was reinforced with other, smaller children, many of the bigger ones, our playmates, no longer came. Agnese had left school because her stepmother was pregnant again and she had to look after the house; and in the meantime one of her elder sisters was teaching her sewing.

Agnese's stepmother was small and thin and despite her forty years had a young girl's face with rosy cheeks and a flat nose. She combed her hair to one side because as a child she had fallen into the charcoal brazier and the burn had become infected, so they had to scrape a hole almost through to the brain. By the time she was four months gone she already had an enormous lemon-shaped belly propped on two little legs knotted with varicose veins; and the knots came up as far as her groin for she showed us one day. She would sit for hours with her legs stretched out in the sun because the old men had told her that it liquefied the blood; and when we told her, Mother lifted her hands in horror and said it was quite the contrary.

Agnese's house was shady, the shutters were always closed and there were green plants in all the rooms and especially in the one where her sister did her dressmaking; and sometimes while I was crouching by Agnese's chair and looking in envy at her precise stitches, clients would come, not just girls from the nearby villages wanting a flowered dress for Easter or their wedding trousseau, but in latter years, not long before our departure, clients from beyond the district, the wives of office workers from Metamunno, or holiday-makers, and even a lady from Corento. They came with fashion magazines and said that vertical stripes suited fat people and horizontal ones thin people, and they were always worried about wedges of buttock or breast that couldn't be made to disappear; and I was left wondering why the finished dresses no longer looked like the models when tried on in front of the big bedroom mirror; and the women, fat or thin, ugly or pretty, took on a stiff, starchy air; which didn't happen to the village girls who came for flowered dresses with a frilly or square neck and short sleeves, and wanted only imperceptible variations on the style worn in our part of the country, for fear of being brutally mocked by their fathers, boyfriends, brothers, told off by the old women and criticized by their friends.

The stepmother sat stiffly in the shade, her great bulging belly looking as if it were full of stones. She had a satisfied and patient look, as if absorbed by her own inwardness, almost as if she were aware of something sucking her from the womb, an expression like that of the cows when they were milked. I knew that stones could be formed in the kidneys or near the liver and imagined that belly full of stones clicking together at the moment of birth to then take on the shape of the desired baby, as happened with the lead which we melted in pans to foretell the future, or with clouds which took on the shape of human faces, of bears, of hortensias. And sitting on a chair in front of her stepmother, sewing and looking after the house, Agnese – who no longer came to school because later she would have to tend the child – suddenly seemed grown-up and almost a stranger to me.

Opposite the main street of the village, to the left of the arch leading to the castle which housed the mozzarella dairy of my friend Maruzza, the cobbler's shop stood on the right. We never went into his house because one of his children always had tuberculosis. That year the cobbler himself fell ill and the

150

shop was closed. Only the mother and the youngest daughters stayed behind. Anna and Immacolatella, both of whom were extremely skinny, played with us all the time in the piazza and when we did too much running about their cheeks took on a hectic red and their eyes shone as if they were more precious than ours. I liked Immacolatella a great deal, and we were linked by the common nickname of 'starveling' because of my thinness.

One day a car came with two nuns to take Anna and Immacolatella to an institution. We weren't present at their going because that day we had gone to a fair in another village, but the women told us of the desperate tears of the two girls who hadn't wanted to leave their mother. Everybody seemed pleased that they'd gone, and that hurt me because I felt cast out as well; and we giggled in distress in front of the shut-up shop and the shuttered windows of the house after the mother had gone to stay with an aunt, so as to be nearer to her sick daughters. From then on, whenever they wanted to take us to the doctor or the dentist, we would run away and hide in the countryside. After the family had gone the neighbours sprinkled lime in front of the house, down the steps as far as the arch and in front of the shop; and from that moment white became for us children the colour of absence and heartless exclusion. We never played near that white threshold, and in the early afternoon, when the piazza was deserted, I would look at its glare through the gap in the shutters, desolate and lost.

Totore's father died, and he was taken out of school and sent to work for his farmer uncle. All the village went to see the dead carter, who had been so merry in life and had dancingly brought us the news that the war was over. That day I went on to the loggia where we kept the chickens and spat on the ground three times, saying, 'I spit in your face, Death'. Before then the other deaths, the young men lying among the lilies, had seemed like voyages towards shining lands. But the carter had been too alive and full of fun for me to be able to hope for a better world for him than the one he had left, with his donkey, his greens and his flask of wine.

151

Totore helped his grandfather with the charcoal-burning. We would come across him sometimes on the steep steps of the shortcut as he and his cousins went up with a sack. The charcoal was heavy and every so often they set it down. But the moment we came by they bunched their muscles proudly and gritted their teeth to show they could make it. At times we gave a hand, not offering our help in any spirit of charity, about which we knew nothing, but rather as if saying: 'Let us into this secret society of workers.'

Our brother was a great friend of Totore's and often went to the charcoal-pit in the woods. They piled up the wood, making sure it was of even length, then covered it with earth, leaving cracks for the moisture to escape; then for seven days and seven nights Totore and his grandfather stayed by it. Under an oak they made up a bed of leaves covered with sacking, and slept in shifts. People going by would stop to pass the time of day with the grandfather. His skin, hair and clothes were the colour of smoke and earth, and the eyes twinkling in his round face could take on the slightly sly look of babies who have just learned to walk and have done some mischief, though when he was engaged in some difficult task requiring all his skill he became frowning and absorbed. He was one of the few country people who weren't becoming specialists and he produced everything for himself: potatoes, lemons, wine, oil, dried figs, charcoal, eggs, a pig, tomatoes, even milk; and did it on his own with his old wife and the help of a small grandchild or two, because when his sons got back from the war they had lowered themselves to become bricklayers in Corento.

On August afternoons the acrid, damped-down smell of the charcoal-pit hung around under the broad dome of the cicadas, while in the evenings it seemed to cut us off from the kindly shadows that descended on the mountains and from the cool of the crickets' singing. We lay on the bed of leaves, sucking grass stalks, and the grandfather sat on the wall by the road chatting to the passers-by, recommending wound-heal to this one, beet soup for kidney-stones to that, laughing hugely as he told the young men who had no access to women how certain leaves applied 'on top there' had a herbal power which would make it all conveniently evaporate in sleep; declaring to another that he had never drunk any wine but his own since coming back from the war in Abyssinia, when he and his squad had been forced to stop in Bari where he had seen them making wine from powder; and everyone who went by asked how the charcoal was doing and he would explain that, unfortunately, it had flared too much on one side and too little on the other, and at that he would shift the sods which were too dried out by then, and there he would sprinkle a little water or fresh grass; and he always found a way of telling everybody: 'Now I'll show you a thing or two.'

When a townee passed, a clerk from Metamunno or a holiday-maker, and they got into conversation, every now and then he would say: 'He's intelligent, the gentleman's caught my drift!' He knew that the townsfolk understood only half of what he said in his thick dialect, and almost nothing of what he knew about the soil and farming, and was therefore startled not to find the total ignorance that he supposed. In that part of the hills there was already beginning to be a lot of deserted land, and he felt himself to be the only one not so much to work it as to plant new trees. He had planted thirty-thousand-lire-worth of lemons that year and his land was like a garden. When we followed him into the fields he always made a point of teaching us something, particularly us three whom he knew to come from the corrupt and ignorant city and doomed to return there; and he would take a turnip stalk and tell us how tasty they were fried up in a bit of batter, and how they cleaned out the bowels when boiled; and now he would pick up a handful of pig-muck in the sty and get us to sniff it, telling us to breath deep because it opened the lungs.

When he heard we were leaving, he was the only person in the village not to show envy. 'Poor things,' he said, 'that's life', as if we were going off to war. Sometimes he would give us a bit of old-fashioned biscuit he kept in his pocket; at other times, when his wife had gone to Corento and he was alone, he let us watch the festive preparations of his salads, interrupting himself with much lip-smacking at the goodness and life-giving properties of the ingredients. They were large salads of green beans, potatoes, onions, tomatoes, sprinkled with the origano he had picked in July dawns in the hills; and when he came out of the kitchen - painted pink from floor to ceiling – carrying the bottle of olive oil in his hand, his face would shine in the high sun and solemnly elevating the bottle he would pour a trickle into the dish; at such moments he seemed like priest at his offices.

He would begin eating with Totore, paying no attention to us; but after the first few mouthfuls he would guess what we wanted, fetch out tin forks and stick them in our hands without a word. Then, almost as if giving us the chance to repay him, he would remind us to collect some salt for him when we went down to the sea, and hand us a little tin pail bodged out of a can of herrings, still with a scrap of coloured label showing a ship. He had lined the inside with the thick absorbent paper fishmongers use. When we brought the salt, he let us climb the mulberry tree to eat our fill, and when we were satisfied we would stain our arms and faces to play actors and heroes. Or he would offer us a glass of sweet wine, and after the first few sips good fellowship seemed to rise from the glass, so that I tipsily imagined myself weaving a wreath of flowers and words round the old man's brow with the message: 'May you live to be a hundred!' When this occurred I would go home with my eyes shining, windmilling my arms, and risk tickling my Mother, who would be puzzled at first and then give in and struggle playfully out of my grasp. Sometimes Mother let my brother spend the night out with Totore at the charcoal-pit. I would return home alone, pale with envy, and to spite the world and her I would take a blanket on to the loggia and fall asleep out there, broadcasting my defiance: 'Down with the foe!'

There were long afternoons that were enervating for no reason, when I felt no wish to shelter in the cool busy room of Agnese's sister, and only repugnance at the thought of finding myself in the reek of the mozzarella dairy, more penetrating since a dully whirring mechanical churner had been installed. The deserted sunlit piazza stared at me; my little sister and some smaller girls were playing in one corner of the room with rags and hanks of wool. Listless and anxious I went out on the balcony, from there to the other end of the room, until, taking shape round the reawakened memory of the acrid, damped-down smell of the charcoal-pit, evoked perhaps by the motionless stagnation of the cicadas' din, the notion of going up the mountain struggled to the surface. Furtively I would creep away, without telling anyone and making no noise, as if on my way to meet some fellow-conspirator; quietly closing the kitchen door, as though afraid that a call from the house would distract me from the still unformed project that, step by step as I left the house and set off, suspiciously peering about for fear of being stopped, took on an ever more definite shape.

I went along in the hope that Totore would not be there but only his grandfather, because all my relations with Totore were mediated by my brother; I felt ashamed of myself in his regard, not only for being a girl, but for being so limp and idle, so I tossed my hair over my eyes in hope of hiding myself and buttoned up my collar and hunched my shoulders to make myself smaller and invisible. I got to the charcoal-pit and sat on the field-wall, dangling my feet as if there by accident, without a care in the world; I didn't dare go any nearer.

Immediately I was enveloped in the acrid smell of damped-down smoke. The grandfather lifted his head and said, 'Ah'. And I stayed where I was, glad to be neither refused nor accepted. The grandfather lifted his head again and said, 'Why don't you get off home?' And I replied, 'They're asleep.' And stayed there stubbornly. He seemed to forget about me then altogether. I got down from the wall and squatted closer, near the bed of leaves, pushing my hair away from my eyes a little. I watched him busily shifting the sods, circling round the tumulus of earth, bending to check the various vents or piling

155

the leaves that served to damp down the fire; and little by little my painful listlessness vanished, and I felt immersed in a vast wave of life which seemed to ebb and flow over all the surrounding country to the rhythm of the cicadas. Only then did I straighten my hair and lift my head; and I followed the grandfather to gather leaves, ignoring his mutterings, until finally, resigned to my presence, he left off talking to his dog and began talking to me, treating me now gruffly and now affectionately, as he did with the animal. I returned home and all evening I was dreamy and soft, I fell asleep early, without calling my mother, in the smell of the smoke with which my clothes and hair were saturated.

As usual that year the three of us were alone in the sea at first because the season had not yet begun for the piazza children. We noticed a lot of changes at the beach; some huts had appeared and umbrellas, and it wasn't just the Marina children who were diving, or the owners of the villas, but whole families of holiday-makers come from Althenopis, and even from the Capital, renting rooms from the fishermen. I was struck by the fact that they seemed to bring the whole house with them, just to have a swim.

Before sitting down they spread out little white, blue or pink towels on the ground, they never walked barefoot on the sand or pebbles, they wore knotted handkerchiefs on their heads or ridiculous little stiff straw hats; they never kept still, they were always having to do something and losing their tempers, either because the umbrella was crooked and threatening to fall or because the deckchair was notched too low or too high; they scratched themselves continuously, rubbed the sand off their backs with towels, complained about the wasps and the horseflies that came to the greasy smells and juices in vigorous swarms, and the more they flapped to drive them away the more the flies and wasps left off their indolent gluttony for fierce attack.

The children weren't used to the sea and became pettish and played constant foolish tricks on one another; and even tried to play them on us); but we stared at them with contempt; if the joke became too heavy we hit them straightaway dead-on with a pebble, and if they tried to chase us we gave them the slip in three quick leaps over the rocks. Of all that tribe, the only ones we had any respect for were the old women, who sometimes bathed in their petticoats and had kept in their faces and manners a trace of peasant decency which made them resemble the women of our villages; perhaps they had moved to the city as brides and had held on to the memory of the countryside, or perhaps they had followed their daughters after their husbands' deaths. They hung on to the boats when they went into the water, for fear of drowning, and often had to ask with humble smiles for a helping hand to get them back to the shore.

Certain hysterical and thunderous pronouncements by the fathers reached us: 'I'm in charge here!' or 'I absolutely forbid you to do it!'; turning to their wives, they said, 'Your son!' The poor women, lying as if glued to the deckchairs, never retorted but went on handing out sandwiches, mineral water, orangeade, and when they had a moment's rest between dishing out and their husbands' or their children's yelling, they stared in stunned fashion at the sea, as if bemused by so large a circle of the world.

The girls from the villas no longer bathed behind the rocks in their bikinis, but were to be seen tanning themselves on the motor launches speeding out to sea as if they had been kidnapped by the bronzed young men; and their eyes, tender and glowing on the rocks, now seemed to hide a grim mystery behind dark glasses. It was as if they had fallen under the spell of magic potions, and I yearned to help them by running over the sea to where the motor launches sped about, drawing futile circles.

A fat old woman came to the beach on her own. She came from the Capital and had been an artiste in the music-hall. I have no idea what hostile force we represented for her, but the fact was that every day she glared and shouted at us and sometimes even called the fisherman who rented her a room to come and protect her from us. We didn't understand at first

157

what wrong we had done her, apart from that of existing, but when we realized that that was an outrage in her eyes, we immediately gave her good reason for hating us with the constant tricks we began playing on her.

She was fat and had a little heart-shaped mouth and wore a tight black latex costume of the kind then worn by emancipated women, who alternated them with their bikinis. It compressed her stomach and back into rolls of fat and made her breasts bulge out at the front; I imagined myself stripping it off, for to me it seemed a penitential garment, and imagined her ample and unhampered in the sea, as dangerously attractive as a Portuguese man-o'-war when, white and purplish, it launches its jelly-like substance into the current. I imagined myself her maid, undoing her costume and firmly but not disrespectfully propelling that flesh of hers into the sea, to float there; for the generous element would be cool and caressing in its welcome. But the more I looked at her, the more I became the focus of her general hate. Once she even made the sign of the horns at me.

At sunset she walked along the beach in the way I had seen actresses do in certain films, just before the epilogue, when, for the last time, the lover prevented by some task from joining her, watches from a distance as she walks away. Or she was continuously massaging her thighs and hips, and since her costume tended to get trapped between her buttocks she tugged it up and down tirelessly to make her breasts stand out, though it wasn't at all clear whether she wanted to increase or reduce the amount of flesh exposed to the sun and the eyes of others. There was a flat rock where she stretched out in a mermaid's pose, the weight of her two large breasts dragging them down to one side, and when she walked along the sand she often used to stroke them. She spoke with a foreign accent and called us 'sons of a bitch', 'peasants', 'Algerians, Blacks, Africans', constantly promising us 'backhanders' and stirring up the holiday-makers against us.

In the evening the young men and the boys from the Marina would sit around her on the beach and begin to make fun of

158

her. They asked if all the women in the Capital were as beautiful as she. She offered ice-cream all round and said: 'What does it matter? I'm swimming in the superfluous.' She massaged the arms and shoulders of the young men and her pet compliment was 'You look like a real fascist officer.' She said she had been in the big hotels at Corento but wanted rustic surroundings for a while; that she was foe to priests and Communists; and that she voted for the party with a 'prick'. She also said that 'you can tell a real gentleman from his physique'; and all this while massaging herself and others, never able to keep still for an instant, getting up from her deckchair, sitting down again, taking out a handkerchief, putting it on her head, screwing it up and stuffing it back in her bag, shifting her bracelets from one arm to the other, taking off her sunglasses, putting them back on; stuffing toffees greedily into her mouth and then spitting them out half-sucked, and rubbing them into the sand with her mules.

Everyone in the fishing village called her 'the madwoman', which put an end to our awe of her; we passed in front of her nonchalantly and once past the deckchair, kicked sand on her. Once I was swimming out on my own when, lifting my head out of the water, I saw an unexpected orange buoy; I tried to heave myself up on to it and discovered to my horror that it was her bathing-cap. I was terror-stricken and fled, swimming till my breath gave out. Later on the beach we collapsed in giggles; and from that day on we children called her 'the buoy'. But for several nights afterwards I dreamed of whales and other sea monsters with the faces of 'the buoy' and my mother. These whale-like beings sometimes took on the appearance of immense buttocks, grey and slimy, or looming tits with blind eyes instead of nipples. Then I dreamt of the young men from the beach, all dressed as soldiers, filing along the edge of a swimming-pool in which I was swimming naked. And in the dream I had the body of a woman.

Mother announced that we would be leaving for the Capital at the end of the summer, and then to a city in France where my father had been posted. And I couldn't imagine the Capital

159

as being different from the woman on the beach. The Capital and the big fat woman on the beach became one thing in my mind. I would climb up to the loggia repeating to myself 'I don't want to go, I don't want to', and it seemed that in the dusk the letters of I DON'T WANT TO formed a black ladder in the sky up which I scrambled to get away from 'the buoy', whose fat arms took hold of the ladder and began shaking it as I vanished weightlessly among the clouds, flying over villages and fields to land in the new city our father had promised us, where blackcurrants blossomed in the snow and the houses did not have loggias but pointed fairytale roofs; and where I would remain a child forever.

That summer, after the arrival of the news, Mother suddenly changed. She no longer had headaches and didn't spend hours lying down in the dark as if to save her life. The windows were thrown wide and the light of day came into the rooms along with the news that put the shadows to flight. In the evenings instead of reading, sweating and listless, by the light of the little lamp, she worked rapidly at the sewing-machine in a room lit up like day, with no thought of the bills, to make the clothes for our departure.

Thus I was no longer afraid to sleep alone and listened from my bed to the rhythm of the machine, interrupted now and then by the steady strides of scissors across cloth. We also had butter instead of dripping, and spread it to our heart's content, and as much sugar on the butter as we wanted. No one scolded us if a little scattered on the table or fell on the floor. Mother went back to haute cuisine and made soufflés, apple tarts, pizza *à la campofranca* crammed with mozzarella. She also took us to the tailor to get a suit and an overcoat each, for she didn't feel up to those herself, and they hung in the wardrobe under a white sheet for the period before our departure, like travellers queueing for their tickets. And when we were in bed of an evening with the lights off, the news drifted our way in the slightly intoxicating smell of mothballs sifting from the wardobe.

One day my brother found some sweets, forgotten in the

160

pocket of his jacket; I found fifty lire in an apron pocket. This serendipity also carried the news.

From the joy coursing through the house in those days I learned that money is life. It seemed we had been left out of its giddying whirl till then, locked away in a fairytale at the centre of which Mother lay on a bed like a queen in enchanted sleep.*

That year Mother often came down to the sea with us, and not to lonely spots either but to the Marina where she joined the company of the villa ladies. And almost every day of that August we went to one villa or another. And she was proud to be sitting in the circle of women, where she belonged at last, nonchalantly crossing one leg over the other, and she scolded us less if we helped ourselves to too much cake or honey. In that period I felt almost like a mother to her, seeing her so contented, but also because – not understanding very well the cause of her happiness – it seemed to me childish.

One corner of our roof was strewn with straw where the biffins were usually set out in rows to dry, but that year we didn't go gathering with baskets on our heads because we were leaving. On certain evenings I would go up to hang the washing and the placed seemed empty without the apples, and the coming winter in an unknown country seemed empty also. I stared long at the moon as it slowly peeked from behind the pine. Often I fell asleep in the straw to the rhythm of the wind stirring among the carob trees, and as I drifted off it occurred to me that the moon would have the same face in the foreign country and that it would look down in the same instant on Santa Maria del Mare and on me far away. I would

* Until that time I had attributed Mother's unhappiness and her ailments to her nature, as it were. Now I understood that the cause was shortage of money, and I began to ruminate about it. From this I went on to consider the saying of Christ that Don Candido so liked to quote in Catechism class: 'Not by bread alone.' It occurred to me that if not by bread alone, then bread was at least necessary. Happy with the revelation, not least because of having grasped the mysterious syntactical links of its language, I ran to tell Mother. 'But nowadays everybody has bread,' was her reply.

go up there when I had had enough of the childish joy running through the house, which seemed like a game that had gone on too long and turned to boredom. Or perhaps the desire to be on my own was the beginning of adolescence. I felt as if growing within me there was some savage and uncontainable beast which was constantly goaded and irritated by the domestic trivia. When Granny was there – a rare thing in those months because in view of our leaving she had moved to Aunt Callista's house in Althenopis – I was quieted by her presence. Sitting on the floor beside her, I breathed in the acrid smell of her clothes and fell asleep to the rhythm of her litanies, so similar to that of the breeze in the carobs at evening. I felt those litanies bore me up on the solemn measured wave of life, cradled me and consoled me for an ill I could not name but which seemed to coincide with the sorrow of leaving. In the breeze among the trees I was aware of nothing solemn, only a soft and muted sound which ignored my distress and merely cradled me , although it could not console.

While at other times I gave the appearance of snubbing the clothes shut away in the wardrobe, on occasions when the house was empty I would set about trying them on. And I also tried Mother's new nightdresses and paraded in front of the mirror. Till I stuck my tongue out at my reflection and ripped them off and would gladly have trampled them on the floor.

We left before we could join in the grape harvest. Maruzza, who had become my closest friend because she was the only village girl who had kept up with me in school, gave me a basket that looked like something out of a doll's game, full of mozzarellas, burrini, small caciocavalli cheeses, all tied up with red ribbons. We promised we would always write to one another.

So we departed, to take up that place in society due to our rank. It was the end of September, 1948.

II

The Homes of the Aunts

Allah brought me to shore to preserve me for further
shipwreck – *The Thousand and One Nights*

1

The arrival at Aunt Callista's

It was raining when we arrived at Frasca, the village of water and dust, lapped by the fabulous humours of the Volcano. The sky was low and full of fleeting shadows. We set our cases down on the mud that had invaded the pavement. Two years before, on our happy departure from Santa Maria del Mare, we had taken the cat with us in a basket. This time it had been a struggle to get ourselves there. Mother hired a cart to take our luggage to the house.

But before coming to Frasca, after my father's death, we had passed through various vicissitudes. We landed up first of all in the house of Aunt Callista, my mother's sister, the usual stopover after an arrival or before a departure.*

The Nobile building stood in a well-to-do and quiet street of Althenopis and had all of two courtyards, shaded by the arabesques of tall palms, which we used to scurry across during the war, with saucepans on our heads to protect us from splinters, as we made for the shelter, or rather, the cellars of the building. But the war and the coming and going of people to the shelter, where the entire neighbourhood took refuge, had finished long ago. The two courtyards were empty of people and the tenants' association wouldn't even allow us children to play there. We would sneak down, until

---

* When Aunt Callista married, Grandmother bought her that enormous flat and, at the same time, got for a bargain a smaller flat for her younger daughter on a different, then very dilapidated, staircase of the same building – as if the gift might induce her to marry as well. But Mother did not marry there and then, and the flat was let. Only in the last years of her life did she manage to get rid of the tenants and move in herself.

the caretaker came and chased us away. Everybody kept to
their own homes, shut up with their miseries, boredom, din.

However we had made friends, so there was another flat we
could visit. There was a big living-room still bearing the scars
of war, where the parents and relations of our friends played
canasta in the evenings; and an immense blonde doll in a pink
silk dress, its head shattered by a bomb, sat upright on a sofa.
The numerous inhabitants of the flat hadn't yet repaired the
drawing-room because they couldn't agree on who was to lay
out the money; an ancient grandfather was still alive and
wouldn't decide on making a will, so no one knew who was
going to get the place; and they weren't even on speaking
terms, passing one another in the corridors like strangers; one
spinster sister saw to the cooking of the various meals which
were eaten at different times by the various family groups. It
was as if the war were still on and that sister, plump, though
light in her movements, was like a carrier pigeon winging
backwards and forwards with peace offerings between enemy
camps.

Here I encountered for the first time a friend who had
menstruated: Vittoria, the friend of our friends, who could go
out in public every day to be offered an ice-cream by the
young men. One day she took off her knickers, splayed her
legs and showed us the blood trickling down. Her clothes
were fashionable and matched her sandals and handbags. She
was always suntanned and went unaccompanied on the trolley
as far as Piazza Cavour★ to visit her friends. Her arms, legs
and the nape of her neck were covered in a light down, and in

★ The Althenopis dialect often gets the accent wrong on foreign words:
Càvour, Fiát, Italsidér, Caflísh. Or bends them to its own purposes and
humours: the 'char a bancs' becomes 'o sciaraball' because in effect one does
bounce about inside; 'Per chi dobbiamo votare?' [for whom should we
vote?] becomes 'Pe chi c'aimmo avuta?' [Where should we turn?]; and
menstruation becomes 'the administration', because it comes every month,
like the building administration which demands the rent, known as 'pesone'
['spesone', large outlay; 'peso', weight] because it does in effect lie heavy on
the family budget.

secret correspondence with this down, with her green eyes, and her jingling gold bracelets, one felt she possessed a knowledge of life that none of us yet had and perhaps might never acquire. She had a dawdling indolent walk that was nevertheless determined, and I gazed in admiration at her beautiful feet, which had the firm grace of acanthus leaves, wide and tanned, solidly planted on the ground, and the little toes like the tender volutes of shells. Her voice was a raucous splashing that opened underwater grottoes in the tidy playroom of our friends. Her visits were always short, she left again immediately, leaving me as under a bell jar, confined to the gelid and artificial world of childishness.

Aunt Callista's apartment was on the top floor of the wing between the two courtyards. Twelve balconies looked out on to the majolica domes of the churches of Althenopis, on to gardens and on to the sea. And this greatly increased the value of the flat.

From a dark anteroom, large as a drawingroom, painted Pompeiian red, with high chairs with leather seats and backs in the Renaissance style,★ and shell-encrusted Roman vases standing on wrought-iron tripods in the four corners of the room – umbrellas were never to be lodged in the vases because it would have broken their shapely lines (art, said Aunt Callista, must be disinterested) – two separate doors led into the other rooms. Not that we could choose any door we liked, because we had to use the one that led into a long dark corridor separating the state rooms from the utilities – the hub of which

★ The furniture in the other rooms, even the 'Louis Seize', claimed not to be imitation. The pieces in the entrance hall – which were relegated there for that reason – were imitations in that so-called Renaissance style whose magisterial dignity furnished the chambers of notaries, barristers, judges, as well as the ante-chambers of the bishops, archbishops, mayors and prefects of Althenopis. They had come from the family of the maternal grandfather (who was a judge, in fact), solid provincial bourgeoisie. This family was never spoken of and rarely frequented because the relationship was only matrilineal; though perhaps also because the sole glory to emerge from that branch was a good and justly famous pastrycook of Castellammare di Stabia.

167

was the big, evil-smelling kitchen, with its yellow flaking walls, followed and preceded by various other rooms given over to ironing, sculleries, storerooms – which were the domain of the two whiskery old maidservants, Carmela and Maria, whose eyes were full of a gentle madness. When we met Aunt Callista on her way back from shopping, however, and she invited us in with her, we went through the great white door, decorated with a blue and gold frieze she herself had painted, as she had painted in their time the drawing-room doors in Uncle Alceste's house.* This door led to the sequence of drawing-rooms terminating in the dining-room and Aunt, who loved regal surroundings, never entered the house along the dark corridor so as to avoid its gloom. Clucking and rustling like a turkey she would throw the door wide open and stand there an instant as if in admiration. Coming from the dark hall, the sunlight in the room would dazzle us, with the gilding on the doors and the luminous cold blue of the divans

---

* Aunt Callista loved to transform houses into royal residences. She even gilded the doors of her 1930s flat opposite the façade of the Stazione Centrale in Milan. The flat had a terrace which Aunt transformed into an Althenopis loggia, painting the walls, which had previously been grey from smog, bourbon red and setting the parapet ablaze with geraniums.

Later, still in Milan, in one of the working-class districts towards Chiaravalle, in a modern two-room flat – her son had come down in the world and was selling books or detergents from door to door – Aunt set about painting the walls and doors in a manner befitting a gentleman's residence. And in the mornings, after painting for a good part of the night because of her insomnia, she complained that the shade of bourbon red with which she had thought to beautify a wooden screen separating the kitchen from the 'drawing-room' did not match up to her expectations when seen in the foggy light of day, so she began all over again. She quarrelled with the decorator she had engaged to distemper the rooms, because he went on using a yellowy or greyish white, while she wanted a dazzling Mediterranean white. And then she would inveigh against the Milanese and their sad taste. For Aunt Callista would like to have transported the hardworking Milan of the 1950s to the Mediterranean and back into the Renaissance. In the Milan of those years everything was possible with the aid of technology, or so it seemed. All that was necessary was to supplement these two qualities with taste. And Aunt Callista felt called to the task.

en style Louis Seize – in that house everything had to be *en style*.

In an elegant little package Aunt Callista carried three hundred grams of mozzarella, supposedly enough for eight people – but perhaps the servants weren't included – and half a kilo of cherries in a paper cone, this time inelegant; but she had been tempted by the beauty of the fruit in the shop. Because generally she shopped for the luxuries, like the mozzarella, while it was the servants' task to get the vegetables, the fruit, the bread. Mewing with joy she emptied the cherries into a stemmed dish of Murano glass and earnestly instructed us not to touch them; though sometimes, if overwhelmed by the beauty of the cherries and our youth she would take a bunch and hang it over our ears, preferably mine or my brother's because we were dark-skinned and they made a better show, while she would thrust one in my little sister's mouth, accompanying it with a light pat on the cheek. And as we went through the last door of the family quarters, which gave on to the sunny corridor and the rooms with the twelve balconies over the sea, her large bosom would strain somewhat in the white dress with the blue dots as she trotted on slightly swollen legs, and in a tone of imperious enthusiasm, summoned our mother, who would be lying down in the dark of her bedroom wearing full mourning or sitting on a straight-backed chair reading or sewing clothes for us.

Mother would then appear in the doorway, fragile and joyful, like a moth drawn to the only light remaining in her life, her children, whose rowdy squealing had reached her. She would turn her myopic eyes toward our smiling faces and her slightly perspiring exuberant sister, with her smeared lipstick, and as if guided by the tinkle of bracelets and rings she would make a dash for the package of mozzarella, anxiously checking its volume and humiliated by its smallness, since she wanted us to eat plentifully in our growing period.

You went from there into the Aunt Callista's workroom, which was halfway between artist's studio and ornate drawing-room. Three of the twelve balconies belonged to this room which seemed to extend boundlessly, not just in the worlds evoked by the strange objects in the row of pictures hanging on the wall, the work of my aunt, but also beyond the balconies, in the gleaming arabesques of the church domes in the palms in the gardens, in the sky and the sea, and nearer, below, in the descending sequence of loggias swarming with chickens and children, women, lines of washing, housemaids, bowls of tomato sauce set out to thicken, the daughters of petty civil servants combing their hair in the sun, lawyers sitting under umbrellas drinking lemonade with their wives, girls teasing the wool of mattresses and old women sitting on stools to supervise the work. But all this swarming life, visible when one peered down from the balcony, the human community in its quality of lowly retainer, left Aunt Callista entirely indifferent.★ Whereas she threw back the shutters with an all-embracing gesture to display the landscape to us; and every arc of that panorama, which began for her at the height of the domes and never descended below the line of the sea and the palms, was represented in her pictures.

On a table in that same room, or on a console or a plinth next to some drapery, arranged in an arbitrary and mysterious way, stood the various precious objects that she put into her still lifes: fruit dishes, candlesticks, dazzling embroidered table-cloths or pieces of yellowed lace, jugs and old crystal, silver teapots. She painted with one eye screwed up and her lips pursed in concentration, or was sometimes shattered by fail-

★ Aunt Callista had no liking for realism or naturalism in painting. Where the Master of Althenopis transformed men into gods, Aunt Callista limited herself to transforming them into gentlemen. She preferred real gentlemen as models, but she couldn't always find them within reach of her brush. To transform captains of industry into Renaissance gentlemen, Aunt Callista had to use the expedient of portraying them in bordeaux red or bottle-green dressing-gowns of silk or damask; in these shining folds the brush could wallow in its element. Or she would paint them in evening dress, but only when worn with style. The captains of industry would telephone at seven in the morning to make or cancel an appointment, and Aunt Callista would get the maid to inform them that she was already out painting, though in fact she slept till eleven. To gain any respect in the Milan of those years one had to give the impression of being continually busy.

ing to reproduce in oil the impalpable effect of silverware on white cloth. Her aspect was more relaxed when she used charcoal or sepia or pastel, for she could erase with a piece of soft bread without having to worry, and the lines in her forehead seemed to vanish along with her mistakes and for an instant a smile dispersed the concentration in her eyes and it seemed to fall away from her brows like the crumbs of bread drifting away into the mote-filled sunbeam that lit up her shining dress. When she painted she wore expensive *mises*, which, though covered in paint, would not have been out of place on a beautiful woman or a priestess.

As a girl and later as a young woman, Aunt Callista had been a celebrated beauty. From the drawing-rooms of town houses, even from the sailing clubs, men had hastened to drink cherry cordial in Grandmother's simple home, simply for a sight of her. At beaches, before 1914, they had bribed attendants to let them spy on her from bathing-huts. Since she had no feminine awareness she carried her beauty awkwardly and this made her even more disturbing to the men. When later she married and became pregnant with Cousin Achille, she seemed pregnant with her own heavy beauty rather than with a human child.

They had dolled her up even as a baby; they did her hair so her head sometimes looked like a flock of netted swallows, or a bunch of wistaria, or the truncated scroll of a capital. From early childhood she had been large and found it difficult to join in the games of her sisters and cousins. She would sit and watch, her limbs idle, but her eyes sharp and watchful. When her family became aware that she had an artistic gift they sent her to study with the great Althenopis master. The master, very old by then and in his right mind again after twenty years of madness, was in the grip of his ancient chimeras. His slovenly family went around the filthy house in dressing-gowns and when they managed to sell a statue they would bake up some macaroni and invite a swarm of cousins and friends. In thick dialect, unpolluted by the national language exalted by the bureaucrats of the Kingdom of Italy and the faculties of polytechnics, the Master would drive them out of the house, scorning their macaroni and their money questions, and of all the people who frequented the house the only one he took pleasure in was a curly-headed nephew who resembled the curly-headed lad he himself had been when he went begging for advice and training from the sculptors of Althenopis, while his playmates were content to beg for a bun or a handful of change in front of the 'Gambrinus'. *

The nephew had lively dark eyes but was very pale in the face, because he was for ever shut away in the foundry breathing the dust from marble and plaster.

When the girl Callista went to the old Master, who was again in the grip of an ideal of classical beauty, she was always accompanied by her mother, or a trusted servant, or her governess so that she might be preserved from his madness and his filth; and under the sly or curious eye of the maid, the governess's watchfulness, her mother's worried look, she would take lessons in chiaroscuro, oils, tempera, watercolour, sculpture. Once when she had failed with a drawing, the Master threw a rag plastered with clay in her face and Grandmother threw up her arms and took her daughter away, vowing never to return. But the girl cried for three days and refused to eat, so they were forced to take her back. This episode was later induced as proof of her vocation. On another occasion the Master kissed her in admiration of something she had done, and it isn't clear whether Grandmother was more worried by the throwing of the rag or by the kiss.

By an alchemical reaction between her imposing beauty, the social position of her family and a mad passion for classical art bequeathed her by the Master, when Aunt Callista reached

* Leopardi used to walk down Toledo from the Museum and enjoy an ice-cream at the 'Gambrinus'. Nowadays the 'Gambrinus' is the meeting-place of Somali, Ethiopian and Filipino domestic servants, of whom there are many in Althenopis, where they are engaged on terms that flout the Italian law on working conditions. In the period in which this novel is set, the villages in the hinterland of Althenopis and in other regions of the South had the present function of Somalia and Ethiopia.

her artistic maturity she found herself painting in a grandiose genre which often lapsed into the oleographic; at times, however, a drawing, a sketch, a detail of an oil-painting or a watercolour, escaped from lushness and gave a glimpse of art's necessity and joy and the fleeting spurt of life.

At two o'clock, abandoning his mysterious and important occupations, Uncle Giobatta arrived for lunch, like a sparrow stricken by the sultry oppression of storm. His hair, face and clothes were grey and he walked with a stoop. He would appear noiselessly in our company, as if resuscitated by our guilty conscience, to take us by surprise and spy on us with malevolent sharp blue eyes. His poor toothless mouth would grimace and whisper barely audible cutting rebukes, for in contrast to the rowdy people of Althenopis, he never dared raise his voice.* And at table Aunt and Uncle never spoke to each other.

* Grey because he came from Turin and Genoa, and because he was an engineer and came from a stern military family, dry, cold, controlled and thin. He had been dazzled by the beauty of the city and also by that of the woman, and through the former dazzlement he had lost his money in rash speculation and through the latter the light of feeling. Thus he had neither an honourable career as an engineer nor an honourable family life.

After the early years of marriage, resigning his last hopes, he had moved into a little room of his own in the house where his wife shone among baroque mirrors, Louis Seize drawing rooms, the palettes and paints of an art that tended to Renaissance pomp, the summery or autumnal splendours of eighteenth-century fruits, the classicizing flights of the old Master (a species of drawing-room art that was the mirror opposite of the crudely sentimental Fogliano stuff for bed- or dining-room so prized by foreigners with a veneer of culture or, as later, *nouveau riche* Milanese industrialists). Aunt Callista shone among her clothes, her jewels and her guests, some of whom came for social afternoons of tea and bridge and others for intellectual afternoons, and yet she had never taken a lover and was, in the last analysis, both a good mother and a good wife thanks to those endowments of restraint and modesty which had passed down to her from generation to generation; thus she could beguile without giving herself; lead into temptation without sinning; bring cheer to her drawing-rooms while saving on the expense, giving even the wateriest of soup a surround of crystal, silver and gentle manners. And she, who had known man and given birth in obtuse patience, reigned despotic over the daytime. But at night the king, an exile

173

When we arrived in the house everyone already knew that whereas Mother wept inconsolably for her dead husband, Aunt Callista was getting ready to abandon hers.

It happens in the lives of many women that the mother's death marks a moment of recollection, of accounting for one's existence, of secret anguishes and anxieties till then held in. So it happened with Aunt Callista. A month before our arrival in the house, a few days after our father, Grandmother died.

For more than thirty years Aunt Callista had been living with her husband, by then no longer in disagreement, but in hatred.

---

in his own house by day, changed into a misshapen predatory beast, at least in the first decades of their marriage, and visited her.

During air-raids, the moment the alarm had gone, Aunt Callista would run to the bathroom to doll herself up for the shelter, and years later the man from the building opposite remembered her thus dolled up, playing cards on a packing-case; meanwhile Uncle Giobatta opened all the twenty-four windows to prevent the glass from shattering inwards, and went back to bed.

He had secluded himself in a room with a bed as narrow as his wife's was large, in a long narrow room with a simple table of unvarnished wood and other simple things, cupboards crammed with rolls of paper and nails, screws, rulers, hammers, drawing-pins and stamps. And there, among so many iron objects (the staplers, the metal calculators, the paper clips, the punches) he exercised his iron will – 'He has a will of iron!' the Great-aunts used to say. He exercised it every day on himself and others in a great many particulars of a sadic-spartan nature, for since his dazzlement had shattered his actual willpower, all that remained to him were little iron rigidities, so that instead of building bridges, he collected nails; and with his slide-rule sticking out of his top pocket he had the air of calculating with daily punctiliousness the meannesses, weaknesses and small faults of others. 'I noticed some drops of urine', he might say to his son, 'at least a metre from the edge of the bowl.'

And he expiated his dazzlement with his sight, for he became almost blind with cataracts. Thus blind and iron-willed he remained alone. And little by little the years transmuted the iron into wax. At times he dropped the telephone book on the floor instead of putting it back on the table; at others, the cousins-in-law might murmur that he had filled out a tax-form wrongly; and finally, in the last days of his life one saw the old man's spirit break its iron bonds and run over the floor, on all fours – thinks he's playing horsy, said the Cousins. Or whispered it rather, out of pity, in each others' ears.

174

In the meantime bad news of her second son had reached her from a northern city. He had been sent to a tuberculosis clinic there in '42 and the Gothic Line had prevented his return. The young man had had a second bout of the illness. Though he had recovered, Aunt imagined him alone in a furnished room with no one to cook for him or iron his shirts. And among other things she blamed her husband for his tight-fistedness with their son. When Grandmother died she decided to go and join him.* None of her relatives was ever

---

* This was in 1950. Italy was starting from the beginning, after Fascism and the war. Aunt Callista was going to do the same and made ready to leave for Milan. Thin, penniless, far from the South and his family, her son worked and studied in his last remaining shirt – a white dress shirt – torn at his handsome bronzed neck. Milan swarmed with young men like him, wrenched from the comforts of the middle-class, ready for action, who did not want to understand the world, were incapable of conquering it, and wanted to change it. Marx and textbooks on hydraulics stood side by side on the shelves of his room, and at night, leaving the Young Communist Federation arm-in-arm with friends, memories of old domestic comforts mingled with comments on the day's politics.

Everything was hard and pure, then hard and painful. Then hard and confused. To each his own reconstruction of the situation, and the sinuous party line for all. But a building worker is not an engineer. And Lenin is not a poet for young men in crisis, no matter how badly stricken.

The boom years in Milan began. Everybody sold everything. A young man still without a degree: a year of the sanatorium, another of work, study, and the Party. A slender girlfriend, from an old Lithuanian family, grown up in the sanatorium like a lily in a greenhouse, elegant, poor, at first. Then go-getting, hard at it selling perfume and toilet-soap, metallic as a coin, enigmatic and fascinating as blind praxis. Her mother, a Lithuanian princess, hard on the servants with her whip; she, the daughter, had enough self-control to have been Queen of England, U.N. interpreter, Pirelli company secretary; but all she could do was sell soap. She loved him and wanted to get ahead in the world with him.

Get ahead they did, fifteen years later. In a brand new flat, with eight rooms, in Milan. They had brought together all the handsome furniture and the bibelots of both their families. And in his studio, high up on the shelves, the works of Lenin stretched alongside old editions of Shakespeare.

He would say: 'Everything depends on the individual', or 'The problem today is leisure'.

'Don't put your elbows on the table,' he admonished his daughter.

able to work out how much the hatred of her husband rather than love for her son had weighted the decision to leave Althenopis and her husband, and sell the flat which had been part of her dowry and where she had lived so long. But what is clear is that on the death of her mother, Aunt Callista realized that for thirty years she had not been living and she wanted to start everything, or as much as she could manage, over again from the beginning. And so she did.

The fact that our arrival coincided with Aunt Callista's decision to leave forever was not a happy circumstance for us.

On our arrival Aunt welcomed us generously with open arms, she even came to meet us on our way there and put three of her twelve rooms at our disposal, but by the time we left she had lost patience and confined us behind a screen.

In the mornings I would take coffee to Aunt as she lay swollen and voluptuous with frills in her great bridal bed, still drifting like a red mullet through the waters of dream. For a couple of hours by then – Aunt took her coffee at ten – I would have been in the kitchen enjoying the company of the maids. For children in such apartments the kitchen became the locus of warmth and affection. There the maids told their bitter, fabulous, obscene stories, there the children gave free rein to their instincts, to the indwelling feelings it wasn't nice to show. Hanging on the wall there were complicated dusty utensils that had served in more prosperous periods; and of all the gadgets of wood and iron that occupied a whole wall, only the rolling-pin came into use every now and again on the occasion of uncomplicated pizza; Aunt mewed with pleasure when it was set on the table and our eyes bulged at its size. In the kitchen the two sisters from Lucania – one brown-haired, small and whiskery, more affable and endowed with an almost mystic joy, the other more severe – told us about the years spent working in the fields, looking after parents and relations, service in convents and the houses of the well-to-do. Aunt Callista had portrayed them in oils; they looked like servants of Philip IV done by Velasquez – Aunt's pictures always looked like the work of some other painter, though

176

never anyone later than 1850. The elder was seated, wearing an aubergine dress and with a look of mischievous innocence in her eye, while the other was standing, wearing a black dress, buxom and virginal; both had their hair done up in a bun, in the fashion of the countrywomen of the South. There was an artful play of white and black in their hair highlighted against red hanging left unfinished – Aunt had other things on her mind at that period – and it seemed like the uncompleted blood-coloured background to their destiny as brides and mothers *manquées*.

I dawdled lazily or messed about all morning. I liked helping them to slice the aubergines, the courgettes, the potatoes, and at such times I felt my clumsy anguish and my futile, adolescent integrity corroded, as it were, by life, and when my fingertips were stained brown and my skin felt wrinkled it seemed that finally something, even if a very small thing, had happened to me. Even more I liked to fry the aubergines and the courgettes, and my vague, wispy, never-ending lack of consistency seemed to condense and become substance, though formless still, in the heavy vapour of the frying oil; and when it spat and a scalding drop fell on my hands, my arms, my neck, at last I seemed to have hands, arms, a neck. In those thick burning vapours and in that acrid soot I seemed to read my future womanliness, and I imagined myself cooking for a large family, future or past, which still lay sleeping the last drowsy sleep of the morning; I seemed to be cooking for my friends from the piazza of Santa Maria del Mare, and for my schoolmates in the foreign country we had returned from, and for my little sister, and for my ever-hungry brother, but most of all for my poor mother in her mourning, and for the courtyard cats who rubbed against the kitchen door all morning long. On other occasions I liked to do the washing-up and dip my voluptuously busy hands into the water, greasy and slippery with soda. I liked feeling the grease melt, and in the grey malodorous water I seemed to glimpse the turbid secrets of life. It was my way of interpreting the mystery of the resurrection of the dead, for in the vapours, the acrid smells, the sweat of the kitchen, I saw the semblance of Grandmother appear, whose absence I was then feeling more, for I was at the onset of adolescence and menstruation was coming on.

When I did in fact menstruate for the first time in those days, I dreamt that Grandmother was resurrected in my blood, whereas the death of my father I was living as a mere social fact: from rich we had fallen poor, from abroad we had returned home, and from juvenile and happy, Mother had become old and sad; or I lived it as a tragic abstraction: the misfortune or the disaster or state of being an orphan.

When the water had percolated, fresh coffee was added to the grounds to make another pot. The lot was then mixed with barley coffee in a jug that lasted for the whole day. Before the mixing, however, some of the fresh, unadulterated stuff was set aside for Aunt Callista, whose only vice this was, though it was more a necessity than a vice, for she suffered from insomnia and couldn't get out of bed in the morning without the stimulus. I would carry her cup along the long corridors of the house, first the dark one then the sunny one, and sometimes I dipped the tip of my tongue into it to see whether it would exercise the same magic effect on me as on my aunt. But I entered into these adult mysteries in vain, as when I had taken a puff of Mother's cigarette and felt only distaste. Thus I connected the bitterness of Aunt's awakening and my mother's bitter life to these two habits.

Often the youngest of the two maids, the cheerful one who was more accommodating to my desires and whims, would read my fortune in the coffee grounds. The grounds were thinned with a little water, turned upside-down on the marble table-top and my fortune read according to the shape they made. And it was a future of love, wealth and children; sometimes the face would appear of a blond young man with blue eyes, a child of the Sun and St Pasquale Bailonne, and those seven streaks like fjords were seven children, and the little whimsical scrolls were loving quarrels; then the line of cholera, but that blob cut off from the rest like a little island meant that I would survive it and that white opening in the black mess, like a pool, were the tears of the Madonna who would save me. The two poor maids had a great devotion to the Madonna, and the worn leather wallet in which they set aside the whole of their pay every month was stuffed with pictures of the Madonna, making it impossible to tell whether what made it bulge was the salary of years or passionate devotion. The mischievous and sunny young man whom Carmela showed me in the coffee grounds bore no relation at all to the grim soldiers who pursued me in my dreams, but rather to the radiant St Antony who kept company with the Crucified Christ over the women's bed, and at whose plump white feet a pig lay stretched, giving me the idea of a pig-breeding farmer husband, in the image perhaps of the one the two women had dreamed of when young. Nor did he resemble my cousin Achille who tried to kiss me one morning when the maids were out shopping and the house was deserted; Aunt Callista had gone with my brother and sister to buy artist's materials and only my mother was in the house, lying on her bed in the dark with a vinegar-soaked rag on her forehead, as often happened again after my father's death.

I carried the cup of coffee along the long corridors to my aunt whom I knew to luxuriate and gurgle on awakening. The room was full of sunlight which entered from the two balconies whose shutters Aunt never closed at night because she loved the light. And if anyone advised her to close the shutters, so that at dawn at least she would be able to fall asleep without disturbance, she quoted Goethe's dying words: 'Mehr Licht!', for she had been taught German as a child, as well as French and English, as if she were an infant prodigy destined for a great future. The cool morning sunlight seemed to slide over the yellow and blue, green and purple majolica of the domes and wash it clean. Aunt was all podgy and clucking, she stroked my chin with fat fingertips backed by painted and scratchy nails. Her voice filled the space with whorls and spirals of snails and shells, she puffed up like an amorous chicken, wriggled along the beam of sunlight like a happy caterpillar, frothed like horses' manes and wave-crests

179

depicted in her tame landscapes. Great disorder reigned on her bedside table, the sign of her nocturnal travail: the stubs of cigarettes, the remains of mint cordial or lemonade, the beaker of water half full, a pill snapped across, a blackened amber cigarette-holder, pads of cottonwool with red or black smears, a piece of bread she had fetched from the kitchen when she had found herself sleepless and famished at one in the morning. Lying on her side, Aunt Callista would gurgle affection at me as she sipped the coffee. Meanwhile I would amuse myself looking at a corner of the room reflected in a mirror which gave a backview of my aunt and myself reflected from another mirror on the opposite wall. Aunt Callista's room, in fact, was full of mirrors and it was possible, without turning round, to see every corner of the room enclosed in frames of gold, velvet, mother-of-pearl, so that everything seemed to be part of a painting and the mirrors seemed kaleidoscopes for 'Nature Morte', 'Portraits', 'Landscapes'; in a slightly sloping mirror one could even glimpse a dome against a background of sea and palms. The bedroom itself seemed like a magical workshop of art, magical because lacking the tools of the trade, the smell of turpentine, the sketches, the paint stains, the pains and toils of the craft. At times I scrutinized my back in the vain attempt to surprise myself as I really was and understand, from behind, the indecipherable enigma that stood in front of me in the likeness of my face. In the same way that after giving birth mothers immediately demand 'How is the baby?' and the doctor or nurse foolishly responds 'It's a boy' or 'It's a pretty little girl', while all the woman wants to know at that moment is whether it is a baby, whether it is healthy, so in the same way when I looked at myself in a mirror, the force of convention impelled me to ask myself whether I was pretty, while the real unformulated question was 'Who, what am I?' It is a futile question to address to mirrors, but sometimes Aunt's mirrors seemed to reply when I involuntarily surprised myself in backview, because at that instant I was not an aping, smirking image, but a gesture, an action: bearing the cup, questing for a lost sandal and slipping it back on with a skilful movement of the foot, bending down to pick up a handkerchief, so that I could say to myself surprised: 'That movement in the world is me'.

Every day after the house was put up for sale, dozens of people came to inspect it, so it always had to be tidy and Mother could not lie in the dark with the vinegar rag on her forehead. Uncle Giobatta was deliberately never at home during visiting times, he accentuated his role of busy man taken up by important things, which, it later emerged, were no more than working by the hour for miserly pay in a draughtsman's office.

Hand-in-hand with the growing anxiety, worries, uncertainty caused by the continual intrusion of potential buyers, who dithered and couldn't make up their minds there and then, and by Aunt's irritation with the unspoken rebuke of family and friends, as the standard of living declined in the house in view of the future expense of setting up in a new city – so the soap in the bathroom became a transparent wafer before being replaced, there was no toilet-paper for days on end and one had to resort to newspaper, and the mozzarella was sliced ever thinner, and the cherries were ever rarer, the meatballs contained ever more bread when, indeed, the meat wasn't entirely replaced by aubergine – as Mother was forced to prolong our stay because of the difficulty of finding a house, so did the living space we had been allotted on our arrival shrink. First my little sister and myself lost our room and went to sleep with Mother, then our brother's went, and finally Mother's, so that at the end of our enforced stay, after the atelier-drawing-room had been partly dismantled and the pictures crated, a curtain was hung at one end and the four of us slept behind it among our piled belongings. And hidden behind there our mother would sometimes cook a supplementary supper for us on a little spirit stove, mostly a piece of meat for my brother because he was then very thin and she was afraid he might get consumption from not eating enough. My sister and I, who enjoyed better health, were allowed to dip our bread into the gravy. This secret operation was conducted with the doors to the balconies wide open so that the smell of roasting meat should not seep through the gaps of the doors into the other rooms and so betray us. During the day, as Aunt Callista went about from room to room ordering the removal men to pack this and the other, Mother got up her courage to follow her, though at some distance. Ten years previously she had entrusted her with much of her furniture, paintings and trinkets, but Aunt seemed to have forgotten that the stuff didn't belong to her, and though Mother didn't dare complain she wanted to know the magnitude of the damage at least. She would become very red in the face during this enterprise and suffer from congestion, and in the afternoons when she went to visit her relations she would give free rein to her recriminations, but no one dared say a word to Aunt Callista at that time, for she seemed possessed and had lost all restraint, as if her sacrilegious decision required it of her. Nor were there the tender gurglings of before, nor did she droop cherries from our ears, but was all imperious commands to get out of the way, not to touch this or that, not to make a muddle.

So one day we left the house.

2

Aunt Cleope's house

We lived for a few weeks dispersed among various relatives. I stayed with Aunt Cleope, also called the Park Aunt, my brother was staying with Uncle Adone, Mother and my little sister with Uncle Chinchino.

She was called the Park Aunt because in the upper reaches of the town the squalid blocks of high-density building that had been going up from the time of the Great War used to be called parks. There were no trees any longer, apart from the planes of the avenue which led there.

Almost everybody in Aunt's building was Calabrian in origin because the government employees belonging to the 'Friends of Calabria' had formed a co-operative to build the flats, which were fifty percent financed by thirty year mortgages. The maids of many of the families were also Calabrian, as was the porter, whose children jostled on the marble entrance steps which were ornamented with evergreen plants in granite vases next to the overflowing rubbish bins always enveloped in a buzzing cloud of flies, a double offence to the decorum of the hall, which was equipped with a creaking art-deco lift. The children were not allowed, however, to eat their spaghetti in the hall and at summer lunchtimes one would see them squashed together round a table in the porter's lodge, the bead curtain of which was looped aside at such times to break the eternal twilight of the room which would hardly have suited the sunny spaghetti, destined to melt in the digestive juice of a watermelon split in two, enthroned in the centre of the table where it cooled by evaporation.*

* In the absence of a fridge or ice-block, the best way of cooling a watermelon is to cut it open and set it out in the sun; rapid evaporation cools it.

In Aunt Cleope's building, as opposed to Aunt Callista's, I was in and out of many homes.

On the first floor there was the flat of Signora Loiarro, an elementary schoolteacher who years before on our arrival from Porto Quì had prepared us for entrance into the Italian school, giving us private lessons out of friendship for our aunt, in a round of obligations and exchange of favours that had lasted for decades. She had taught us that 'oca' and 'madonna' are pronounced with a broad *o*, that the farmer 'polled' his pear trees in straight rows, and that one should 'compose' oneself in front of a book. But since we were considered of superior social standing because of the nobility on our mother's side and our father's diplomatic post, Signora Loiarro, who was small and extremely fat, put up with our bad manners and negligence, and came out with indulgent little giggles and sighs of satisfaction at our waywardness, rewarding every passage read in one breath, every dictation without a mistake, with a comfit or a caramel. At the end of the lesson, from a plate which showed two shepherd-boys at the centre, she offered us little biscuits in the shape of letters of the alphabet and barley-water or sparkling orangeade.

The schoolmistress had a beautiful daughter, pale and curly-haired, with heavy rings, bracelets and earrings in solid gold. She had bright stubborn eyes, lips painted the same purple as the nails on her diaphanous hands, and all in white crossed the hall to disappear into a dark bedroom.

It seemed that this daughter – married to a young engineer, respected and amiable, already co-owner of the firm where he worked – had the habit of stopping strangers in the street and going off with them; and after lunatic hours or days of perdition and madness she would fall into a state of utter exhaustion and guilt, and not daring to appear before her husband, fled to

---

The Althenopis 'mellone' is of two kinds, the 'bread melon' and the 'watermelon' (the double-l spelling, less common according to the dictionary, is the only one used in Southern Italy); this method of cooling is not to be advised for the bread melon, the flesh of which is insufficiently watery: since evaporation is slow, it heats up instead of cooling.

her mother's house, to the room she had had as a girl, and remained there without saying a word, refusing even to eat. The husband, who was a man of broad views and had no wish to lose her, sent her to specialists instead of throwing her out. Her mother and Aunt Cleope said she was sick, but when they spoke of that good man the husband, little smiles on their faces betrayed a knowingness, a disapproving scorn, which was immediately and duly corrected by their almost simultaneous agreement that he was a very handsome young man, a fine young man, and in particular, had a very good job. The thing that he lacked had, in their conversation, the ambiguous character of being considered the very basis of marriage on the one hand, and a mere, though not indispensable, adjunct on the other.

When the young woman – all in white, with white legs, slightly hairy in summer – crossed the living-room in high-heeled sandals, the two women fell silent and bent over for a biscuit – both were stout – in greedy concentration and unthinking vagueness. The girl sliced through the dimness of the hall and one heard the thud of the door followed by a smothered rattling of glass because all the hallways of those flats had two doors, one of wood and the other of frosted glass with the initials of the head of the family etched in the middle of a roundel, either plain or with a floral motif. That rattle used to throw me into a state of unspeakable anxiety; I would like to have gone after her, hiding behind the trees in the avenue, and got to my feet impatient with the mother's gossiping, and always when she said goodbye she gave me a pinch on the cheek with her plump hairy hand. And I, who would like to have been maid to her white witch daughter!

A tax-collector lived on the second floor with his wife and three daughters. Their flat was really two put together and so was larger than the rest. The wife, who came from a remote northern province, was blonde and extremely thin and had dyed and redyed her hair so often that it had various tints going from ash blonde to gingery, and when she bent down one could see the scalp in several places. Her movements had a constant tremor; her eyes were dilated and gleaming from living constantly in the dim house. She crossed and uncrossed her knees all the time and I was struck by their lunar pallor kindling at the knee to pink, as if from fever. The three daughters were tall, brown-haired, of a sickly beauty, fair-skinned or rather, pallid, as their mother and wore strange old-fashioned frocks which were somewhat worn and made of pink or blue organza or of satin, covered in bows and frills, with a slight hint of dirt at the seams. They sat stiffly on the worn-out sofas in the drawing-room, even in summer wearing closed shoes of black or white patent leather on their large feet. The row of six skinny calves looked like the Arab portico of a cloister, shining in the dark of the room. I stared in silence at that elegant frieze and would like to have taken off their shoes to check that their feet were flesh like mine. At a word from the mother one of the girls sketched a ballet step, another went to fetch her violin. They had the cult of art in that house and the father regularly enrolled his daughters in contests and competitions, but as their health was uncertain, and to pre-serve them from life's ugliness, they were given lessons at home. My aunt's teacher friends took turns at it, and in exchange were rewarded with the father's advice and some-times a blind eye in regard to the income from some piece of land or other in Calabria, or in regard to some relative of theirs – prodigal then in sausages, sheep cheese and aubergines in oil. All the members of the family spoke in terms of overblown rapture, which seemed to spread beyond the house to the world of the daughters' would-be fiancés, who couldn't go beyond gazes and sighs since none of them yet had jobs.

On the ground floor lived a schoolmistress who always went out in headscarf and dark glasses. If one met her on the stairs she immediately drew aside and walked hugging the wall when she was out in the street. She had a mongol son who had been living with her for twenty years. Coming down the stairs, I often heard him scratching at the door, and looking up in fear, I would see his mild and lucid eye in the roundel of the glass.

My aunt's apartment was on the third floor. When you rang, a pair of wary eyes could be seen trying to make out the caller through the transparent whorls of the initials. Before belonging to Aunt Cleope and her family, the flat had been my grandparents'. Grandfather had received the keys in 1925 when his children were already set up on their own: my father had moved to China in 1921, Aunt Cleope had married, and only Uncle Adone, the eldest, then still a bachelor, lived with his parents. But the moment Grandfather took possession, he decided that his duties towards the family were done, and left them. As a young man he had been a socialist sympathiser, but later he restricted himself to being a mason. Before '14 he had even incited the mob in the piazza to rise up from its material and moral poverty, but after '14 he exhorted them to fight for the liberation of the Italian territories still under the foreigner. His conception of socialism was all verbiage and conspiracy.

The centre of any conspiracy of course could only be the Capital. So in great secrecy, after the marriage of his already twenty-five-year-old daughter, viewed by him as the kidnapping of flesh of his flesh, he applied to transfer from the Althenopis high school where he had ended up after various stints in Sicilian and Calabrian towns, to a school in the Capital, and given his seniority, the transfer was granted. He justified it to his pale stern wife on the pretext of having to get to work on the Ministry if he wanted a headmaster's job, and of the obligations he had contracted in getting himself nominated to a high rank in the Masons. Grandmother pretended to believe him. Thus decorum was maintained both within the family and in the public eye. It is not true that once women are past fifty they no longer need love. Widowed in this way, Grandmother began to fade and fell ill of an obscure slow malady and so, to look after her and cheer her up, Aunt Cleope moved into the flat with her family, and the flat took on the look it was to maintain for more than twenty years.

The hall was papered with green and gold vine tendrils on a brown background, and bentwood chairs and divans with holes in the seats stood against the walls. There were plants and hatstands, again in bentwood, and in a corner there was a heap which grew by the year of Italian, Latin and Greek anthologies, dictionaries, grammars, editions of the classics and collections of irregular verbs, sent out by publishers to the teaching profession. For some time in another corner there stood a cageful of parakeets, given to Aunt Cleope's soldier husband by a fellow soldier in the colonies.

On the right-hand side of the hall was the door to Grand-father's study, which later became Uncle Adone's, and then when he married it was turned into a child's bedroom. Though Aunt Cleope was a teacher she had no right to a study, nor did she seem to demand it, and gave her lessons in the dining-room, in the comfort of the noises and smells from the adjoining kitchen, where an ageless maid went around invisibly, as if flattened against the walls or dissolved in the vapours from the cooking. Nevertheless, to keep up appearances, Grandfather returned every now and then and installed himself in the study, making it necessary for Uncle Adone to go out for interminable walks. Grandfather didn't just come for appearances' sake but also to recuperate and find comfort. When he arrived he looked as though he hadn't been to a barber for months. The moment he was through the door, despite the protests of his wife and daughter, he set about doing his washing, almost as if he were afraid of its being seen, and hung it out on the balconies to dry in the sun, declaring that at last it would be rid of the stink of kitchen and toilet. During the night or at dawn, the two women stealthily washed it again, alternating insults with concern as they scrub-bed.

After hanging out his clothes, Grandfather would empty the books and papers from his leather briefcase, rummage among the piles of books in the hall, give a rapid glance at the prefaces and commentaries to the classics and begin to swear; howling at his anguished wife he would demand matches to set fire to them; it drove him wild to see Martial and Petronius bowdlerized, but Catullus above all.

Two walls of Grandfather's study were lined with books, and despite the changing history of the room which was invaded by heaps of plastic toys, the books were kept in their old order. Under the window there was a Savonarola chair with a twentieth-century writing-table, in front of which generations of pupils had succeeded one another, the children of office-workers, shopkeepers who had made money, aristocrats come down in the world between the two wars. They came mostly in summer to prepare for the re-sits, pimply and limp in the afternoon heat, almost always on their own, sometimes accompanied by a maid or by a relative who sat outside in the hall on a bentwood chair, where, fleeing the boredom of the afternoon nap, I would come to join them and listen to the halting Latin scansion, interrupted at times by the sonorous declamation of Aunt or Uncle in the grip of an enthusiasm which went beyond the task in hand, rising above the reek of broccoli which had escaped from the kitchen and dining-room and liked to hang about in the hallway.

A room led off the hall which had been Grandmother's bedroom during my early childhood, but had then become Aunt Cleope's and her husband's when Grandmother's husband abandoned her. The furniture was of solid walnut, ornate in style, and there was even a *chaise-longue* which waited in vain for a feminine form, because Aunt Cleope was an active woman, endowed with good health and an honest aversion to loose and abandoned poses. Only after her husband's death did the room become more accessible to us children and the other inhabitants of the house. Before then we were not to know about the marital rituals celebrated there, which included the trimming of each other's toenails. Financial worries were given outlet in that room, not just the most secret rites, and worries about health and about promotion; it was perhaps there and only there that politics were ever discussed, in the run-up to some election. In front of the mirror in this room, on the marble top of the chest, the bonbonnières from weddings and christenings finished up, here letters, telegrams (only rarely telegrams of congratulation, one could hardly go to all that expense just for a piece of good news), and the money were kept; the laundry of the house was also stored there: the bathroom towels which were changed once a week, the sheets which were changed once a fortnight, and the tablecloths. All the laundry was white and never in that house did it smell like fresh linen. It had instead the reassuring mustiness of generations; certain pale stains on it seemed like the mark of the mouldering of those industrious lives, as if in the changing history of the family each person had been required to leave his mark before departure. And only after fulfilling that requirement had Grandfather been able to give free rein to his folly, only to return – having abandoned Masonic intrigues and the chorus-girl – sad and broken, to stamp the white banners of the family with the signs of senility. Because the fugitives always returned. And so it was with Iris, Aunt Cleope's daughter.

Cousin Iris was seventeen in 1939 and a very beautiful girl. All the more beautiful in Althenopis where tall and shapely blondes are rare; and she herself felt all the more beautiful not merely because of the youthful splendour which the young men of the Park district ran to admire when she came out of school, following her to the very door of the building, but because – responsive at least in this to the propaganda of the Ally over the Alps – she felt herself to be of pure Aryan stock among the small dark Southerners. In a black and white check frock, with a black bow at the neck in sign of mourning for Grandfather, sweating slightly under her armpits from the exuberance of her pace, she went to school swinging her books at the end of a strap. Her hair, to tell the truth, was chestnut, but she bleached it in secret with peroxide. Uncle Adone, who had married in the meantime to get away from the strangers invading the house, nicknamed her Nausicaa, after being persuaded by Aunt Cleope to stop calling her 'Helen of Troy' which didn't seem respectable to her.*

The beautiful high-school girl had a university student

* 'Troia' also means 'whore' – *Trans.*

boyfriend who waited for her outside school. Apart from his enthusiasm for Italy's splendid destiny in the world, he cultivated, as a song much in vogue in those years had it, an overflowing vein of poetry.

No one ever found out where the two young people got together for their encounters; the fact remains that no sooner had Cousin Iris finished high school, than she found herself pregnant.

An immediate marriage made an honest woman of her and the study of which Grandfather and Uncle Adone had been co-tenants became the bedroom of the young couple, who imported a touch of modernity with a flowered cretonne bedspread and photographs on the wall of the actress Luisa Ferida and of the Duce as farmer standing in a heap of corn and hoisting a boy child into the air. The baby, however, was not called Benito, but Ermanno. The son-in-law and the father-in-law used to meet in the hall without greeting each other and ate in the dining-room at different hours, until the young man was called up and posted to a barracks in Rome. In the Capital he came across subversive ideas and another woman.

Iris went to join her husband but was forced to flee because of this double plot, so she seemed destined to the precocious continuation of her Grandmother's fate, and the conviction became rooted in the family that Masonry and Bolshevism were all one with the destruction of the family and sexual impropriety.

Poor Iris, blonde and Aryan at least in appearance, crossed the Gothic Line with her freckled nurseling at her breast. She resisted for three days in the train without a shit or a piss because she could never have done it in the proximity of men, let alone soldiers, but the child's given name of Ermanno was of great help in her tribulation for it brought her offerings of food and drink from the Germans, though she continually refused, foreseeing that she would then be unable to cope with evacuating them. Swollen with urine and shit, stained with menstrual blood and milk, her gaze dark and watchful, she returned to her father's house and did not move from it again.

In August Iris took us to the sea. Coming from the various houses where we stayed, we all met up at nine in the morning in front of the Domizia railway. Iris sat next to the window, blonde and tanned in a low-cut dress with red and white stripes and two big ornamental buttons on the shoulders; her breasts rose above the line of the lowered window and merged with the line of the hills. She wore a coral necklace which, rather than matching the stripes of her dress, set off the glowing felicity of her roseate flesh. She was jammed between two big straw bags, one of which held our bathing costumes, and in the other Aunt Cleope had packed an abundant picnic. Her son sat near to her and after amusing himself a little with us he tried to clamber over the bag to reach the warmth of his mother's side, until finally the bag had to be moved and he clung to her lap and seemed to melt into it.

We sat in front of them. But the moment we got up to stroll in the corridor or look through another window our seat was taken by a dark, smiling young man wearing a medallion of the Madonna or his patron saint on a gold chain round his neck. The young man sat down, gazed out at the landscape with an indifferent air, and then stared at Cousin Iris with ostentatious determination. Back in the compartment we glared down at the usurper; then quite decided to reconquer our seat, three of us squashed in where there had only been two of us. Under the young man's insistent gaze all Iris did was pet her son and let him cling to her. And over his head she looked at us in sly rebuke, as if we had deserted the battlements of a fortress under siege, and hugged her son as if to say that he was her sole remaining defender. Urged by Iris' gaze and our uncomfortable position one of us would finally pluck up the courage to assert our rights and say to the young man, 'You're sitting in our seat.' The man would get up then and go to sit motionless on one of the lateral seats, from where he fixed Iris with eyes so liquid they seemed about to melt. He swapped comments about the weather in a strained Italian with a friend, while negligently turning a heavy gold ring round and round upon his finger. Quite at her ease, Iris smiled at us and kept up

192

a continual chatter, straightening by turns a curl, a pleat of her frock, a ribbon, her collar.

At the beach she was always surrounded by male stares and by clouds of flies attracted by the picnic basket and the creams with which she covered herself. In the bathing-hut I helped her fasten her bra and do up the zip of her latex costume, black or purple with green stripes. And as she pulled her stomach in I tried to keep the two edges together with one hand and pull the zip up with the other; then you had to flatten and stuff into the costume the roll of flesh which had worked its way up her back to her shoulders, and perform the same operation under her armpits, taking care not to pull the curly blonde hair, while in front she herself managed to stuff her breasts in and shape them to the fabric and the stiffening. A cretonne bed-cover and the towels were then spread on the sand under the umbrella. Before sitting down Iris went over to the mirror by the huts to bunch her hair at the back of her neck and put on her sunglasses. Cushioned on the towel, she scrutinised the sea in all directions and in a wailing tone, which seemed to contain a permanent anxiety, called us in for fear we would drown. We ran up, hooting, holding her son by the hand and she wrapped him in a beach-robe and rubbed his hair with a towel and hugged him again and again as if he had narrowly escaped danger.

As we sat round the bedcover eating, a group of young men came up to lie on the sand near us. After the picnic Iris sent us off to get ice-creams, because she was so overwhelmed by the business of digesting that she didn't have the strength to get up. Struggling against sleep, the lashes of her screwed-up lids fluttered and met, but a little start restored her to watchful duty. As we ate our ice-creams, we too made indolent by that slow lapping, a tune came across from the group of young men clustered round the radio of the bathing establishment, rising up through the sultry air above the whorls of cigarette smoke. Iris smoked a Marlborough to shake herself awake. She lay on her side with her belly slightly swollen from the food, her mild eyes fixed on the grey and motionless expanse of water; on her neck, which the sun had turned amber with the aid of her creams, her coral necklace caught the light, filling me with nostalgia for the transparent and lively sea at Santa Maria.

On the train coming back we licked the salt off each other's skin. Iris smiled in the cool evening breeze from the open window. Her small son's head resting in her lap sank into the soft swelling of her crossed thighs. I left my brother and sister, who were playing cards on a seat with some other children, and came to sit opposite her.

Iris stroked me lazily under the chin. The young man came to sit next to me and offered me a sweet; in distress I closed my eyes and pretended to sleep, and sometimes I really did fall asleep to escape the unease. I seemed to hear people talking as I drowsed. Afterwards Iris told me that he was a friend of her brother's.

After dragging myself upstairs – I was afraid of the lift – I would become wide awake in the shady house. I locked myself in the bathroom with her, where, unknown to her father, she depilated her legs. I passed her a towel and the soap, and watched her. I followed her then to her bedroom where, with a towel wrapped round her head like a turban, she did her nails and her eyebrows.

At eight o'clock a modulated whistle came from the dining-room indicating the start of the news; meanwhile Aunt Cleope would loom in the doorway dressed all in black for the death of her brother, and in the steady voice which always seemed to be admonishing and exhorting as if she were in school, she summoned us in to dinner.

Aunt Cleope's table was the opposite of Aunt Callista's. In the one place, starched lace-trimmed napkins, china, crystal and silver waited in vain for lavish food, whereas what came was miserly, while here, cheap crockery was laid out on the stained cloth in any old fashion, waiting for someone to set it straight, but one rich course followed another: peppers stuffed with meat or macaroni, the breaded cutlets an inch thick at least and on the bone, the artichokes and the cabbage fried in batter, the boiled fish, the ragouts and parmesan sauces. And there was always a carved fruit-dish in the centre of the table piled with the season's fruit and often along with it a tray of pastries. My cousin poured me wine and water, alternating his courtesy with hard thumps on my back to make me sit up straight, and Aunt Cleope, while my back was turned, slipped more tidbits on to my plate. It was an insult to health and to the family not to have appetite.

It wasn't disgust I felt in front of the remains of a *parmigiana* surrounded by a thick layer of grease, or in front of the remains of a mozzarella in its whey, next to the moulded cream cheese and the slabs of butter; what I felt was a sense of stubborn detachment, sharpened and exasperated by the lyrics of a tune put out over the radio which seemed to evoke nostalgia for an insipid past or anticipate with its rowdy truculence a banal and peevish future. As stuffed with food I rocked in the bentwood chair which had been mine since I was a baby, I became lazily aware of a secret affinity between the deceit in those lyrics and the red-varnished nails, bleached hair and painted mouth of Iris, wrapped in a white dressing-gown with red spots and wagging her pink plush slipper in time to the music, while the smoke from her Marlborough mingled with the eau-de-cologne dabbed under her arms. At her feet the child played, hidden by dunes and promontories of toys of painted tin and plastic which, as the years passed, had overflowed from the room where they were meant to be kept into the hall and corridor. Cradled by the rocking I imagined rows of Doric or Corinthian columns, similar to the ones Aunt Cleope had made me copy the day before in preparation for my drawing exam, rising up against the clouds of cirrus which the smoke of Iris' cigarette had turned into, or that from our cousin's pipe who sometimes came to dinner, and then his mellow voice would waft over the silence of my aunt and cousin, slightly sing-song like all the voices in that family.

In the discreet lament of those voices I seemed to be aware, in that drowsy rocking, of a placid nostalgia for a life less burdensome and more intense; and in the long pauses of the

195

conversation I looked at all those thoughtful gloomy eyes which little Ermanno looked up at every now and then in astonishment. 'For what do we live?' I asked myself. 'Today we went to the grotto of the Sybil,' I said to break the silence. Because, when the sea was rough, Iris took us for a walk to the lake of Acheron. At that moment Aunt Cleope, her head nodding from sleep, in a voice that itself seemed to hover between the family circle and the grandeur of ancient times, murmured: *Apothanein thelo*; and her gaze lit up with liquefied light.

Later, lying on the big bed beside Iris – she was hugging her son to her on the other side – I fell asleep immediately, listening to the fairytale she was telling the child in charmless fashion.

When I had homework to do I was shut into the drawing-room. The slovenliness that ruled in the rest of the house was excluded from there. Two Chinese vases, a present from my father, were displayed on an out-of-tune piano. The backs of settees and armchairs upholstered in damask with an arabesque pattern were protected with antimacassars decorated with dancing cherubs. Above the divan, in the centre, hung a Nativity which Grandfather had found in a Calabrian attic and which a painter friend of his had restored badly. There was much fantasizing about the worth of that daub which various family friends attributed to one seventeenth-century painter after another – just as they fantasized about the worth of a little flat in a working-class area of Althenopis that Aunt Cleope had inherited and for which she was paid no rent, while still paying the rates, because the people who lived there were too poor.

As in the foyer of the building, on the landings and in the hall, the corners of the drawing-room were made fresh by potted plants. But in the shade of that room they were fleshy and sensual, of a rare species made more precious by a red flower that bloomed once every five years, and which I had never seen, but on whose beauty and fleetingness relatives and family friends, who often came round five in the afternoon, made long disquisitions, alternating descriptions of the flower with maxims on youth and death.

One of the first to arrive was Professor Perfetti, whom Aunt Cleope begged to come early to check on the training she was giving me in the Humanities. Since she herself had studied Modern Languages she felt a sense of inferiority in his regard. Professor Perfetti offered some amiable criticism: 'Too much grammar, too much syntax,' he said. And he regarded me ironically, almost scornfully, when he noticed that after a rapid read-through and translation I hadn't the slightest idea of what it was about.

He was small, squat, very dark-skinned, with a dried-up, extremely agile body. The few remaining curls on the nape of his neck and over his ears were still black. His face was Samnite. Despite his veneration for the classics, he spoke of them with scorn. Sometimes he would contemptuously call the Greeks 'Merchants!' and the Romans he called barbarians, or rather, and it made Aunt Cleope blush, 'big pricks'. And then of Manzoni - and I had to read eighteen chapters of him - he broke into dialect to say: 'He's like a pig! Nothing gets thrown away!'

It annoyed him to hear my mechanical reading of Latin metres; he would stop me in midstream with an imperious gesture, prop himself lightly on the piano, and begin to recite, waving his hand rhythmically as the verse required. Still reciting he would begin walking up and down the room and since there wasn't much space because of the furniture, he opened the doors to the balcony, leant for a moment on the railing and with his hand still raised came to a halt facing us; but there still wasn't room enough for him, so he opened the other leaf of the drawing-room door; his voice swelled out into the hall and the glass rattled in the door. Then he slumped on to the divan and wiped the sweat from his face and neck with a large handkerchief, immaculately clean and pressed - the only clean thing he had about him. He would then ask Aunt Cleope's permission to make himself comfortable and wrench off his tie and undo his collar. Long after he was sitting down his

197

voice went on floating through the rooms.

One night, after his patrol through the house had been longer than usual, I dreamt a sentence in Latin, the meaning of which I could not grasp; the Cumean Sybil, standing before her high rock, gave me this response: *Tibi manet tua sponte videre Eum. Eum*, naturally enough, I saw written with a capital letter.★

Some years later Aunt Cleope again entrusted me to Professor Perfetti for the preparation of my philosophy exams. Of all the philosophers of antiquity he preferred Epicurus. And jokingly he would say: 'Ah, if only your aunt had been epicurean!'.

From this and other insistent allusions, I was able to deduce that as a young man Professor Perfetti had been secretly in love with my aunt, but had had to marry a poor cousin who had been brought up in his father's house from childhood, to whom he had contracted some obligation while still adolescent.

Every time I entered his dark, book-lined study, from which the cats were constantly having to be shoo-ed, the Professor scrutinized me at length and I would hear his disappointed murmur: 'You don't resemble your aunt', and he seemed to regret the fullness of the figure that had won him, the high luminous brow and the limpid gaze, whereas I reminded him of his young wife, dark and thin, who now when she opened the door to me seemed an evanescent shadow immediately swallowed up by the domestic walls.

Despite this, he gave me an impassioned commentary on each of the single fragments of Epicurus, neglecting the rest of the syllabus and deriding all the other philosophers of antiquity.

★ The dream in question was a 'great dream'. The fact that the oracle was in Latin increased its solemnity. But it is better not to interpret dreams: interpretation is death to them. The greatest rationality lies precisely in the knowledge of their function as unspoken ferment.

3
Uncle Chinchino

Homesick and full of loving passion I went to visit Mother and my little sister, who were staying with Uncle Chinchino. Aunt Diletta, Uncle Chinchino's wife, was my mother's first cousin and daughter of the most beautiful, perhaps the most foolish – so the word was – of Grandmother's sisters, the one who had the beauty of a swan and the foolishness of a goose. In the ten years of her marriage she had received on the threshold the guests of her Admiral husband, and cut the ribbon at the launching of the ships which in those days came in numbers from the yards of Donnammare and Althenopis. In the grandiose apartment of her widowhood, where the lights of receptions had given way to the penumbra of a retired existence, the bashful beauty of Aunt Diletta flowered. Throughout her long life she never shone for artistic gifts, nonconformity, *savoir-faire*, culture, intelligence, elegance, as did the other cousins, but only for her modesty, her diligence, her stubborn patience, her childishly unformed surges of tenderness and a generosity so obscure that it seemed to border on egotism. Her beauty did not stay in the memory with the intensity of a detail: a statuesque or slender body, raven, blonde or tawny hair (it was soft chestnut in fact), intense green or violet eyes; her voice had no gravelly or crystalline tones, in conversation she lacked brio, and she did not know how to sing on yachts at night. Her beauty was so natural that only after long observation or much frequentation did it dawn on those who had a happy rapport with life, something hardly ever the case with the men in the social set to which she belonged, not by wealth but high birth.

She wore her hair in a loose bun at the back of her neck, in the modest fashion of countrywomen. Even at fifty, when getting ready to go to a ball shortly after the death of her mother, she stunned my mother by asking whether a white silk dress with black trim could be considered mourning (Mother was stunned because she believed mourning excluded dancing, but poor Aunt Diletta had to go to keep up with the dizzying tempo of her husband's life), she seemed like a young maiden being led by King Theseus to face the terrible Minotaur. Her hair, still waiting to be done up, hung down in ringlets on her shoulders, her face, which had never known make-up, shone without a wrinkle, her patient eyes smiled, sad and awkward. Only a necklace, a brooch or diamond pendants could give her a more sophisticated, grown-up look.

Thus it was that as a girl Aunt Diletta, without piquant qualities or money to attract the disenchanted young men of her day, had not found many admirers.

But the boisterous and vulgar geniality of Uncle Chinchino, who had not had occasion to be blinded by the refined obtuseness then reigning in the drawing-rooms of Althenopis, glimpsed the essence of that beauty and was taken by it.

Like a whirlwind he burst open the doors of that apartment, his friends in train, to lay siege to the meek young woman.

He was fat and greasy, with a sharp, greedy look; he wore showy silk shirts with diamond cufflinks and was followed everywhere by a loud retinue of relations and friends of both sexes.

The shadows in the widow's apartment were slashed away, the windows on the sea thrown wide. He tickled Great-Aunt Ada, who was a swan and a goose, laying at her feet baskets of out-of-season fruit, marzipan, chocolates; he decked her table with spumante and French wines, lost generously to her at cards, relegated the porcelain vases and the family silver to unused drawing-rooms and replaced them on the side-tables with radios and gramophones. During the engagement, he sent a team of workmen to install a telephone in Great-Aunt

Ada's bedroom and another lot to take down the dusty curtains obstructing the light from the thirty windows and take them to Papoff's laundry.★

Unexpected and presumptuous, at all hours of the day, trays of pastries or ice-cream arrived, or tripe and shell-fish, ordered according to his whim when he was in the house between one business deal and another. Uncle Ubaldo, Aunt Diletta's brother, was immediately co-opted into a giddy whirl of wheeler-dealing.

Aunt Diletta married the whirlwind which had turned the house topsy-turvy, yielding passively like a cow led to the bull, but as the years passed she fell ever more in love, though fruitlessly, for they never had children.

It was into this family that my mother and my little sister were received after the disaster.

I found Mother lying down on a settee, wrapped in a sumptuous cashmere shawl given her by Uncle Chinchino, who could not bear to have sadness, poverty, mourning and misfortune around him; on a small table next to the settee the gramophone was softly playing a jazz tune; whenever Uncle Chinchino went by he slyly turned up the volume. My sister was beautiful enough not to have need of colourful dresses and shawls, though Uncle Chinchino had insisted on giving her a little coral necklace, and only after the repeated protests of my mother had he been prevented from taking her to the doctor's to get her ears pierced† because of a pair of mother-of-pearl and gold earrings he had given her and dearly wanted her to wear. He also sent her to dancing class, enrolling her

★ From the end of the eighteenth century much foreign capital was invested in Althenopis. Testimony to this are the many English, Swiss, French, Dutch, Belgian family names, the descendants of bankers, industrialists, financiers: Caflish, Papoff, Stevens, Winspeare, Gay-Odin, etc. Papoff was a chain of laundries. Under Fascism the foreign firms that still survived were nationalized or forced to sell out to Italians.

† It was considered vulgar in those years to have pierced ears. Women with pierced ears were considered provincial, on a level with women who went to mass or who had too many children.

even though it was the last month because he wanted her in the performance at the end of the course. Along with fifty of her companions the child appeared in the Dance of the Carillon: all the relatives were in ecstasies, except our mother who did not like cuteness in children, and amongst all those mothers, aunties, grannies, like a shopful of artificial flowers, she stood out sad and ironic, wearing her mourning like too clearminded a thought.

When Uncle Chinchino was at home, the drinks cupboard in the drawing-room where mother, Aunt Diletta and the visiting cousins were sitting or lying, was constantly open and Uncle would send round a young maid with trays of soft drinks, canapés and spirits because, in his obstinate intention of bringing them over into his camp and of using his opulent generosity to contaminate and cheapen the whole lot of women on his wife's side of the family, who had so criticized her marriage to a parvenu, he would have liked them all drunk and disorderly, or freer, at least, in arranging their legs and with bolder eyes and conversation.

Before dinner he offered caviare and champagne.

Uncle would have liked the maids to have worn colourful and elegant uniforms, especially with low necks, but Aunt Diletta had imposed – she managed to impose so little on him – a black dress with a white apron. But he had managed to get a woman friend of his who had a shop making women's underwear to go wild on the frills and the cut of the blouses, so they finished up looking more like chorus-girls than maids. Poor old Teresa, Aunt Diletta's old maid, wife of Uncle Chinchino's enterprising and sun-scorched sea captain of the wobbly walk – not so much from his time at sea as from the ambiguity of his moral principles, given over as he was to illicit trafficking of all kinds – even Teresa was forced into that travesty. The neck of the blouse plunged in a deep laced-trimmed V, giving glimpses of the furthest whites and reds, but on the pretext of a weak throat which lasted well beyond winter and gave her no peace even in August, Teresa wore a white chiffon scarf; the apron was a masterpiece of lace, nylon this time, while all of them wore a string of coral like an evil talisman around their necks; whereas Aunt wore pearls during the day and diamonds in the evening.

Thus got up, poor Teresa would come in with a tray, followed by the youngest maid, and raise her eyebrows at the aunts as if to say, 'I obey the Sultan's orders.' And the aunts smiled in collusion and pretended to be scandalized, though underneath they were pleased with so much gratification. Greedy and disapproving, they lowered their eyelashes to mask timid sidelong glances at the caviare, the champagne, the olives. Sitting for hours in the flowered armchairs, so ample and comfortable that not one but three of those aunts could have sat there together, they passed the time gossiping and sewing; Mother was making us clothes, while Aunt Diletta worked on shawls with a silk thread running through, after the fashion of the shawls of Corento, black interwoven with silver, or white interwoven with gold, red with black stitching, and Mother would disapprove, finding the combination of colours and materials vulgar – especially the gold and silver thread – since she preferred the mix of vivid colours and patterns used in the East or by certain peasant peoples. *

★ Although fashion was not then a mass phenomenon as it is today, good taste in no way – or only slightly – entered into it. Everything Gallimard published was in good taste, the whole of Wilde and Shaw; the Greek and Latin classics were for pedants. Lace (bedcovers, doilies, collars, cushion covers) were no longer appreciated; instead oriental and peasant fabrics were; not *chinoiserie* however. Nineteenth-century furniture was allowed, other styles, unless in old noble houses, were suspect; art deco and the art of the 1930s was for the nouveaux riches, for friends of Fascist dignitaries not those of the ex-ruling house. Ladies who went to church hid their weakness. Babies were no longer to be nursed by women from Ciocaria but by Swiss swesters. Dogs were in but cats were not. Cameos and coral were tabu. One listened to Wagner and jazz, but not Verdi and Beethoven. Pianists were no longer appreciated except, in private, Renato Caccioppoli, a mathematician of international repute. Dialect could only be tolerated in aristocrats whose nobility went back a long way. Women's suits were tweed, large checks were abolished. Wild mink, not astrakhan. Having more than three children was vulgar. It was no longer chic to die of consumption.

When Aunt Diletta put aside her shawls she began to mend the servants' sheets since she would never have dared put mended linen on her husband's bed. She indulged her modesty by destining a mended sheet or two for her own bed, but when her husband stopped visiting her at nights and even toyed for a period with the idea of leaving her for another woman – for a long time after, the unexpected strength and ferocity she showed in that time of crisis was whispered about in the family – poor Aunt began covering her bed with the finest new linen, she put on her diamonds, pearls and drapes again, even to the extreme of going to balls during a period of mourning; and in her husband's presence, she forced herself to drink champagne.

Thus amid that great luxury Aunt's domestic virtues nevertheless found a place to shine, and the greatest of them was thrift. Despite everything that was thrown away in that house, scraps of bread were jealously saved.

She found Mother and her other cousins allies in this mentality. Mother had the advantage of enjoying much credit with Uncle Chinchino because of her splendid past as woman of the world, and because of her status as mother and widow, so she could busy herself openly in the kitchen putting up preserves, while Aunt Diletta had to do it secretly on her own in the house because Uncle Chinchino wouldn't put up with it. And chattering away, the two women put up peaches, apricots, tomatoes and aubergines for the winter in front of our little family, and Aunt Diletta seemed happy to find herself a busy housewife again, as her mother had taught her, and to cast off the role of ornament assigned her by Uncle Chinchino.

In her two-month stay in that house Mother had occasion to notice the baskets piled with food that came daily out of the kitchen to go weaving down the service stairs on the shoulder of a young lad; but Aunt Diletta didn't dare intervene because her friendship with the trusty Teresa would have turned to unfriendliness; in fact it was just the sense of thrift and the memory of old lessons imparted – something that bound the

204

two women strongly together – which drove Teresa to make away with those heaped baskets; and Aunt Diletta preferred to think of that food finishing up in Teresa's crowded alley with her hundreds of relations and their children rather than in the revels of the young maids and their men friends. Thus Aunt Diletta let things pass, wanting to hold on to the sole friend and accomplice she had in that luxurious desert of a house. And then, the trusty servant tried to make good her defect in her own way, both by saving on the household expenses, beating down the tradesmen, and by offering Aunt – more especially all her relatives, since Aunt was very frugal – various cut-price goods which she sneaked from her husband's smuggling.

She sold Mother cut-price cigarettes and good quality cotton fabric and wool for our clothes. Every morning she gave Aunt a bunch of wild flowers which she ordered from a relative of hers who came in from the country; and canaries and parakeets, as if to console her for her lack of children. Teresa herself was without children and this common barrenness also united the two women. But more than anything the thing which bound them was the resemblance between their sultan husbands.

Aunt never had any cash because the tradesmen were paid at the end of the month by Uncle Chinchino in a paperchase of checks. And given the life of luxury she led, she didn't dare ask her husband for money, with the result that she could never give money to poor relations or some old school friend or some less radiant niece who would never attract the prodigal concern of the uncle; and the trusty maid filled up the gap with loans, and they would put their heads together to find a way of slipping it on to some tradesman's bill. Poor Teresa, in fact, in her luxurious, childless slum didn't know what to do with the money she had piled up. With the result that her two rooms in the seafront district of Chiaiola had become a bazaar: apart from the mounds of stuff her husband smuggled, not so much out of need any longer but from the sheer spirit of adventure, bottles of spirits were piling up, cigarette cases, ornaments, stacks of new linen, electrical appliances, gramophones, radios; and sometimes she even bought baby clothes for some particular pet, which she gave away every so often to some luckier woman in the neighbouring tenements, with an envy and a generosity that were never at odds. Relatives sometimes asked why, with all her affluence, she didn't retire from service, and she replied: 'No, poor lady, and then how would she get on without me!' And the relatives made no further comment, knowing that the childless must in some way 'sbarià'.*

All the communicating doors in the great apartment were left wide open. Uncle Chinchino's room was like a real corridor; he had chosen a connecting room because he loathed solitude, concentration, silence, which to him seemed akin to death. He had a large round bed made and set it in the centre of the room, and from there on waking he loved to listen to the clamour from the kitchen of the maids and the tradesmen following on each other's heels, the postmen delivering telegrams and parcels, the nuns come to beg alms, and the more discreet coming and going of nieces and nephews and habitués of the house who used the main entrance instead. From bed he would whistle to his dog, which would jump up on top of him. Sometimes in the evening when he was giving a reception he would leave before the end to go to bed, for it gave him pleasure to fall asleep amidst the muffled noise from the party. And when the house was too quiet he pressed a button and listened to the gramophone, pressed another and listened to the radio, or reached for the telephone to call someone. He often got cravings. Then he would phone the local greengrocer – who was a friend of his because he liked sailing, but then all the local shopkeepers were his friends for one reason or another, as were all the concierges, all the delivery men, all the taxi drivers, all the tobacconists, the beggars, the prosti-

---

* From the Castilian *desvariar*: to ramble, to talk deliriously. In the Althenopis verb *sbarià* the sense of rambling talk has been attenuated, yielding to the idea of futile effort, an end in itself. Those who feel the most need to *sbarià* are boys, the old, and the unhappy.

tutes and above all the smugglers, the fishermen and the sailors – and get him to send up a basket of figs; then he would call his wife and the servants on the house phone to come and eat them with him. And he would eat one or two, rarely more, because he was personally abstemious, but it rejoiced him to see the loaded basket of figs and his friends eating them. Or he would get the pizza man to send some croquettes; and everybody, knowing the generosity of his tips, came running in answer to his slightest whim, solicitous even as far as the bed where he lay wrapped in plaid blankets and furs.

In those afternoon hours when I came to visit my mother, he was rarely at home.

Thus I had no difficulty in examining his room in every particular. The walls were covered in photographs, paintings, strange objects. One photo showed Uncle Chinchino dressed as a pasha, another as a rajah, yet another half-naked on his sailing yacht; in another he was standing with some other people in front of an oil rig; in another he was a child, already round as a balloon, next to his sisters plumped out with frills and heavy jewellery. But I was particularly struck by one photo in which he was dressed as Buddha; he was sitting naked, shiny, his legs crossed, his great belly covered his pudenda, a tiara on his head and long pendants on his ears. His arms were stretched out to the side in a hieratic pose. Two smiling women stood behind him stroking his shoulders and flanks; another leant over his shoulder to suck his nipple. Underneath was written: 'Carnival 1939'.

The furniture lining the walls of the room was of polished ebony, glass and metal, like office furniture, and on the flat surfaces at various levels incredible objects were arranged. Next to the usual kind of knick-knack, probably put there at the time of Aunt's wedding, there were chamberpots, lavatory bowls, miniature turds, dozens of phalluses in plaster, clay, even plastic, and a red-painted one from Thailand; there were little silver or enamelled boxes full of cigarettes, cigars, comfits, salted almonds, marrow and pistacchio seeds; and colourful boxes of chocolates or candied fruit; and he loved opening those boxes and offering them round. Many of his friends and habitués of the house took drugs; and it amused him to tease them by hiding among his handkerchiefs and socks little sachets of what looked like cocaine, but which was only harmless powder, or sometimes more mischievous powder that made them sneeze. He had a pastry-cook friend who made pricks out of marzipan for him and he got his lady friends to suck them.

He had a collection of shells in a glass case and in another a collection of bone and ivory skeletons with silver screws at the joints, and dolls, puppets, marionettes and masks representing death naked and laughing. Many years later, Aunt Cleope summoned me and the other nieces to Uncle Chinchino's bedside as he lay dying, to entertain and distract him with our youthful voices and appearance. I was present then at an extraordinary spectacle: an old puppeteer, by then almost out of work, had been called to the bedside to animate the collection of marionettes, masks and skeletons. And before Uncle Chinchino, ever more deformed by metastasis, but who followed him attentively with round green eyes, tiny in his swollen face, the puppeteer put on a performance partly improvised, partly following scripts dusted off the night before. He had come for the handsome tip but also out of liking for the sick man, who even in his last hour showed such appreciation of his art; and the skeletons and the other personae representing death danced the tarantella, choked themselves on mozzarella and spaghetti, made love, blasphemed; they despaired at sea of ever finding a public house, and after incredible shipwrecks, they swam for days in the waves of a sea done with great mastery by the puppeteer, the sounding roar, the calm, and the fresh, light, regular wash of the wave on the pebbles of the beach which gently received the exhausted castaway.

Once Uncle Chinchino invited us for a trip on his boat. The yacht was furnished in identical fashion to his bedroom, but in that narrow space the objects seemed even more obsessive and grotesque. They lacked the echo spreading through the open doors of the sequence of rooms, voices of tradesmen, friends, relations, down-and-outs, prostitutes, out-of-work actors; and they seemed to wallow like hulks in the roar of the sea.

Shiny, fat, suntanned, Uncle sat aft with his legs crossed; the wind filled out his white pyjamas like a balloon. He stared at the vacuity of the sea with his shark's eyes. A staggering steward with a tray, out of whose back pocket stuck a wad of banknotes held by an elastic band, offered pastries and champagne to Mother and the aunts who, refreshed by the breeze and memories of youth, remained quite unaware of his presence.

4
Frasca, Frascone, Fraschetella

Since we had no money to rent a house, Uncle Chinchino made us free of a villa at Frasca. The villa had belonged to his mother and in the division of her property had come to him, though it was a place he never went for holidays because the only thing that distracted and lulled him was the motion of the sea, constant and boundless as on land was the movement of capital; whereas Frasca, a place of water and dust, was more fitted to the exaction of rent and the enjoyment of landed income. In fact, it had been from the rents of its soil that the capital for his dizzying investments had germinated. There Uncle Chinchino's ancestors, factors administering a vast holding, had so racked the tenants and swindled the owners that the property had become theirs and today part of it is still known as 'I Parlati' from the name of a branch of his uninhibited forefathers. There his numerous sisters had been conveyed in marriage to their landowning peers, while Uncle Chinchino himself had soared like a young eagle to the city, where first he had invested his rents in army supplies, then in construction, and finally in the nascent oil industry, until the home-grown Italian six-legged greyhound of AGIP had put him out of business, for it had been in the shadow of the Seven Sisters that he had prospered.

Uncle Chinchino's sisters were fat and ruddy, and early on in life began wearing dresses of black moire in sign of mourning for various deaths in the family. They couldn't manage to cross their legs when they sat down, and stuck out little swollen feet in patent leather shoes. They relished telling stories of the tortures the peasants had inflicted on a friend of

210

theirs during the land troubles, and how she had been tied by the hair to the tail of a horse, to be dragged over the countryside. On Sundays they went to the noon Mass after supervising the cooking of the meat sauce and inspecting the maids' hair. Incredible self-will was concentrated in their gaze.

The house had been shut up at the time of their marriage and it had been the air-raids which had forced a relative or two to take refuge there.

Frasca was not limited, as was Santa Maria del Mare, to a single piazza but had as many as seven.

The first was the Infrescata piazza, which had been the nucleus of the original village, once called Frasca, but because houses large and small had begun multiplying from the last century onwards in the plain below, popular usage had changed it to Fraschetella. Climbing vines shaded the little square in front of the church, which was always locked except for an hour on Sunday. The vines belonged to the parish, but the grapes were always mitched by children, as if to compensate for the sketchy pastoral care they received. In the old houses around the church lived the village poor, those who every morning offered themselves for hire in Piazza dei Mulini as day-labourers on the farms or building sites, and whose only hope of improving their lot was to emigrate. The sand of the volcano lapped around those houses, where small tomatoes and yellow marguerites grew on the balconies in large tin-cans. In the evenings the children rolled about in the sand that had covered the *basoli*★ and stirred up a dust-storm as they played.

In the mornings a cart stopped in the piazza, selling vegetables so wretched they looked like the garbage of the fertile fields below. The women rarely came out of the houses and when they did so, wore headscarves, their eyes sullen and reddened by the sand if there was wind. When the water-cart arrived at midday and their vain shouts for their children to

★ Volcanic rock used for paving the streets of Althenopis.

come and help brought no reply, they looked like women possessed.

The once-numerous shops in the piazza had closed, and the only one remaining was the tinsmith's. People came to him from the village, from the farms, and even from other little villages in the area. Gennaro did not work copper, brass, or other valuable metals, he only repaired them; instead he worked tin. Once a week his two sons went around the houses and the countryside with a cart to buy, sort out from the rubbish, or be given, tins that had held tomatoes, oil or other preserves. From the tin he would make things: oil jugs, measures, cups, bowls, beakers, oil-lamps, candlesticks, even ashtrays. On a shelf of his workshop stood a beautiful chalice and a monstrance that looked like gold. He made all kinds of children's toys. With the bigger tins he would make buckets; when the containers were not intended for oil he soldered them on the inside, while inside the toys and the ones for oil you could see the trademarks picked out in a variety of vivid colours, because his technique was to turn the tin inside-out so that the outer surface was always gold or silver. I passed hours and hours with my brother in Gennaro's workshop watching him at work; and my brother even tried to imitate him at home and make some of those marvels for himself. But during our last year at Frasca plastic stuff began to arrive; cheap glass and aluminium were already available; and by then only the pizzerias wanted the tinsmith's work, though the moment business improved they replaced them with copper. Thus he was left without employment. That inert and indestructible material provoked his scorn, and he would angrily burn pieces of it to let us smell the stink. One day he shut up shop and said: 'I'm off to find out where all this plastic comes from.' And off he went to the North, to work as a building labourer in Milan or Germany, I don't remember which.

The Piazza del Mercato, the Piazza dei Mulini, the Collegiata piazza were located at the southern end of the village, the part called Frasca. When, in the second half of last century, the government built the state highway along that axis, a

212

covered wholesale market was erected at the bottom of the village where once a week the produce of the fertile countryside round about was taken to be sold. Little by little, houses and blocks of flats went up around the market. The Mulini were so called because the site had been originally occupied by the grain mills, and later the pasta factories; but when after the war Frasca, like other places, was inundated with UNRRA flour and pasta, the mills went out of business. For some years, however, other factories had been going up: a jute factory, a canning factory for tomatoes and peaches, the rope mill, the fireworks factory. The neighbourhood rich – the landowners, ex-factors of the large estates, who still lived in Frasca, the dealers and merchants, the manufacturers – made a collection and the Collegiata, a Jesuit boarding-school, was built for their sons. The architect and committee decided it should be designed on the lines of the shrine of St James of Compostella. I was awed by its steep steps on which the sun always beat down, while the rest of the piazza was deep in the shadow of the imposing mass of church and college buildings. And just opposite the Collegiata stood the gate of our villa, which had its garden at the back.

It had been in the last twenty years that Frascone had come into being, around the town hall, the station, the sanctuary. The town in fact continued to grow. The town hall and the station had been built under the Fascists and the sanctuary had been consecrated recently – it was the time of pilgrimages to Our Lady – and given its proximity, it had been modelled on the lines of the Madonna di Pompeii, not so much in scale as in the profusion of white marble. It had been built from the contributions of rich French people, in thanksgiving for the men who had survived the war.

Frascone, Frasca, even Fraschetella* had grown up as

---

* The dialect speaks of the old village with a diminutive and inflects it as feminine, whereas the enlarged village of today is seen as masculine. The feminine inflection often indicates something wide and thick, as opposed to the masculine long and thin; for example, 'pettene' and 'pettenessa' [the ordinary comb and the Spanish comb].

deformed offspring of the fat volcanic soil. How different the countryside was from the peninsula on which Santa Maria del Mare stood. There the vegetation, the animals, the men, and even their implements, seemed to live in harmony; everything here instead took on a monstrous and domineering aspect: the tractors, the mechanical reapers, the diggers, the huge water-pumps, the interminable lines of trucks on the state highway, bringing in fertilizer and pesticides and leaving loaded with fruit and vegetables from fields of tomato, beans, potatoes and jute which seemed to go on for ever, boundless as were the rows of peach trees and even the fields of carnations, whose scent was not concentrated and pungent, but stagnant and nauseating like the cheap perfumes sold in department stores.

The people also were multitudinous: the mass of farm labourers setting off along the highway in the morning, the workers going to the Mulini factories. The processions and the religious feasts wove in and out of political rallies and demonstrations, to the point where, in '53, to celebrate the defeat of the *Legge Truffa*★ after three days of negotiations and quarrels with the clergy, who didn't want to join in with them, the Socialists went by themselves en masse to the shrine of the Madonna della Montagna.

I, too, joined the morning crowd, in the students' train.

There was no bridge then between me and a world which seemed to have gone up overnight like the stalls of a fun-fair, in which I was supposed to act out a part that no one had assigned me, the lines of which were barely sketched in.

After our arrival in Frasca my body had grown, almost as if to keep the promise I had made to Mother to be her support in my father's place. And with that body, so much bigger that everybody said it was the body of a grown-up girl or woman, I seemed to have adapted myself with cheerfulness and diligence to our new life in the village. But there was something

---

★ Swindle Law: an attempt to favour the ruling Christian Democrats by changing election regulations – *Trans.*

in that body of mine that diminished as I grew. And I did not know what it was. I could become absorbed in the daily round, stay out playing childish games or throw myself into friendships which were already teenage, but in the pauses, or at night, I felt the guttering and insistent call of the thing that was diminishing and dying, to which I could give no name. I called it my friend, my kitten, my little plant, my jewel, that flickered ever more dimly. I returned to the language of my early childhood and called it by the stately name of 'Vida de mi vida', or the pet-name 'mi videcita'. When I imagined it, or saw it in my dreams and fantasies, I could not make out whether it was something very old and close to death, or some extremely tender thing, as yet unshaped, which had all of life before it.

In the house we had an old cat that had fallen sick after producing a litter and I dreamt of it in the shape of this cat, much smaller though, and wrinkled, all grey, curled up in a corner, its fur all wet, with the birth waters or a mortal sweat I didn't know, with a point of liquid light in its dim eyes that might have been an indication of imminent death or of recovery. Or I would see it as a precious stone with a vivid white reflex, and I couldn't make out whether the gleam was the last flare of the worn-out stone or the sign of its miraculous growth. Or it would appear in the likeness of a young male friend or of Mother, suddenly wrinkled and skinny, and from a distance, seeing them, I couldn't make out whether they had become young again or were decrepit old people. But in those imaginings there was always something that gave out a gleam of light, of an unknown kind, similar perhaps to that of a saint's halo, as I remembered our bodies gleaming with the woolly substance from the prickly-pears in the grotto of Santa Maria del Mare.

These thoughts of mine I could confide to no one, not even my closest friend, and they tormented me and filled me with immeasurable joy.

On the train to school the whole band of students from Frasca travelled in the same compartment, and after the usual joking, laughter and jostling, the girls huddled together to play a game. Each of them had to give an imaginary description of their boyfriend. Some really had them, and we knew it, but they decked them out with such marvellous qualities that we had difficulty in recognizing them. Others didn't, and we sought to imagine which of our friends corresponded to the halting description, for their whispering led us to believe it was someone we knew well, somebody in the compartment perhaps; we would look round and one of our male companions would always be staring at us. Some of the girls blushed as they spoke, the eyes of others would shine, and as they whispered their mouths would seem to change into a juicy cherry. One of them, beautiful, tranquil, upright and smiling in her seat, invariably responded, 'Like Peppino', who had been officially accepted by her parents. Her reply irritated me at first, but then I began to wait for it in trepidation, in fear almost that it might change, for I had fallen in love with her placid and awkward beauty.

I joined in the game and in the beginning adopted a dramatic role but soon turned into a comic actress because the lover I evoked slipped from prince and warrior to gay or grotesque mummer, and I was accused of not keeping to the rules. Furious or ashamed I would protest, for it was the truth that I couldn't believe in my lovers. The more I conjured them, the more they seemed insubstantial phantoms compared to my secret company. The future with such creatures, always within the context of marriage, seemed tedious to me and it occurred to me that all those dreams and fantasies had the purpose of embellishing and disguising a future modelled on the family life of my friends; even if there were those who were really eager for it.

One year I too had a flesh-and-blood boyfriend to describe; but I had chosen one so far off in space and one probably so far from me in mind and so foreign to our world that for a certain time I was able to make him coincide with my secret company. Only, one day in the train I committed the sacrilege of describing him and surprised myself, thinking on what I had

216

said, at how banal he was. Thus the young man from the realm of my spirit entered that of the world, and though I continued to think of him, he had become totally distinct from the secret company with which I had managed for a certain time to confuse him.

There were certain mornings in May when, approaching the school along the avenue of acacias, I hoped until the very last bend that some magician had spirited it away on a flying carpet. Listlessly I passed inside and during composition (the only school activity that sometimes stirred a spark of passion in me), I observed a fly land on the still blank page and watched as in the play of levels, page against desk, white against black, it took on a metallic purity almost as if a mineral life had taken the air. I drew a circle on the spot the fly had landed and wrote, 'Here my life came to rest'. And I would have liked to dedicate a poem to it in the manner of Ariosto, but I had to limit myself to underlining that as title and after bringing my mind back with difficulty from its looping flight, get down with passive diligence to 'development'.

Certain summer mornings while I was lying in the armchair in the shade of the drawing-room, Mother would announce that lunch was ready. Suddenly the smell of barbecued steak reached me, and what on other occasions had gladdened me, now filled me with disgust. 'I don't want to eat,' I thought, but didn't dare say so for fear of a row that would have snatched me from my world. Listlessly I would sit at table and reply in monosyllables. 'It's the heat,' said my aunts, and Mother would sigh at the thought that she couldn't afford a holiday for us where the sea or mountain air would have overcome my lack of appetite, brought on, according to her, by the stifling humidity of Frasca. Stretched out in the arm-chair, I had been imagining my 'vivecita' like a plant set to grow in a bottle; at a certain moment it seemed that the plant was shooting up at an exaggerated pace, stems thick with leaves and buds climbed in tight spirals in their restricted space until a bud almost managed to pass the neck of the bottle and reach the free air; but just at that moment they had summoned me to lunch! From then on I abandoned the childish nicknames and called the thing inside me the Vegetative Principle, and then simply the Principle.

One summer day I walked round and round the garden with nothing to do. The concrete statues of nymphs, satyrs and other mythological creatures wore homely expressions; the half-naked nymphs seemed intent on ablutions in small bathrooms rather than in lonely streams; the sculptor had turned the satyrs' goat-grin into the smirk of certain shop-keepers when they scent a good customer. All the possible styles of garden had been imitated in that tangle of vegetation: the branches of two weeping-willows smothered a small pond sprinkled with waterlilies; a thicket of oleanders hemmed in a little temple with a stone seat in pride of place in the centre; giant cacti rimmed a canyon of fake rocks that led to an abandoned stable, and in the very middle a poor jasmine aroused in me the memory of the gardens of Santa Maria del Mare.

I climbed over the wooden fence that had taken the place of the gate which had disappeared during the war; a sandy path, lined with broom, climbed towards the volcano. I halted in a little copse of sambuco trees shaded by an immense carob, the last big tree on the slopes of the mountain. I loved that copse when, at the end of the spring, I was surrounded by the scent of the trees in flower, blown by the wind to hold me in a cool vortex, away from the dusty or humid sultriness which weighed on Frasca from the end of May like the heat from an incubator ripening the fruits of the fat countryside.

But on that August day the air was motionless. Weighed down by the heat and the grotesque forms in the garden, I headed for the wood, guided by a dumb instinct like that which brings a dog back to his master's empty house. To justify myself I carried a book to read in the shade. I had picked it up at random, attracted by the binding which was decorated like the wallpaper of a child's bedroom, with rab-bits, bears and little pigs on a background of flowers. But when I reached the shade of the carob I didn't even have the

218

strength to open it and fell straight asleep. I dreamt of a tall olive-skinned woman with black hair coiled tightly round her head who held out a small stone goddess with a concave belly. Putting the gift into my hands, she opened a black book lying on a rock which gave out sulphurous vapour, and read:

La clef que tu cherche n'est pas là:
jette-toi dans la vie et tu la trouveras.

On waking I knew that she had been addressing my secret company, my Principle. For a long time I lay there in a drowse, gripped and pinned to the ground by a happiness I had never known. 'But why should I get up? Where do I have to get to?' And I remained lying there. The scirocco made my legs and cheeks burn. My hands were buried in the sandy soil and laughing foolishly I thought: 'This is the earth.'* And I also thought: 'I am alone', and it didn't disturb me as at other times but instead filled me with bliss. A stream of images flowed before my eyes, one of which I remember: the rose. It grew out of the arid sandy soil and at the top of a strong straight stem opened out drenched in dew. It was of an intense pink; the precise pride of that colour was that it had no wish to fade towards white nor to deepen towards red. A thousand childish blandishments rose to my lips, which remained dumb as if refusing to pronounce them. And my hands remained paralysed in the sand. With the force of desire I saw myself with hands of glass, not two but a hundred, cupping the rose in wonder and rapture. I called it the Initial Rose.

I remember a strange detail from that day: the sirocco stirred up the sand and the grains which blew into my eyes gave me no trouble. My eyes burned, but I felt the burning not as sensation but as memory. For a long time, after that, I felt myself to be invulnerable.

---

* It is from that day, I believe, that the foolish smile dates which often appears on my face and irritates others – those at least whose every relationship with people and things is predatory.

5

The counsellors

As we grew older and the day approached for us to leave the family and face the world on our own – the world that our mother saw as a pathless maze, similar to the officialdom she had dealings with in the years of her widowhood, to get her pension, to obtain reparation for war damage, for questions of taxes, social security, the birth certificates of her children who had been born in a foreign country – certain members of the family, knowledgeable about the world, dispensers of advice, suggestions and help, came to assume importance.

While the aunts and Mother sat gathered round a small lamp in the evening twilight, sewing, knitting, reading French novels and essays, as if the merciless light had fled them to blend into the pastel shades of dusk like a childish memory or the presage of a future as yet vague – and the passion I felt towards them gave way to a *pietas* not yet saddened by separation – other relations appeared like meteors in the drawing room at Frasca, portents sometimes of threat and danger, at others of promise, novelty and adventure.

Uncle Nini, light-minded and dissipated, still extremely handsome, entered the drawing-room with a paternal and winning smile for his unfortunate sister and absentminded pats on the cheek for us, his nieces and nephew, who had neither his own children's beauty and grace – the only virtues he valued – nor that of friends' children. He threw open windows and shutters, took a look round, and remained standing – sitting down would have meant a long visit – to smoke a cigar in contemplation of the landscape. He came to preach to our mother the need, utterly vital in the modern world, of freeing herself from the slow, slack workings of the laws of landed income and of plucking up courage to launch into the money market; and he invited her to invest her 'capital' in 'profitable mutuals' which was a euphemism for a certain kind of loan, made at usurious rates of interest, to enterprising spirits – in Althenopis, at that time, the building contractors.

Mother hesitated; – in this case, as in many others, her moral scruples supported her fear of risks. But Uncle Nini, who had been very wild as a young man, had become an excellent father and moreover had shown a brotherly concern in passing on to his widowed sister the income from a small inheritance. Thus the risk was seen to lie within the reassuring limits of the proverb: 'Cast your bread upon the waters'. How was it possible to have doubts about the brother who every month passed over a small bit of income though his children were in the exorbitant phase of growing-up? And how, on the other hand, was it possible to stay ahead, or rather, see that one's children stayed ahead (not of illness or poverty, needless to say, but of other children)? Glimpsing the interest that might accrue, Mother's eyes shone: the holidays, the language, dancing, tennis lessons she would be able to afford! She gave in. And from then on, for years to come, there was talk in the house of 'worries' about the 'mutual' and plans for the lessons and holidays it should make possible.

Uncle Giobatta – Aunt Callista's abandoned husband – would sit down when he came, as if to give notice that the visit would be long and painful and that he had no intention of sparing us the smallest troublesome detail; and if he ever had a piece of good news then it was only at the door that he would give it to us, at the moment of leaving, as he rubbed his broad white hands together, whether out of satisfaction (not at the good news, but at the delay in communicating it) or from cold, who was to know. For, thin and bony as he was, he gave the impression of suffering cold, and of bringing it with him. He was always dressed in shiny grey, like the trees in winter, his hair sparse and grey, his face pale and white, miserly with his smiles, and with a laugh that sounded like ice breaking, not as it thawed, but to augur catastrophe. He was the administrator of the property and came to give his account. Among the properties there was one that had never been divided up and on which eighty-four heirs had claim. He would dwell at length on the revenue from this eighty-fourth (it would then have been three thousand lire), and only then would he pass on to the more substantial revenues from which, he would immediately add, various sums had to be subtracted for rates, wear and tear, litigation. After his long and minutiose visits, gloom descended on the house.

On other questions the person consulted was Aunt Ea. Our family had been full of beautiful women, but Ea was without peer. For various reasons she had been born in Athens, and the limpid purity of that sky seemed to have clarified and exalted the beauty she had inherited from her mother, the least statuesque but perhaps the most resplendent of grandmother's sisters, whose actual shape is smothered in surviving portraits by the nineteenth-century clothing whose elegance manages to vanquish her beauty. Her daughter Ea instead seemed permanently nude. The fashions of the time allowed her to bare her arms and legs and so dazzling was her skin that even elaborate dresses seemed to melt away. Her small head was helmeted in copper-coloured hair, cut very short and curling on the back of her neck, while the lobes of her ears, shapely as the handles of tiny china cups, reiterated the delicate force of her curls. There was something breathtaking in the colour of her hair, in that shade of blonde, which didn't decline into tow, nor fade into ash nor even surge into red, but which shone transparent and compact as a fruit, and curved with the constant caprice of a wavelet.

Her violet eyes, shaded by thick, dark gold lashes, soothing but steady, smiling when she was serious, thoughtful when she laughed, were deeply set, expressing not torment, but an occult secret of being; and the wrinkles which came with the years seemed to make them the more gentle. It was the family's view that she had given birth to insignificant and fatuous children, but she remained as untroubled as Nature, believing that the world has place for all.

When she frequented our drawing-room in Frasca she was a rich relation, married to someone very high-up in a bank. How else would Mother have been able to ask her advice?

With a knowing lightness she set down the elegantly packaged gifts on the circular drawing-room table and in her presence, radiant in a rainy November, the dust, the boredom, the meanness of daily chores disappeared: even the molecules of fat in the broth that scented the late hours of the morning seemed to have yielded to subtler celery and carrot. She sat calmly, proffering advice, while Mother seemed the Moon to her Sun. Might the girls go out with boys? Might they go to the sea with the boys from Frasca? Was it permissible to frequent young socialists, or communists, even? And – a more delicate, almost whispered question this – might a girlfriend sleep in the same bed as her daughter, or was it better that the sisters sleep together when the friend came to stay?

Her smiling advice lit up the room. Certainly one might. And the anxieties, in part provoked by the other aunts, sterner or merely less knowledgeable, would blow away. And later in a peremptory tone Mother would tell them, speaking German to avoid our understanding – whereas it was French in front of the maids – just what might be done and what might not, concluding with the declaration; 'Aunt Ea said so.'

When the business concerned Rome it was Uncle Serafino who was called in.★ At Mother's least request he would arrive from Rome, for when he did a favour he gave the impression of having waited his whole life just for that chance of being

★ Every Southern family, even those from the most remote provinces, has a relation in Rome, in a government ministry, working for a public body – he may be a doorkeeper or member of parliament – especially in the police or at the Palace of Justice. The entire traffic of papers, seals, documents, application forms, files must sooner or later pass through their hands, and full of trust, people place themselves in those hands.

useful, of having nothing else to do with his time except come rushing to be consulted.

Uncle Serafino arrived, small and stooped in a great black overcoat with an umbrella hooked over his arm and attached by a small chain for safety's sake. The soft light in the black eyes set in a round frog's face, wise and jovial, made visible his urge to perform chaste acts of charity. Having undone the chain on his umbrella, he took off his overcoat and folded it carefully inside-out. The lining was a silvery blue check, while the lining of his coat, which he also took off, was a brown and blue herringbone. The clothes he wore had belonged to his father, and showed, at least in the lining, the mark of the more ornate fashions of the last century. Out of his attaché case came a pullover with leather patches at the elbows, once the property of his nephew. He then sat down, took off his galoshes, and undid the laces that had held his turn-ups to his shins, after the manner of cyclists who don't want them to get muddy. These operations took place in absolute silence and required studied care, and meanwhile his round eyes scrutinized us.

Uncle Serafino was the son of Uncle Goffredo, Grandmother's only brother, the one whom as a girl she had lovingly helped off the toilet where he had fallen asleep. That male branch of the family was the Italian branch; but as if to relieve the Italianness of its power to impress, it was the bizarre or, as they said, the 'extravagant' branch of the family. In this branch, as opposed to the Althenopis one, the women died once they had finished childbearing. Uncle Serafino, almost prophetically, hadn't even married. And then found himself with four children to bring up after the death of his sister and her husband. Four males. That male environment, lacking feminine warmth to smooth out spikiness of character and feminine skill in preserving the species, was bound to go off into freakishness. And clucking maternally, the Althenopis coven sometimes showed concern for the distant Italian, or rather, Umbrian branch of the family. Uncle Goffredo, Uncle Serafino's father, after the truce between the papist and

224

Garibaldian branches, had made the acquaintance of a cousin while on a courtesy visit to his relations, and later married her.* She had followed him to set up home in Assisi.

At the beginning of the century Goffredo had invented a lamp-kettle, an item of tableware which was capable of providing lighting for the dinner table and of making poached eggs – apt food for a light and dimly lit dinner – and many other machines for which, being a gentleman, he had never claimed the patent.

It was murmured in the family that Uncle Serafino was a bigwig in the Foreign Ministry, within the walls of which he had passed his life. It was murmured because his modesty prevented him from giving further explanation. To tell the truth would have meant boasting. That he was a bigwig was deducible not least from the flexibility of his hours. He left messages, for example, asking to be telephoned between ten in the morning and midnight, or between one and four in the afternoon, notoriously hours in which the bustling population of the ministries slumbers in the armchair or in bed, and not in the office. It was also deduced from the fact that he went to the Ministry on a bicycle. Would, in fact, a petty official, or even a doorkeeper, ever have gone on a bicycle, in the early '50s, in Rome, the capital of social appearances? In Milan perhaps, but not in Rome. (And not in Althenopis, where the frequent ups and downs and the road surface of lava slabs counsel against it.†) On occasion, one or other of the aunts would telephone

---

* To consecrate the reconciliation in a carnal way as well. Much of the freakishness of that branch was attributed not so much to the consanguinity of the marriage partners as to union with bloodless papist stock. The great-aunts, who had iron constitutions, spoke of the Assisi relations as decadent in body and spirit. They claimed to be the continuation of that line nevertheless, and employed skilled Althenopis craftsmen to inlay the little wooden boxes in which they kept their sewing and correspondence with the family crest.

† As I became well aware when I decided to do what I had been doing in Alpine valleys, and cycle as far as the Park where Aunt Cleope lived. Apart from the effort, the catcalls, the wisecracks! But I was above everything, untouchable!

about something that couldn't be put off – but this only happened in the second half of the 1960s★ – asking the switchboard to put her through to the 'Count'. A secretary would reply: 'I'll put you through now,' adding confidentially, 'For goodness sake, if you're asking a favour, don't call him Count, it upsets him.' Thus one could also deduce Uncle Serafino's high position from this reverential respect for what the great-aunts called his whim. And apart from the concern, from the whim itself, which only a bigwig would have been able to permit himself.

More than a counsellor, Uncle Serafino was, like the knights of old, a faithful servant obedient to the behests of the women of the family, provided of course the behests weren't in conflict with his obscure battle against favouritism – obscure, indeed very obscure, in the Capital – and when with mole-like insistence it emerged into the light, it was immediately cast back into the darkness, or when all efforts at that failed, you had to account it one of his oddities. But it was already a great favour that he should come from Rome to explain the regulations in force, these to be dealt with on ordinary paper, those on special stamped paper, in regard to pensions, applications for, obtaining of, regular payment and increase of same; or in regard to plans for setting someone's foot on the first rung of a 'career'.

For his dinner Uncle Serafino liked the broccoli of Campania, spinach or beet-tops, accompanied by humble *fior di latte* cheese – mozzarella was too expensive – so that then with untroubled digestions he and Mother, sunk and almost submerged in armchairs covered in green cretonne with a pattern

---

★ It was only in that period that, one by one, the aunts installed the telephone. Thus the paying of calls, so good for the health of the body, and letter-writing, so good for that of the soul, became more infrequent. But only towards the mid 1960s did they manage to relax about it, even when they made long-distance calls. Until then, relatives who received long-distant calls immediately imagined some disaster, as they had done with telegrams previously.

of smirking poppies,* could examine the Ministry circulars; pedantic explanation and alarmed questions yielding every now and then to a pathetic duet on the subject of other relatives. Where now were the one-time 'careers' and the promising childhoods? The thick long braids of Aunt Mafalda, the accurate, objective memos and reports poor Attilio (my father) had sent to the Ministry from abroad? Where? they asked. Curled up behind them in another armchair, upholstered in brown velvet whose worn and dirty patches no one had bothered to hide with cretonne – thus cradled I often nodded off, for I loved more than anything to fall asleep reassured by voices soothing the passage to sleep.

When Cousin Achille was to arrive, preparations for taking a bath began from the moment of waking. I would put three pans of water on three gas-rings and when they were near boiling, yelling at everybody to stand clear, I carried them up staircases and corridors to empty into the bath. The shower, and the availability of hot and cold running water, have eliminated from among the objects of the *contemplatio mortis* those floating residues of body dirt which, united – glued, rather – with soap, adhered so persistently to the white enamel sides, making a straight grey line, a frontier almost, between organic and inorganic life, which could then only be got rid of by insistent scrubbing with a pan-scrub – and the rows with my brother who looked down on scrubbing as a woman's job and could climb out of the bath regenerated and uncaring.

I had improvised, I don't know how, picking up clothes here and there, an outfit: blue pleated skirt, red T-shirt, red canvas shoes. Clean and thus decked out I set off for the station. Meanwhile Mother scurried round preparing lunch; my sister repeated the bathing rite, with less disturbance, and

* A vain attempt had been made to reproduce on the cretonne the poppy's flame, something whose felicitous ambiguity I have seen reproduced only on antique Chinese silks and art-deco fabrics. On the cretonne it was painted as in spelling-books. The Italian (*papavero*) and the German (*Mohn*) have caught the secret of the flower, while the French (*coquelicot*) catches only its surface gaiety.

our idle brother, perplexed, lying in a sunny corner of the garden, worked out unconvincing explanations for his poor performance at school. Wasn't it true, perhaps, that Cousin Achille demanded a pitiless accounting from him and a masculine fellowship from which my brother's panic spirit withdrew, lost in the garden in the splashing of the fountain, the flight of a butterfly, the ceaseless labour of a caterpillar?

I set off for the station. Cousin Achille kissed me, and I dodged his lips. He found my outfit decent, my looks almost improved.

He got to the house and began telling everyone how to get on in the world. The world in those times seemed to be situated entirely in the North. Not designed by God but by a designer. It was there one had to go. Cousin Achille asked me whether I had any boyfriends, in the plural naturally, like money. I answered no, half proud and half guilty. He looked at me, puzzled and curious, whether more concerned or pleased at the lack I don't know. Love in fact was only possible in the North, in scientific copulation, without commotion.

But in the North above all you could get on.

And thus it was that one November at the beginning of the 1950s, I set off like the tinsmith of Frasca to the land where the plastic came from.

Bestelle dein Haus*

Denn wir haben keine bleibende Statt,
sondern die zukunftige suchen wir.
  Siehe, ich sage euch ein Geheimnis: wir
werden nicht alle entschlafen, wir werden
aber alle verwandelt werden und dasselbige
plötzlich, in einem Augenblick, zu der Zeit
der letzten Posaune.

— Brahms, *Eine Deutsches Requiem*†

* 'Set thy house in order' – Bach, Cantata BWV 106 [Thus saith the Lord, Set thy house in order; for thou shalt die, and not live – Isaiah 38:1]

† For here we have no continuing city, but we seek one to come [Hebrews 13:14];

Behold, I shew you a mystery; We shall not all sleep, but we shall all be changed,

In a moment, in the twinkling of an eye, at the last trump [1 Corinthians 15:51–2].

1

Return from the North

Unexpectedly the Daughter returned from the North, to the house of other returns, of other peripeteia, prepared for further shipwreck.

Palms on grey untended ground, American soldiers from whom one was not to accept money, but only smiles and sweets, the maw of the shelter by now resigned to swallowing old bicycles, the doll torn apart by a bomb; and the internal courtyard florid as an Alhambra for the games of richer children returned from the Isles of the Gulf; vast drawing-rooms in shadow; ancient kitchens and ancient women come from Lucanian villages with greasy hair, moustaches and intact litanies; cupboards jammed with tins of stale biscuits bought in pounds, heavy with moisture or too light, almost dust.

The autumnal light of Althenopis lay upon the stairs. But the smell of the banister was the same as in that August at the end of the war; the lurking cat seemed to scent it, slow to catch its more secret ingredients, making a spiral approach with its tail, rubbing against the railings, passive and appealing, still unwilling to catch it, to make a bound and lay hold of leaping life. Catlike, concentrated and hesitant, she bent close to perceive the smell.

She, the returned Daughter. With bones grown on placenta, on milk, on cures, and eyes without a squint, nor swollen face, nor six fingers, nor a leaking valve in her heart, nor the hangover of meningitis, but altogether a human machine in good condition, which had begun to operate on its own account.

By now the Daughter and the Mother no longer spoke in words but in signs. And the signs were clouded, a malign

231

Logos, uncontainable by reason, by moderation. The Mother spoke at the front door with a hug fragile as the last ring made in the water by a stone. How often they had played, and the game was cruel, squeezing the roots of life.

The Mother seemed to personify weakness, privation, the tremulous hesitation and fragility of a caged bird which mimics an attenuated instinct instead of killing itself against the bars. And the Daughter had arrived, with her perfect biological machine, to hurl against her an 'I' which, because it was the fruit of personal experience of the world, was mean and irreducible.

At that door, recently re-varnished, the umbilical cord was cut a second time. It was necessary to learn to breathe in a different way, and the Daughter fell sick in her breathing. Up till then the Mother had carried the Daughter in her womb, from then on the Daughter began to bear the Mother on her shoulders.

It was in a wintry season, the distraction of the sun was lacking.

The house of many houses was perfect Mannerism. Recently renovated by the Mother, cleaned of the tenant's sweats, and the myriads of summer cockroaches which crept in through gaps left by negligence, and the splashes of sauce on the walls where the flies swarmed. With marble floors in the reception rooms, majolica in the bathrooms, the doors and walls dazzling white, and the corridors freed of their clutter; a great many bedrooms (for whom?) and the usual kitchen, a little dilapidated, where the dressmaker of two generations recognized in the Daughter the Grandmother's nervous slenderness; and swapped gossipy threads and pins to stitch the present to the past. And yet the anguish of the throat gaping in sleep.

The Daughter's Mannerisms. She behaved like an autonomous modern woman of advanced ideas. The first days, the night on the divan in the big drawing-room. Then she became afraid of being swallowed by the emptiness of the room. And she made a lair for herself of dirty things, ashtrays, books and blankets, in the farthest corner of the house, a recess not meant even for a maid but for old paralytic relations. Furniture everywhere to reaffirm the Mannerism from wall to wall, but they were as foreign between those dazzling walls, marble and tiles as visitors to a clinic. You too can have them, if you work, if you settle down with a family. They're only waiting for your nod. Perhaps that furniture once breathed a larger air, as well as dust; but only while he, the father, had been alive. Then they had become signs of the past, dragged after them in their wanderings from flat to flat.

A great solitude, distant, especially from oneself. The sheets, too new like everything in the new house, seemed to belong on a poster advertising happiness. Even coloured sheets had been admitted to the house, in the attempt to abolish the frontier between waking and sleep, or rather in a pretence at an eternal, overriding day. The blankets still had family stains. But the stains were someone else's past.

See it like this: a child on the outskirts of the city possessed only a bird. Possessed, to put it another way, only its own heart; the rest still didn't exist except as an enemy entrenched behind an endless Maginot of prohibition. It spoke in tachycardia, gaps, sudden halts, bursts. But was something at least alive. And its throat. A sea of affections, all the embraces in the world, the caresses, the melting, the explorations: imprisoned. In the catch in the throat, bars between heaven and gaol.

Defeated she had come back to the Mother, almost as if to ask her the reason for living. She was nothing, outside of her Mannerisms, but toil and a stumbling heart. To Mannerisms she replied with other Mannerisms. To hieroglyphs with hieroglyphs. Meanwhile the world crumbled around piece by piece. Lifts could crash. Power cables come down in the street. Coaches leave the road. Cars and trams run you down. And the high sloping buildings leaned towards each other like giants in combat. The heart in cruel jest stops.*

* In the psychiatry manuals this 'end of the world' sensation is the prelude to schizophrenic crisis. See also Nerval's *Aurélie*.

In greeting her, immediately after the hug, the Mother had said: 'Now that you've shown us you don't know how to work, learn to sew at least.' This was the way they spoke to each other, doing violence.

But she grasped the Mother's dumb love. She began to eat. She diligently set semolina, cheese, steak, fruit on a tray for herself and ate in solitude in that remote little room, nurse to herself. And an obtuse biological process, more tenacious than love, conquered her.

They survived, but their fates divided. They had become two, but in an unequal way, like Austria-Hungary, a kingdom within an empire: when Hungary faced its destiny, nothing remained of the Austro-Hungarian Empire. The Daughter discovered her destiny, but the Mother vanished.

Thus she came to feel pity towards the Mother.

Plan of a house: the Drawing-Room

The cult of triads: a sofa in the middle and two armchairs, a large painting flanked by two little ones, two inkpots on the silver tray and the penholder in the middle . . . For various generations a pompous bilateral symmetry shaped the Drawing-Room, one that celebrated the rites of order; and the notion governing the order was that of making visible, even if only in drawing-room fashion, the position at the centre of the universe, not of Man, but of the Family.

So much so that the inheritors could be classified into those who had consciously continued to pay their dues to the cult of the drawing-room Triad, those who had merely respected it unconsciously as an inveterate custom or had made attempts at hybrid rebellion, always of a drawing-room kind, and those, finally, who had been driven by some wind of change to profane the simulcra of number in iconoclastic fashion, sapping the very roots of Drawing-Room Being, and thus of Order and the Family; in the houses of these latter, the maternal welcome of sofa-armchairs (lap and arms) was lacking.

In infants and schoolchildren sitting in those drawing-rooms, nothing, not schooling nor digression nor reasoning, contributed as much to the development of the faculty of (undetermined) abstraction and an idealistic conception of the world as their mere presence, thus seated, in that environment. Because normal chairs – so put upon, with holes when made of cane, scuffed and coming unstitched if upholstered, stained, grooved, carved, scratched – are still chairs; while the Drawing-Room chairs are ideas of chairs; and the paintings which, given the constant dimness reigning to prevent their fading, could barely be made out there where they hung in their high stations, are ideas of paintings only. And every object was the idea of itself. And the child, its mind darkened by so much mystery, consoled itself by inspecting, when it could, the trace of dust on its finger, or the furrow it had made on a surface, placating its anxiety for the concrete as best it might.

And then a drawing-room of this kind had to be kept closed to too much everyday profanation – never should a child leave a crust of bread on the leaf of the writing-desk, nor a boy scribble or make an inverted double-v with his carbon stick on the walls, nor a thirteen-year-old daughter shut herself away there with her exercise book and her yearnings; but above all else it must remain fixed and stable, always in the same place, in the same house, with the same people if possible.

However, given shortness of money and various other vic-issitudes, the Drawing-Room was constantly being profaned and was constantly on the move, not only in space but also in time: for some years, for example, it was swallowed up by a cellar, though it remained there in ambush, ready to strike various square yards of a new flat. And one might see it dismembered on the shoulders of gigantic removal men (or the other kind, thin and tiny, all sinew and shining scornful eyes), weaving down the stairs, passing time in the entrance halls of buildings; and the aunts or other familiar figures convoked for the occasion sat in the hall to supervise the removal, unrelaxed and watchful in armchairs wrapped in newspaper and sheets, stripped of their decorum, while about their feet, blown by the wind which often blew on these occasions – because the weather was seldom favourable to removals and swung round just when the loading began* –

* It was the custom to move house on 4th May, when annual leases fell through. But April, sometimes too mild and uniform, handed on to May the downpours it had held back. At the time when transport was horse-drawn, for reasons of hygiene people used to wrap the animal's tail in newspaper to prevent it brushing against the furniture, especially the mattresses.

swirled wads of straw and balls of newspaper (those sheets of newspaper softened by the many times they had wrapped brandy glasses, salt-cellars, Chinese plates, Bohemian bottles, Capodimonte cherubs; and here blew a *Figaro* 1950, there a *Franc-tireur des Alpes* 1948, there a headless Cardinal Mindzenty, and there an envelope with Haitian stamps containing keys that might have been described as 'lost in the removal of 19 . . . from Via . . . to Via . . .').

And then one would see the furniture and the ornaments, or rather *bibelots*, rearrange themselves in a different location as if nothing had happened; and the Daughter, a teenager by now, sadly noticed that the space destined for reception rooms swallowed up what had been intended for her – for she desperately wanted a room of her own.

The Drawing-Room had neither conviction nor any air, despite the fact that it wanted to give the impression of both: meaning the conviction given off by the family furniture of industrious professional men from Calabria, or even Frasca, settled in Althenopis after diligent and dignified efforts in jurisprudence or Carduccian studies – furniture bought out of small savings or gifts of money from better-off close relations after long and passionate engagements, to serve as surround to the monogamic monolith and the children to be proud of, and thirty or forty years later, provide the setting for the onset of illnesses and deaths. And meaning the air, the airiness, of certain upper-class living-rooms (no longer really drawing-rooms therefore) which certain ladies of the Isles of the Gulf or Althenopis had furnished in the roaring years (baying, instead, where we were) with contemporary and other pieces giving witness to the 'mentalité primitive' present, and not just as nostalgia, in the members of civilized society also; the setting for extra-marital loves, jazz records, books by Gide or Tagore, portraits of beautiful young men, and one of them will have become famous and another of them will have died young.

Instead it was a hybrid, an imitation of a conviction that had belonged to others, Spanish sacristies, for example, Provençal *mas*, the dwellings of ancestors who had been wealthy and professional men for generations. And its air was not festive, not that of freedom of the spirit, but of vacuum, an empty curtsy to certain fashions in vogue after the First World War, so that some rustic item or piece of peasant embroidery took on an inane overblown look, as if belonging in the house of the nobles or bourgeoisie who governed them. There were 'period' pieces of furniture and bibelots – Louis Quinze and Empire – but they were all on top of each other in a bric-à-brac of stubborn decorum, stripped not only of their cultural nexus but of their function as well – though they had once had it – because what counted was the fact that they were 'period' and represented, not so much the Family's present condition, as its past splendours and those yet to come. Thus the Drawing-Room served to admonish the children of the need to get on in society and to get out of the hard times of the Widowhood.

From removal to removal the Drawing-Room became more and more the shadow of its former self, losing not only the function it had had for previous generations, but also that of admonition to the children, since, in one way or another, they had all betrayed the Family; and increasingly its character was marked by obstinate stubbornness, a neurotic compulsion to repeat its ancient moment of life. It was – while the bathroom was Purgatory and Paradise one's own corner or converted storeroom – the Hell of the house, if Hell is dusty boredom and an inability to communicate. Upper Hell it was when the shutters were closed and the door was closed to keep it from wear and tear, and Lower and Deeper Hell it was when one 'got together again' for after-lunch coffee with some relative; or on New Year's Eve when, out of compassion, one of the children opened the champagne with the Mother pretending gaiety and both of them reflecting in their eyes and in their smiles the lights of the candelabra lit for the occasion and those of the houses across the road, where perhaps happier rituals were being celebrated in other drawing-rooms.

In the last years, the years of Loneliness, stubbornly and coldly intent on perpetuating the drawing-room entity, the

238

Mother's ever more diaphanous face hovered there, her eyes bent over a hand of solitaire; or bulging with ever rarer anger in a face congested by high pressure; or very remote, the eyes, vague, of a tender blue in the trembling face, bent over the chances in Napoleon's solitaire; and the gesture with which she laid out the cards as unconsidered as the movements of babes.

3

The bathroom

There had never been any faith in that house. Not even the negation of it – or the false religion – that manifests itself in the making of money, and constant accumulation, calculation, investment. Nor had there been, come the time of Widowhood, even the cult of the Family, neither past nor to come. Nor that of Science. Nor that of Art. Nor that highest of religions that manifests itself as compassion. Nor were there passions. In males, aridity becomes cynical, it softens at times and veils itself as scepticism. Aridity in woman does not offend but abolish. The Mother withdrew ever further into her own entrails, as water into the depths of the earth.

She had annulled herself in her children. In a mute and biological way. Hence her values became ever coarser and more limited. Religion: yes, but only on the occasion of weddings, christenings, confirmations (not indispensable these last), first communions, extreme unctions (if begged for insistently); mass, no, a hymn-tune or two for small children of the kind. 'Our Lady plucks a flower and she plucks it for Jesus', to be sung absentmindedly, however, in with all the other nursery tunes come down to her; but decided disapproval if the child, all shining dress, yearning and Sacred Heart, seemed to believe the prophecies of the nun who wanted her to take the veil. Work: yes, but it was only worth the trouble if one earned a great deal and in the public eye; how one was supposed to achieve this remained a puzzle given that the effort, dedication, sacrifice required in getting there were held in the greatest contempt; it was taken for granted, in fact, that her offspring would come out on top though this of course contradicted her rooted conviction that they were good for nothing, and suffered in addition the hidden anguish of the difficulty – inherited from generations of widows and rentiers helpless in the face of currency devaluations enacted by the Terrible Leveller, God – of achieving themselves in work. Death: it seemed not to exist out of respect for caste privilege, but also because of some doom-laden extension of the duties of history: it was the males in fact who died, in the trenches, in warfare, at work; the women's deaths did not count; the women disappeared, cancelled themselves out, 's'effaçaient', in French; nevertheless the Mother, who had been forced in her Widowhood to make herself somewhat male, had the habit of saying – 'Après moi, the atom bomb'; whereon the children would have a sense of being stifled, almost as if they wanted to demand of her; 'Then why did you give us life?',* apart from the Little Sister, who had always been told that she was a mistake. Sex: as long as possible its existence was denied; when one could no longer fail to notice its mischief, it was immediately brutalized and cut off from any possible communion with thought and feeling; it was a kind of savage beast that had to be kept caged up; and this done even as a kind of going one better, as if to say: you think you're the first to discover it? I could teach you a thing or two!

And the things she could teach were: 'You're dripping blood too, here, these are the towels!' Or: 'You've wet the bed, you dirty thing!'† to her teenage son. And 'Put a plastic cover under the sheet!' to her Married Daughter. As one attacks diseases with hygiene, so with sex. Freedom to go out: certainly, one knew that the daughters 'would never get up to

---

* This, in any case, is an altogether improper thing for children to use against their parents, and vice versa. It is life, in fact, that has given us parents and not vice versa, despite them and ourselves.

† Literally 'wet', out of the precise wish to mistake nocturnal ejaculation for enuresis and thus mortify the adolescent boy by reducing him to an infant, reminding him in the same instant that as a boy he had behaved as if still on the breast. But perhaps it was also woman's nemesis against the male in her son.

certain things'; and it was better that the son did them out of the house. Art, literature: adoration, yes, but devoted entirely to the spirit, woe if the spirit be made flesh, especially family flesh. Politics: stay with the government you have, the next one might be worse. Money: contempt for those who had only money; pudeur and shame about the facts of money, but sparkling energy when it came. And money worthy of the name came only from money (she invested secretly in shrewd unit trusts) or from property. The small sums earned by her children were treated with scorn. In fact they were small, and immediately went on buying things. Whereas money was the sublimation of savings into increased capital.

Every one of these principles was limited, so to speak, and denied by another.

Only shit was shit. Whence the importance of the privy as location of truth, of pure reality, neither brutal nor ideal, of a sure and serene link through constant bodily need with one's being just so and at odds with the world.* And here, if merely in an unspoken way, the hope might arise, by analogy with bodily functions, of purging yourself of quite different waste. Here also, beyond any principle or history, you might hope not to be forgotten by life, alert for when the occasion might present itself. Here you could go apart from others when they became unbearable.

* In the majority of houses there is no other place where one can be alone, not just materially, but even legitimately.

242

4
The dining-room

Of the dining-rooms of Widowhood, only that in the house in the country, made available by a relative in the early days of mourning, had ever been such. Vivid in memory of it were the charcoal braziers in winter; and the children with their reddened legs, around the table with its green cover, this one sewing, the other reading, that one studying, that one disturbing the rest with idle chatter, brought together by the central fire; and outside the sheet frost cracking in the afternoon, and on the peak of the volcano the fluffiest snow in which to roll around when they climbed up in the Christmas holidays; and vivid in that room are the steaks, essential to teenage hunger, just turned over on the fire, blood and black scorch, and the smell that spread through the house from the kitchen, redolent of log fires in the country; and the rustic nineteenth-century furniture of that room creating more than anything the illusion of living in a novel, in someone else's life, and therefore of being uprooted from one's own, able to enter a fantastic future. Almost as if it was a veranda, broad windows opened on to the garden where statues of nymphs alternated with Campanian broccoli: the industrious country people planted vegetables in the flower beds when the house was uninhabited; and there were palm trees and creepers to clothe deserted loggias in mystery, and the voices of locals rose from below to animate and enrich the mystery, voices rising up the iron art–deco staircase, furtive and whispering at times, at times snatched from their privacy by the playful breeze on the stairs, and intimidating also, at times, so that it seemed the very glass trembled in the french windows of the loggias. And in summer, in that garden, idle adolescence gave itself to sunny gymnastics – but the Mother deplored those legs which were at their awkward age, tensing for the high-jump, tomboyishly lacking softness in shorts and socks, and contrasted them with her own when young which had been 'superb' – or became clouded over by distress and fled among the loggias hedged with wistaria and lined on the inside by the sealed apartments of relatives in age-old lawsuits; or revisited perilous headlands of childhood peopled by musketeers and mohicans; or tormented itself at the unhappy loves of 'Le lys dans la vallée'; but the Mother was blind and dumb to the torments and the loss of weight, ironical about the adventures, scornful of the curiosity, because what she had burnt out in herself, she considered burnt out in all the world.

Then came the other dining-rooms – when the cellars opened to release the furniture bought in the period of wedded bliss and economic prosperity – always situated next to the Drawing-Room in city apartments. And because Keeping Up Appearances in the city was very much more expensive than in the country, the food was coarser and less nutritious: disdainfully the slender crystal fruit dish received the humble strawberry grape, the worm-eaten pear; the wide and generous blades of the steel knives never gave back the festive gleam of wine; the silver laid out on side tables had forgotten even the memory of slices of roast beef nestling on beds of purée and the tenderest *petits pois*, or of mayonnaise, or roast chickens garnished with new potatoes, or of bechamel sauces, cakes, salted almonds and pistachios, but seemed the funereal gifts of royal tombs. That dining-room exuded a special kind of poverty: that of those who continually lament a more resplendent past.

'Why don't we eat in the kitchen?' asked one of the daughters, with youthful contempt for family customs. But mothers, the dispensers of milk, afterwards like to keep their children in subjection, in a state of continual need. So that the continual contrast between the splendour of the dining-room and the humble nature of the food served to inform them that what they had – and it wasn't little when you thought about it – was nothing compared to what they had had, and especially compared to what the obligations of their social position would require of them in the future. Thus the Dining-Room was not an accident of form but a baroque obstinacy of substance; and that it really was a matter of substance turned out to be the case many years later, when the children sold off the glasses one by one and the silverware – this by weight, because the dealers refused to allow them any antique value. But altogether more substantial was the children's rooted conviction that they must manage to restore the family fortunes. And this conviction was not as easily got rid of as the silver; sacrilege in fact is negative proof of the existence – obsession rather – with the sacred in those who commit it.

5
Scissors, glasses, keys

In latter years the Mother was forgetful, we were always having to find her glasses, scissors, keys.

Oh, they weren't Quaker glasses set on the bridge of the nose to read the Bible in the evening in the family circle. Nor were they typesetter's glasses. Those glasses were akin to the tremble in her hands in latter years, chastisement for the wide blue happiness of the wifely gaze in the days following childbirth – days when the body, with just a hint of opulence, was draped in the Japanese folds of a shiny pink dressing-gown with a sea-shell pattern similar to that stencilled on the plaster of the seaside house that had been hers as a bride – similar also to the petals of the orange capucine, her Favourite Flower. Chastisement also for the over-sharp, inquisitive gaze, ingenuous and yet pitiless, of the eleven-year-old girl – so different from the velvet gaze of her sister which was saved from any external labour by being turned entirely on her own beauty and upon its echo in others.

In her latter years, their steel frames (she scorned coquetry and, bent on saving, contented herself with what the health service provided) gave them the look of prison windows, a templar's shield; they were all the iron and the hardness and the hospital and the sanitary-equipment shop of the world; instruments of the world's torture also because they froze objects, took away their shadow, depth, breathing-space, playfulness, made them bare, lifeless flesh.

The scissors were black and so were the keys – then came stainless steel scissors as well, and a Yale key or two.

The scissors were something extraordinary. They were

intelligent. They cut everything, even impossible knots. The glasses were malevolent instead, cold, meant for better vision, all the better to establish the proper distance.

The keys, tight-fisted, nervous in the act of entering the right keyhole and groping for the click, in vain. The scissors, instead, hard-working. But hateful the curved nail-scissors, mannered like an oriental empress. In the latter years they were the only ones, because the Mother no longer did any sewing for her ungrateful children, nor did the rooms ring with grandchildren, to recall at least the dumb and lifeless entwining of time. There was in some box or drawer a pair of steel scissors, dead new like the merchandise in stores before need or desire has bent over it and use quickened it; along with old cotton reels, buttons ordinary or bizarre, some still attached to the material from a youthful costume, brooches of imitation diamonds or horn, suspender-belts with a scrap of lace still hanging; and the scissors, stainless steel and new, among those old mute things, were crude and arrogant, scissors for other hands, for other mothers. The others – a little institutional, prison-like, in Peabody Trust style, or even of the iron wedding-rings of Fascism, after the shapely curves of Granny's Mozartian ones – were perhaps in the kitchen, perhaps for the fish, or under the table comforting the maid's neglected child.

The beautiful house without keys – after the four years of leanness, cramped rooms, thin omelettes; but the geraniums, the flowers dear to her! – the beautiful French house, among the beeches and the hedges of redcurrant and blackberry and the lawn with flowerbeds trimmed with roses, setting for the snapshot of the Beautiful Daughter of the fluttering sleeves (the Little Sister), her eyes happy with grace and promise; but that same happy day came an echo of sombre fate, she saw crows fly over the roof and in the attic, while putting away the travelling trunks, an owl.

A house without keys it was, and when during the first days there were no servants, the kitchen for the children was a paradise of mothers and abundance, because when wealth first came it was nursemaids who looked after them and not the Mother, who tended them only in times of poverty, though it was just at such times that want prevented her maternal tenderness from reaching full flower. And she led the children into the big larder which also had no key, where bananas hung in bunches and on the shelves there were rows of tins of Marie biscuits and apricot and blackcurrant jam.

She could never find her scissors, glasses, keys in the last house, or found them where the others should have been. In the last dysphasic years she confused their names, though the children nevertheless understood, ironically fetching the thing she was looking for with the proud precision of their youth. Young is what they were, clocking any sign of decay.

And in the last years the tragic glasses; white cataracts had fallen over her eyes – oh, still perhaps in order not to see – dark glasses and, underneath, steel glasses; and the Daughter helping her with a barely intuited compassion for her suffering. The bitter gift to the Daughter: a fridge; bitter because subject to the laws of calculation, even though given in gratitude and *a posteriori*, with no preceding contract, as if to say: you didn't deserve it before; and received with obscene delight – because the fridge filled a need – as the calculation was obscene and obscene the hiatus in feeling.

6
The clothes

The clothes looked as though they were left over from a cataclysm: like those in the houses on the island of Umo left behind on beds and chests, companions of the dusty and mouldering bottles of vinegar and Marsala in the cupboards, abandoned, on receipt of a postcard from an Australian or New Zealand consulate, to await return. Yet those clothes of the Mother weren't poor but expensive, not like those on the island of Umo, a harlequinade of patches sewn together, the various colours harmonized by a greenish or faded purple shawl, nor like the work-trousers for the fields once rich in olives and vines, but clothes, instead, for formal occasions, the ceremonies of the 1930s, at the time of Althenopean elegance, snapshot on the seafront or the tennis club or at Villa Gluck, short skirts already out of fashion and frilly underwear back in; or the ceremonies of the trousseau, and the bed-jacket for the birth of the longed-for Daughter, pink with seashells set in hexagons and kimono sleeves; and the brown suit, an elegant discreet colour, because supreme refinement had the power to cancel the colour's Franciscan overtones of votive habits in country districts or the aura of sad toil that envelops certain women in the towns of the South.

And shoes with very high heels – the green shoes that the Mother imposed on the sixteen-year-old daughter for her first dance, and at the dance she hid her feet because they were awkward in their unaccustomed elegance and in any case not given to dancing, or she displayed them nonchalantly in a surge of goodwill while stretching out her charms in an armchair; and the evening dresses, one of cardinal red and the other purple, coming down to her feet, from the period of biological fertility in the lands of Godamighty, the former moth-eaten and the latter taken in for the Daughter when she got her scholarship for study abroad; and the French intellectual – *Cimetière marin* and well-mannered anti-Poujadism – pitilessly disinterred, its origins in amusement: 'Est-ce la robe de votre mère?'; but nevertheless she felt herself to be beautiful then – and perhaps she was, out of the strength of her youth – and unassailable as her handsome belt of diamantés, splendour and defence, difficult to undo, of the familiar clasp (I'm letting you go, but I know there are some things you won't ever do'); and the frock with black and white dots (fortuitous colours, but prophetic), back in the days of the Paterfamilias, run up by an Althenopean dressmaker – the only dressmakers in the world! – so that it was long with a great many pleats in front, because there was to be no sparing of silk; and then it became unexpectedly more useful than her other dresses, in the third year of Widowhood (when she went from deep black to black and white, to grey, to purple), and which the Daughter in the end took over, wearing it with a red rose at the neck.

She wore it in that way on her last return from the North, under the jacket with the awkward fit at the armpits the Mother had got wrong; with a sick heart and painful breathing she had put on that dress with its generous yards of silk in order to hide herself, and the Mother had met her at the Railway Station (they were knocking down the old one which had been damaged in the war, and the fakir's spikes of the new one didn't yet stand out against the background of the volcano). Later the sister commented on her swollen face, the ancient dress and her wild-eyed gaze ('psychopathic' was her word for it, from when she had learned to describe an unknown caller who phoned with obscenities and offers of love).★

★ Because of the predilection that Mother nurtured for me I was permitted a certain madness or at least extravagance, so that my younger sister was forced to give proofs of equilibrium and good sense. Families like ours, just as they could afford for only one child to study, could only permit themselves one case of madness.

And here the heroic age of clothes comes to an end.

For the Mother there came the time of make-do clothes – synthetic wool immediately threadbare, imitation silk and a great deal of black poplin – or of clothes passed on by rich relations, the black ones left after the daughters had taken what they wanted, for it was their privilege to take first pick.

Black chosen out of too much heart, but without tradition; among the country people who eternally wear the black of religion and ritual, pain, should it outlast toil, has no uniform of its own. But in her there was the terrible decision of the heart, terrible for the children.

And then came more recent times, the last times, the times of respectability. Sad clothes. With neither the ostentatious splendour of the relations by marriage, nor the refined elegance of her own kin, a nugatory elegance, superior to the accidents of life, menstruation, childbirth, sicknesses, pains and even joys; nor had they the cosmopolitan fantasy of certain old foreign ladies on the islands of the Bay of Althenopis; nor the pastel shades for all age-groups of the American tourists; nor the sublime, almost mystically inhuman clothes, black with green lights, shiny with wear, of the women stooping in the fields for capers. But respectable and miserable, because of poor material and always in dark colours (after the blacks came the purples, the greys, once a timid bordeaux appeared), and almost always homemade; like the last two pullovers of her life, the ones that on the morning of the thrombosis were still draped over the back of the chair, and the heavy bordeaux suit, no longer the product of thrift or of dash for her young daughters, because in her last years she had lost her fondness for what were futile chores by then.

And she even gave away the sewing-machine, the venerable Singer, to the maid (replacement daughter, malleable to her wishes and advice, and her painful regrets), because her tailor husband had pawned his own.

A lace collar, an edging of fur, a jewel at the breast, a new belt transformed them into clothes for a Lady – a sad, scrawny lady with thin white and blue legs, the calves still somewhat plump, however, with obstinate youth (only in their seventies did the women of the family lose these final markers) – for a sad Lady, stiff-backed among future in-laws – well-off in villas, freelance professions and ecclesiastic vocations – and at the tenants' meeting.

Respectable street clothes in the mornings, the shopping-bag, of which she wasn't ashamed, on her arm; or visiting the doctor or some relation in the afternoon; latterly she crossed the road trembling because of her cataracts and the tremor in her legs, and one day the desolate Daughter saw the impatient motorist cursing at the 'old woman'.

After her death her clothes were passed on to the maid and her hats finished up crushed under old books. Her horrible hats. Respectability and distinction worn on the head. But at the time of the war in Spain – so the student friends of the son related – ladies didn't wear hats for years, so as not to be distinguished.

7
The dinners

The Mother by then ate alone in the deserted kitchen.

Off the chipped plate, white with a thin gold-border, not china but a glazed terracotta imitation, her broccoli, once aggressive, an outrage committed by good health on the nervous stomachs of the daughters and on the (aristocratically, proudly) suffering stomach of her son-in-law; sodden, glinting, heaped-up, fried in oil and garlic, with the deadly snare of a pinch of red pimento, except for the son-in-law, while the daughters liked the burning purity which cancelled the grease. She then set it on the stove for the son who came home late at night, in the big frying-pan for vegetables, black with a bolted handle as tradition requires, its rim sometimes encrusted with lumps and craters of hardened fat incorporating irreconcilable scraps of aubergine and potato – Pompeiian finds almost – because of the maid's slovenliness; at others scratched with pan-scrubs and detergents from the maid's angry reaction to the mistress's scolding; it rusted then on the wall for the strong drying sun of the country didn't reach that kitchen.

When her high blood pressure got worse, broccoli with crude olive oil, salt and lemon – light for the stomach, the kidneys, the heart, her rheumatism – despised by the daughters as over-simple.

In her last trembling diaphanous years (her anxiety no longer red, sudden and strong, but ever-present, blue) the evening greens were replaced by milk, with a light dusting of cocoa, lukewarm, however, without the ritual of the steaming cup; and by bread spread with orange marmalade and apricot jam put up on one of her good days; but on the transparent surface

253

spots of green mould, in confirmation of the dust on the lids of the jars: a futile spurt of life in a larder otherwise empty of food.

On the bowed figure sitting alone, and on the diaphanous arm – where on the elbow there was a circular bruise, like the mark of a malign fate, which she had received at birth – the harsh insult of the strip-lighting, as if her desolation did not seek refuge in the twilight, where we like to imagine old people, but cried out lividly and then slumped in small movements under the inscrutable gaze of the neighbours across the way, and of God, in order that He see, that He not forget.

The harshness of that light: in the same way she tendered the things of the instinct lifeless and intrusive to the Daughter who glimpsed the love frozen in the sexes; the secret union which had preceded her birth, broken then for ever by impatient rejection, was remote as buried waters.

A cockroach sometimes appeared in that light and terrified her; she burst out on such occasions into the low screams and smothered gestures of a child neglected by a mother who has covered her other children with tendernesses; and it had always been like that, as a girl, as a woman, even as a widow. Or sometimes on summer nights an insect drawn by the light would cause a flutter in those hands, those wrists, those eyes, which lost their reassuring maternal calm to reveal the intimate insecurity of the bride's possession – a small lascivious victory for the Daughter; and the warm nocturnal hum, when one has intimations of ample ripenings and repose outside oneself – of families, in poor farmsteads or in alleyways, around the dinner table, the television or the youngest child – was broken by those tremulous averting gestures, votives offered to the goddesses Anguish, Worry, Uncertainty, Insomnia, as they loomed in the strip-light dividing the window from the night.

Fat bustling maids or pale skinny ones with some hidden village craziness, women with no home to go to, on call night and day, sometimes set out those dinners – when she still ate broccoli – in the dining-room, under the draining light of an ornate chandelier with no candlepower; and among furniture and ornaments inherited after muted quarrels with relations, or bought with thrift and delight in the happy epoch of the bride and bride-mother, it was not a dinner but the staging of a dinner, the consummation of all past rituals; anyone could watch her from the windows opposite – like students on the tiers of an anatomy lecture theatre – as if the undertow of loneliness had drained bread and water of their ordinariness (there was no wine to turn to vinegar) and even the smell and the dirt of the stained tablecloth or the bleached stiffness of her napkin – when it was ironed – of theirs. Never did measured, 'Mozartian' gaiety play over the three Capodimonte cherubs, one-time centrepiece of formal dinners.

Later, at the time of the pallid milk with cocoa, the maid would bring it on a little silver tray as she lay in bed, the bed on which her husband had taken his repose and died, between sheets that many years before, soft and life-giving, new from the shop and fresh from dreams, had wrapped her baby children of marvellous birth and promise. There the new commodities of the day surrounded her: the little radio, a present from her younger cousin, 'to keep her company' (even the advisability of television was discussed), and the handsome English plaid, a present from her future daughter-in-law, as a luxury to brighten that period so poor in presents received and given, not only by her children, by friends and by relations, but also by life and by God.

8
The pastimes

No one was ever less given to, or taken with, the pleasures of affluence: the industrious and property-owning thrift of her parental family in Castellammare di Stabia, the tightness of money later on, being the cause. But a further reason was her knowledge that she couldn't buy the stars in the sky, nor her vanished strength, nor her sweet youth. So she bought *Puzzle Weekly* which passes so much time for a hundred lire. And she plunged into that lower middle-class world so foreign to her, not for the sake of the jokes, the childish puzzles – piazzas of Italy, ridiculous records, utensils with queer names – but for love of the small economies that induced her to smoke simple Nazionali, like workers and farm-labourers, and later Alfa cigarettes, when she discovered they cost less. And also for the metaphysico-rational pleasure of those black and white mosaics which she preferred to a rebus; she put the letters in the empty squares as if performing some ritual of reparation, and the lightly traced grids set off her slim spaced characters – which later came out in the younger daughter's hand, after the clear tidy writing required by school, by one of those passages of the blood that don't limit themselves to the eyes and the voice, and which give a sense of the miraculous, or of anguish.

And around her lay the garish covers of thrillers – another inexpensive pastime, because one could buy them second-hand at the kiosks and sell them back again in a chain of tiny losses and gains equal to the wear of the pages – in which there was as much activity as there was time in bed for her, a dynamic toing-and-froing of whisky, steaks, lifts, super-shiny and super-powerful cars, as fast getting to the scrapyard as the corpses to the cemeteries along the page.

The world of affluence and efficiency was brought near that bed for a couple of hundred lire: the important, meaningful hundred lire, the patient, humble, substantial hundred lire of mountain villages; less essential, nevertheless, than those of the time she was left alone with the children after her husband's death and spent on rare butter gaily spread on the startled children's bread, on pencils she got the maids to buy in stealth the eve of the Epiphany, and on her Nazionali, the vice of a woman suffragette – suffragette at least in her clothes when young, and in her *garçonne* hairstyle – a vice now no longer genteel but brutal and stubborn, more that of an Amsterdam news-hawker, an Israeli girl-soldier, or some poor labourer in a mountain village.

In the last two years a stainless-steel lighter came into the house – a present from her cousin – relegated to die as an ornament in the gelid wintry drawing-room, when the paternal certainty of the family doctor and her inner tremors forced her to give up smoking.

She often showed regret at never having cultivated her love – so in keeping with her square face and clear eyes – for numbers and science. And that love and that regret, which had found no outlet, overflowed into her account books and business papers; but the too familiar-human justification of shortness of money and of finding herself on her own with the children nevertheless gave some vent to her smothered interest, such was the precision lavished on those figures and on those papers and such her enlivenment from them. The furniture round the bed was covered with her account books, campaign maps compiled in solitude under the covers – because there was no heating – as if she were the general in his tent. Bread, sugar, rice, pasta, frozen fish, mincemeat, and the five lire less paid to a street vendor for broccoli or oranges were the infantry and the trenches of a war fought for thrift and the children's future.

And when the children left home the Mother retired to that bed for ever longer hours, so as not to hear herself resounding through the echoing house.

257

9

Die mit Tränen säen, werden mit Freude ernten *

The restless little girl of the frail and tremulous movements, of the faltering giggles, of the milk darkened already by the mystery of blood, was born without frills from the womb of the dying Mother and prattled in the lap of an old woman falling apart. The little girl who had been her mother was born again in the last days of her life. For each of us has another buried self which awaits its day with blanketed spark. She now received her cue – and almost always the prompter is Satan, and sometimes the contrary.

And there were beside the bed all the things requisite for these occasions: the medicines for the heart and for blood pressure, the teat for liquid food taken from the maid's baby just in that period, that, in any case terrestrial, drying up of hope, the oxygen cylinder, and the extremely slender spaceship tubes to be inserted in the rebellious nostrils, the bedpan which 'every home should have', because if it is a home you don't merely live in it but fall ill and die there; the catheter for the aetherial urine, no longer clouded, purified by fasting and the fear of death; the greedy leeches, like a witch-burning in the booking-hall of Termini station, swift, sure, slimy as a rat's belly, then afterwards drooping and swollen; and the many sheets, some of them stained for ever with iodine and rejected blood, terrible in the wardrobe later as in memory a cruel childhood

* 'They that sow in tears shall reap in joy', Brahms, *Ein Deutsches Requiem* [Psalm 126:5].

story; and the doctors, grim and fat the family doctor, and guilty also, as if feeling himself accused, but bolstered by his embonpoint as by the certainty that in the long run death goes beyond the limits of the human. And the consultant, at twenty thousand lire, man of science, thin and old, ennobled by his high fees.

And the sorrowing relations, male and female cousins, sisters, brothers, who at every death saw the mirror of time reflect not the agreeable and everyday rituals of the present but turn to the past, to the ever more shrivelled bagpipes of joy, of when . . . and there, a piece of furniture, there a photo, there an olive tree, always the one on the road to Santa Maria, and a villa, always that one, the first visible from the steamer going to the Island . . . or turn instead to their own deaths; and as they went by they breathed on the mirror so as not to see.

And into that death agony, without heirs greedy for rings or inheritances, a woman managed to insert herself, a meteoric presence because foreign to the family planet, a woman who had come not so much to rifle the handbags of the sorrowing aunts and the wallets of the disoriented children, as to seize the chance of filling her spare time with returnable favours, of taking over a mother, though not her own and dying, she whose mother had not been loving; and of getting her teeth into life in the closeness of death, as is said to happen to necrophiliacs by one of the profoundest mysteries of being; and in fact her cheeks were red, her voice strident and her gaze bright.

Nor was the person of the maid lacking, quick to wash sheets and rinse bedpans, between preparing the baby's pap and a fleeting smile in the direction of the play-pen – the mistress had taken her on as an unmarried mother with a month-old baby – who afterwards got herself given many of the mistress's possessions and helped herself to others and caused trouble with the union when the children had to sack her after closing up the house – that was the period of transition between family servants and unionized ones, or a period like every one so far, in which the weak have to fight without quarter or scruples against the strong, and so as well as being the unfortunate will also be the crooks – and who then married a fifty-year-old gaolbird who venerated her and the child in a way the lover and father had never done and who looked after her in that crisis and who had the added attraction of a large car, an out-of-date limousine, the kind one often sees being driven by market-traders whose wretched distant cousin he was.

That death, which decided to get busy from Sunday night to Saturday – a working rather than a holy week – decked itself with the proper accoutrements – children, relations, doctors, friends – in night watches and in anxieties, to rise up as thing in itself, with its own dignity; but decided not to outstay its welcome and left off before anyone had got used to it. A statement rather than a lamentation. Just as she had been. Not one of those sudden deaths which drag the living for an instant down into the eddies of the void and leave them marked for ever by anguish; nor one of those which wear them out; but like the deaths of tribal chiefs, who withdraw when their task is done to make way for others, because the protection of their own kind prevails over every other impulse.

And they always leave something behind them, a gesture, an amulet, a word of counsel for those coming after, who are not always ready to accept the gift or understand the sign; to become receptacle or target, or beacon lit from that torch, or soil or wind to transport that seed and make it fertile. They are a guide, these gifts. But from her, until that moment dominated by a crude and arrogant reason, no achieved oracle might come forth: barely four faltering words to go with a gesture. Only an unstable sign which the person who had to grasp it could well confuse with the signs of death. Turmoil or fondness could burn up or devour the meaning. Or one could deny it, dishonestly, by fleeing it. But to her who received it – straining forward from the start, now almost panting, in futile listening, or in failed embrace – it seemed a clear voice, admonitory, n⊃t faked, though grotesque and strange. Nor did the gesture seem like the flight of the dove which alights on the shoulder of the predestined, but rather the blind flight of the bat, zigzag but responsive to its promptings. Not the kingdom of heaven, therefore, for the chosen, but the nether one. And all of it to cross.

Without shame, insistently, in the first days she touched her sex. The older female cousins tried to distract her by taking hold of her hand and chanting over and over in the tone they had used in childhood, when the five or ten years difference counts: 'You don't do that, you don't do that', and in that voice, faltering as if snipped by scissors, she replied; 'I'm a baby girl, I'm a baby girl.'

That gesture which had remained buried for so many years alighted in her lap, to reclaim her rights and assert them, to peel away from the old dying body and enter the soul of her who grasped it, to lift the ban and make her fertile, that others born of woman might see the light.

Italian fiction from Carcanet

ALDO BUSI   *Seminar on Youth*

DINO BUZZATI   *Restless Nights*
                             The Tartar Steppe

NATALIA GINZBURG   *Family Sayings*
                             All Our Yesterdays
                             The City and the House
                             The Manzoni Family
                             Valentino & Sagittarius
                             Family

ELSA MORANTE   *Arturo's Island*

PIER PAOLO PASOLINI   *A Violent Life*
                             The Ragazzi

FABRIZIA RAMONDINO   *Althenopis*

UMBERTO SABA   *Ernesto*

LEONARDO SCIASCIA   *Candido*
                             The Wine-Dark Sea
                             Sicilian Uncles
                             *The Moro Affair & The Mystery
                                of Majorana*
                             One Way or Another
                             The Council of Egypt